"Anna Solomon has created a singular heroine, whose story of dashed dreams and eventual triumph is a wise and timeless wonder. Intense and gorgeous, *The Little Bride* gives us an unparalleled snapshot of the West." —JENNIFER GILMORE, author of *Golden Country* and *Something Red*

"This is a very intensely imagined book, an elegantly written pocket of forgotten history." —AUDREY NIFFENEGGER, *New York Times* bestselling author of *The Time Traveler's Wife*

"A stirring love story and an unsettling, original portrait of the New World." —SANA KRASIKOV, author of *One More Year*

D1054021

THE

Little

Bride

Anna Solomon

RIVERHEAD BOOKS, NEW YORK

RIVERHEAD BOOKS
Published by the Penguin Group
Penguin Group (USA) Inc.
375 Hudson Street, New York, New York 10014, USA
Penguin Group (Canada), 90 Eglinton Avenue East, Suite 700, Toronto, Ontario M4P 2Y3, Canada
(a division of Pearson Penguin Canada Inc.)
Penguin Books Ltd., 80 Strand, London WC2R 0RL, England
Penguin Group Ireland, 25 St. Stephen's Green, Dublin 2, Ireland (a division of Penguin Books Ltd.)
Penguin Group (Australia), 250 Camberwell Road, Camberwell, Victoria 3124, Australia
(a division of Pearson Australia Group Pty. Ltd.)
Penguin Books India Pvt. Ltd., 11 Community Centre, Panchsheel Park, New Delhi—110 017, India
Penguin Group (NZ), 67 Apollo Drive, Rosedale, Auckland 0632, New Zealand
(a division of Pearson New Zealand Ltd.)
Penguin Books (South Africa) (Pty.) Ltd., 24 Sturdee Avenue, Rosebank, Johannesburg 2196,
South Africa

Penguin Books Ltd., Registered Offices: 80 Strand, London WC2R 0RL, England

This is a work of fiction. Names, characters, places, and incidents either are the product of the author's imagination
or are used fictitiously, and any resemblance to actual persons, living or dead, business establishments, events, or
locales is entirely coincidental. The publisher does not have any contol over and does not assume any responsibility
for author or third-party websites or their content.

Copyright © 2011 Anna Solomon
Book design by Kristin del Rosario

First Riverhead trade paperback edition: September 2011

Library of Congress Cataloging-in-Publication Data

Solomon, Anna.
    The little bride / Anna Solomon.
       p.   cm.
    ISBN 978-1-59448-535-0
    1. Jewish girls–Fiction.   2. Mail order brides–Fiction.   3. Jews–South Dakota–Fiction.   I. Title.
    PS3619.O4329L57 2011
    813'.6–dc22
                            2010054194

PRINTED IN THE UNITED STATES OF AMERICA

10   9   8   7   6   5   4   3   2   1

For my parents

וכאשר אבדתי אבדתי

V'ka'asher ovadeti ovadeti.

And if I perish, I perish.

or . . .

Since we are lost already,
we might just as well defend ourselves.

Look

ONE

ODESSA, 188-

THE physical inspection was first. Eyes. Nose. On her chin, a thumb opened her jaw. The woman's hands weren't soft but they were dry, at least, like salted fish. Minna closed her eyes, then worried she looked afraid and opened them. The fingers tugged at her earlobes. They prowled at her nape.

All this, she decided, was normal enough. She had been to doctors, twice, men who accepted milk for their services. The first time, she was six, and still living with her father—the milk came from his goat—and she was still a boy then, in her mind, and did not mind undressing, or standing in the cold, and was not ashamed of her unwitting body: the foot kicking out, the throat gagging. Then she was thirteen, and already in Odessa, and she had seen her breasts in Galina's dressing-room mirror, sideways and from the front, and she carried the milk—stolen from the dairy boy's cart—with disgrace, made worse by the reason she went: a smell of beer, a heat, a terrible itching. She was sure something in her own touching had damaged her inside, and as she walked she took a long looping detour: out Suvorovskaya, past the hospitals, through the cemeteries. She decided to say a man had done it to her, whatever "it" was—to have hurt herself seemed worse than to have been hurt by someone else. But as it turned out, the doctor asked nothing. He didn't even make her lie on his table. He looked at her tongue, that was all. Then he gave her back the milk, telling her to let it sour into yogurt and smear it on herself at night.

But now the woman ordered Minna to take everything off, and when Minna had stripped down to her underclothes, she ordered her to take these off, too. Minna felt dizzy. The room was unheated, in a basement, in a municipal building, after hours. The only color came from orange patches of rust on the walls.

The door opened. A man entered the room, followed by another woman, followed by a tall metal contraption she rolled behind her. She held a flame to it; gas flared; white light flooded the room. Minna's skin went taut. The lamp was the sort they brought to the mines after an accident, the sort they'd used when they pulled her father out. Its cold glare missed nothing. The stone floor was crumbling.

"Off," the woman said again.

The man waited, a pipe in his mouth. His beard was red and tattered, as if it housed moths. Maybe he was a real doctor. Maybe he wasn't. Minna chose to concentrate on his thin shoulders under his thin shirt, on how he kept his eyes on his fingernails, which he appeared to be cleaning with his thumbnails. He could almost look—if she looked right—apologetic.

She unknotted her bodice and folded it in half. She folded it again, then again, then set it on top of her other clothing, on the floor. Order, she thought, willing her arms not to shake. Show them order. A wife is meant to create order.

"Get on with it," said the woman. "Drawers."

Minna concentrated on her feet. Her toes were purple; her soles stung. She would have to sneak out to Galina's vodka late tonight and siphon off spoonfuls for the cuts. She wouldn't dare pump any water. The pump made a noise like a cat in heat.

"Might as well know. Hard of hearing's a mark against you."

The woman's breath was close, and sharp, like seawater crossed with wine. Minna fended off her desire to pull away. She would never, she told herself, have to smell this smell again. She would live across oceans, she would have a husband, she would have her own house. Her own sink and bath, made of zinc or copper—even stone would do—in which she could wash whatever and whenever she pleased.

She slipped her drawers off her hips. She planned to catch them but her body stayed stiff: the idea of bending over now was unbearable. The man's pipe nodded as the white cloth fell to her ankles and now her eyes closed, she couldn't stop them; between her legs, the hairs stood. The lamp gave no heat. She concentrated on the worms of light across her eyelids, on seeing sunlight, sky. In the house, above the zinc or copper sink, would be a window, which she would dress with a lace curtain. The days would sift through the lace as a silent, dustless light.

Her eyes startled open when the fish hands cupped her breasts and lifted. At her stomach she felt a tickle: the man's beard. He drew so close he might have been sniffing her.

"You're sixteen?" he asked her navel.

Minna nodded.

"Your event comes every month, yes?"

She nodded again. Though sometimes she bled for a whole month straight, and sometimes not once in a year.

The tickle withdrew. "Arms," said the man as he sucked on his pipe, and as the smoke from his exhalation swam up Minna's front, smelling of her father, she couldn't help but breathe it in. The woman told her, "Lift," and started slipping her fingers around in Minna's underarms, pressing, kneading, turning sweat to ice. At last they stopped. Slipped away. The woman nodded.

"Unremarkable," said the man.

The woman who'd brought in the lamp scratched something in a large book.

"Fat," declared the doctor, and the fish woman's hands began to squeeze at Minna's waist. The doctor circled her, observing. He was thin in the way of cellar insects, as if made to slip through cracks. Minna tried to blur her eyes. She focused instead on the pattern emerging: he questioned her, yes, but he did not command her, and he did not touch. There was a woman to perform these functions, and another to take notes. It was all part of a procedure, Minna reminded herself, a system. Rosenfeld's Bridal Service. An underground operation, yes—but the doctor, the women, they were all Jewish. Her jaw clenched as the hands grabbed her hips, but she did not squirm. It was a service, a system, run by Jews for Jews. There was nothing personal here.

Nothing to squirm from. Every bride was given her Look. Usually by the groom's family, admittedly—but so many families had already left. Perhaps it was better this way. She'd never have to see these people again. There was a method; there were rules; there was a prize.

"Recommend more nutrition en route," said the man, and disappeared behind her. "Legs."

The hands tugged her drawers from around her feet. Minna started to shiver. She tried to control it, tried to breathe through her teeth so they did not rattle, to calm her limbs into stillness—but when the fingers poked the soft spot at the back of her knee, her foot swung back. Her heel struck something soft. The doctor swore.

"I'm sorry!" she cried. "I didn't mean . . ." But her voice had come out sounding like a child's, and she did not turn to face him. She feared seeming too aggressive, or skittish, or ingratiating.

"Do you work on your knees?"

Minna didn't reply. Did they want her to have worked on her knees? Did they want humility? Or did too much kneeling cause injury? She had knelt too much, she knew this with certainty.

"Must he repeat the question?" asked the woman.

But perhaps the doctor had already seen some sign of it. Perhaps she was marked, and he was only testing her.

"Sometimes," Minna said.

"Bring the lamp closer."

The lamp was brought closer.

"Have her bend over."

The hands nudged Minna's shoulders forward. And now the

tears that had been waiting ran into her mouth. She pushed back with her shoulder blades, but the hands were firm—then she was folded, upside down, her nostrils stinging. The hands pulled apart her buttocks. Except for the man's teeth on his pipe, there was silence.

Minna had not been able to wash herself for days. She'd eaten almost nothing but the beets Galina had asked her to buy for a borscht before deciding she didn't want it; this morning she'd shat water bright as Oriental silk. Her tears poured up and out her nose, then down into her hair.

"Unremarkable," said the man. "Lay her down."

O N the floor, at least, she no longer had to hold herself up. Through her tears she saw water stains on the ceiling, so old their centers were clean again. She bit her tongue as the hands spread her knees, as her own hands slid under her back— an automatic, pitiful bid for shelter.

"Speculum," said the man.

Cold inside. Minna kept her mouth closed, her nose closed. Cold metal, cold air. Everything that could be closed, closed, her chest pounding like soldiers' drums, as if—her mind pounding: what they must think.

When the metal withdrew, Minna moved to sit up, but the hands pressed on her feet, *stay*, then there was a prodding— Minna brought her head back down, hard, and tried to focus on the pain. Yet she couldn't block out—was that a stick? another piece of metal? It was searching for the place that always eluded

Minna, the place she tried never to think of because when she did it was gone, and when she found it again, it didn't seem to recognize her. She approached on tiptoe—or she circumvented, pretending not to care. She'd spent years playing those games, trying mostly not even to try, and now this object was going straight for the place, as if it was—but it was—it was found. The object tapped, twice. Minna clenched her teeth. The object stroked, three times. In her right leg, a muscle twitched.

"Unremarkable," said the doctor, and the hands closed Minna's legs.

T HE room was dim again. Minna was dressed, and alone. She heard the lamp clatter as it was wheeled into another room, then heard boots on the stairs. Another girl's, she could tell, and felt a mean relief. Someone else would be humiliated now. Someone else was stupid or desperate or brave enough—and which was it?—to have come here.

The steps vanished, a door closed. When Minna's door opened again, a different man walked in, short and dark, in a tattered coat that looked like it had once been expensive. It was too heavy a coat for late July, which it was. Or which it had been when Minna walked here; it seemed possible now, down in the basement, that summer was already gone. The man didn't take off his coat, or look at Minna, but motioned for her to sit on the room's one furnishing, a desk so chewed with knife marks it was nearly blank again. When Minna sat, she felt the ridges of old letters through her skirt: names of the bureaucrats, she guessed, who spent their days here, whistling and sighing, wading through files labeled with other people's names. They wouldn't try to under-stand the people, Minna thought, and she didn't particularly blame them. There was rarely any advantage, as far as she could see, to understanding another person. She'd been sent to serve Galina when she was eleven, after her father died, but in the five years she'd spent scrubbing Galina's underclothes, holding her head while she vomited, bringing her soup when she was heart-broken, she'd been careful never to ask questions, or listen too well.

"Psychology," said the man, and opened a large black bag.

T HERE were three tests.

One: a tangle of yarn, to be unknotted. Minna had heard of this at least, a puzzle of patience for the bride-to-be, and tak-ing the yarn into her hands, she was comforted by the notion that anything in this room corresponded with the world outside it. Maybe, she thought, her mother had to do it at her own Look, in front of her father's sisters, all five of them with their black hair and long, black nostrils. When Minna's aunts spoke, you might have believed God Himself was upon you. If you believed in God. Yet her mother must have made herself undaunted. She was a rug maker; she knew knots. And unlike Minna, she knew who she was marrying. She knew how the wedding would be, knew the wet wood scent of the old shul, the sweet breads she would eat, the face of the fiddler who would play at her dance. The night she married, she must have believed that she would stay married. Or perhaps she tricked herself into believing this, as she must have tricked the aunts at her Look. She must have fooled them into thinking she was patient, and would stay. She must have unknotted the knot.

The yarn was coarse and thin, all the same dark gray—dyed, Minna suspected, to make it harder to see its edges. She wanted the mining lamp back. Her fingers were stiff, and stumbled. It took five minutes just to find one end and take it between her teeth, then she thought better of it—teeth were bone, mannish, the man was watching—and used her lips instead. She fumbled the yarn apart from itself. When her eyes began to pulse, she closed them and felt, and when they stopped pulsing, she opened them and looked.

After an hour, the yarn had become a dream of yarn, a gray trail passing through her fingers, which had started to blister. It was enough yarn, she thought, to knit a muff. Or maybe—more practically—a shawl. The yarn drifted across her skin like a long, supple knife. She decided upon the muff. She could see herself walking with it, or rather behind it, her bearing stately and slow, the muff drawing her along in an effortless glide. For every foot of yarn she rescued, another inch of muff became itself, and the fantasy grew closer: a winter afternoon in America, floating along a city street, her ever-expanding muff parting the crowd like an enormous jewel, leaving the people's mouths agape. They'd never seen anything like it. And so she reached the other end.

———

Two: two glasses of water, loud with chunks of ice. Minna put her fingers in, like the man told her. At first they were soothed, after the yarn. Then they ached. The numbness, when it came, was preferable. One glass, she thought, was enough to wet her throat for a week. The other was enough to wash her body. She saw dirt lifting from skin. Ash from stone. Galina's tea leaves from wherever she'd thrown them.

Was this a test of endurance?

Her fingers, when he told her to lift them out, were limp as fish fat, and as white blue and dripping.

THREE: a bird, small, on a plate. Stunned by something, woozy on its feet, its wings flitting then forgetting.

A rock. A knife. A fork. A nail.

The man started with a nail. He picked out one of the bird's eyes and let it fall onto the plate. The bird opened its beak, but made no cry, only a gasp, a shuddering. Sinews, vessels, blood wrestled the air.

Minna did not cry out. She did not close her eyes. Endurance, she thought. Again. They wanted to see if she could endure endurance. It was worse—far worse—than anything her aunts might have dreamed up.

The nail stabbed. The other eye fell. The bird fell next to it.

The man put down the nail, and picked up the rock. He placed the rock over the bird's feet, and with his other hand, pulled. The bird stretched, soundless, until it broke from its feet and started to convulse.

The man put down the rock, and picked up the fork and

knife. He looked Minna in the eye for the first time, and she saw, suddenly, that he had a napkin tucked into the collar of his coat.

And then she saw nothing, she made no choice, her hands moved to the bird, they twisted until the neck snapped. The head hung loose. The bird was light, and warm.

"Brava," said the man, in his dry, dead voice. "Kindness."

TWO

S HE was late.

Late to serve supper, late for shock to set in, late for what must be her real life to begin, Minna Losk ran. Off the steps of the municipal building, past another girl heading in, through Sobornaya Plaza, across Moldavanka's dry streets, her feet calling up dust, for it was indeed still July, the city's acacias in full bloom, her lizards asleep in the last sun, the scent of tomato plants coming up off the piers, all Odessa in a peaceful late-day glory Minna had never stopped to notice and now, too, she could not stop, she ran in the heedless way of the newly free, and confused, and guilty. She was never late. Soon she would always be late, she would leave and be married and be late to serve dinner forevermore and Galina would have the nightly pleasure of reprimanding her for her absence. It would hardly be any different from when Minna arrived, five years ago, after a long day's travel, carrying only a pillow, a change of undergarments, and an extra dress. Galina had glanced at her, glanced away. "You might have come sooner," she said.

Oh, the hope Minna put in that small bundle. She'd carried so little not because those items were all that she possessed, or all that she could carry, but because they were all she hoped to need. Minna had an idea (she did not think of it as a superstition) that whatever one prepared for would happen, that if she packed even somewhat adequately, nothing would be provided to her. And she had a precocious mistrust of sentimental objects, for she had seen her father attempt to keep her mother in the form of dresses hung at even intervals along the closet rod, and jewelry clasped and dusted on the table by the bed, and her mother's two shawls hung precariously over the bedposts as if she'd been there, that morning, and tried on both before deciding to wear neither. When really she'd left when Minna was five, after a second child was born, a boy, already dying. This much, everyone agreed about. Also, nearly everyone agreed that she'd left with a yellow ticket. A ticket to sell herself to men. What they didn't agree on was the reason for this behavior. Minna's aunts said she'd gone off to become a *kurve* because she was one. Minna's father said she bought the yellow ticket because *kurve*s were the only Jews allowed to leave the Pale of Settlement, and that her plan, once she'd crossed the border, was to send for him and Minna. A woman Minna barely knew told her that the baby boy was the reason, that all Minna's mother had ever wanted was a son and that his weakness, his *toyt*, had driven her out of her mind.

Minna didn't understand. *Out of her mind.* As if her mind had been their house.

Her mother's name was Roza. Her father hid the few photographs of her, saying they made it seem as though she were dead, and instructed Minna, each week, to buy Roza's favorite almonds, which he kept in a bowl on the table, though he didn't like them and Minna didn't dare eat them. When Minna got older, and recognized the despair born out of such hoarding, she dared suggest to her father that they stop "wasting" the money. She hadn't meant to be rude. Or maybe she had—she frequently felt so desirous of her mother that she wanted to hurt her. "She's gone," Minna said. "She doesn't need fresh."

Two weeks later a far chamber of the salt mine collapsed with her father in it. Her aunts came like crows, pecking and squacking, and in their presence, Minna was still. But once they'd concluded their *shiva* and gone back to their better towns—moaning and squeezing her cheeks and weeping, a great billowing cloud of relief trying to pose as misery—Minna set to work packing away her parents' belongings into her mother's old rug shop. She threw out the almonds, and the bowl. The only thing she wanted to keep was the only thing she never found: the photographs of her mother, which her father had hidden too well.

For a time, she was content in her father's house, rummaging and rearranging, doing what needed doing each day. She ate frugally to make her father's small savings last. She washed the windows, as he'd never encouraged her to do. She sold his goat for money and a writing table. She would keep books, she thought, for various businesses in Beltsy. Her father had sent her to school with the boys after all. Only for a couple years, but still; surely he wouldn't mind if she put it to some use. Minna liked the idea of the sharp black ink, the rows and columns, the questions answered, the answers in place. She found an old ledger of her mother's, made a list of the men who owned various businesses, and of the women who actually ran them, and prepared the speech she would deliver to convince them of her use.

Then the Charity Women began to visit, pride and suspicion beaming from their faces. Minna served them tea, and mandel-brodt she'd bought at market, and dusted off the chairs—which were not dusty—before she let them sit down. They must have been slightly terrified. They knew about her schooling, knew she could read and write better than they. Yet they also knew—everyone knew—all she had not learned, without a mother. And so they managed to puff themselves up and address her with pity, as they must have addressed the gentile peasants outside town. Minna was like an old woman, they said, already rangy, solitary, unpredictable. She ought to make good of herself. When Minna told them of her bookkeeping plans, they looked at her as they might look at a rolling pin that had warped—and in the same way that they might give such a rolling pin to a child as a toy, to bestow upon it a new purpose, they seemed to think that if they could give Minna away with her own new purpose, she, too, might not go entirely to waste. They would save her. Or at least they would not have sinned for not trying.

They convinced her to hire herself out to clean houses. Any girl could do that, they said. Women in Beltsy cleaned their own houses—this was a source of pride, a permissible fury, a suffering to hold over a man's head—but they knew of Minna's misfortune (once upon a time, before her mother had departed, they might even have known Minna, as a young girl), and they gave her work. In their houses, on their floors, were the rugs Minna's mother had made—old now, stained, worn thin or to holes. Minna had not been taught to clean from the top down, and so she started with the rugs. She dragged them outside, shook them, beat them with brooms, shook them again, beat them harder, dragged them back inside. Then she quit the jobs, one by one, giving no explanation, even to herself. She would simply walk out, midmorning, and go home. She loved that sensation, of ceasing to try.

The Charity Women shook their heads. They were polite—they appeared patient—but Minna could see anguish in their faces: *what will you do with yourself,* they seemed to cry, *apart from shame us?* One suggested that Minna would be better off leaving Beltsy, and starting over. Eleven was not too old to start over. She had a cousin in Odessa, who knew of a situation, a wealthy, finely bred Jewess by the name of Galina Hurwitz. Wouldn't Minna prefer that?

Minna said nothing. She couldn't know what she preferred. Her father hadn't intended for her to be a maidservant, but what he had intended was never clear. He raised her to be his dead son, yet to cook for him—to be his gone wife, yet pure.

She served tea and mandelbrodt and showed the women out the door with crumbs still on their chins. And this exchange became as much a part of her routine as sweeping the steps or feeding the birds or boiling the chickens' eggs. If it weren't for her father's money dwindling, she thought she could go on like this for a long time.

Then she received a letter from her aunts informing her that as a minor, she held no rights to the house and that, as compensation for her upkeep, they would soon have to sell. It would "behoove" her, they advised, to find a more permanent "arrangement."

Then the explosions started, deep in the forest, far enough away you could only feel them, a feral shudder, and smell them, long after, if the wind blew right. A taste of coal but sweeter. A railroad, the women said, to connect east and west—though it would not stop anywhere near Beltsy; though they had taken young men to build it and promised no return. Ah, railroads, sighed the more worldly of the women, for they already knew these to be the ways of railroads everywhere. The explosions grew close enough that the tree line visibly trembled.

And then one day the birds were gone, and it seemed to make no less sense for Minna to leave than it did for her to stay.

So a decision was made. Or rather a decision was not not-made, and she came to Odessa by not not-coming. She believed— she had to believe—that her mother had left in the same way, without meditation or clear will. Even when she caught herself wondering if her aunts were right, and her mother had become a *kurve*, she thought of her as a good woman who'd been stolen. To believe otherwise would have been to give in to her grief; it would have been like starting to die herself. Which would have made her good, like her brother, but also gone. Which was the one thing she'd always succeeded in *not* being for her father. After her brother died, Minna stayed home for weeks—months. Other children knocked at the door to invite her outside to play, but she didn't go. She watched her father close up her mother's shop. He'd worked by his wife's side, done as he was told, learned well enough to keep the business going on his own. Instead, he began walking out of town, across the Low Bridge, toward the mines. At the mines there were no other Jews, no one to remind him of his shame, and the work left him with little time to go study at the *beis medrash*, where he would have had to see the other men, who slept, still, beside their wives. Soon he stopped going to *shul* altogether. Minna heard people say he'd lost his faith, but it seemed to her simpler than that. His sadness would lift sometimes, and there he would be, as before, strong and straight and seeming to know her when she spoke, but she could never predict when the next bout would come. He was like two men, the miner and the mined, the one who still believed his wife would return and the one who believed she was a whore—and the mined man was two men, too, one stripped empty, the other filled back up with rage. During the filling-up times, there was a way he looked at her, with a certain warning in his face, a kind of beggary: don't become your mother.

What would Minna say to him now? She'd reached the edge of Moldavanka, the wide, stately dusk of the wealthier Jewish streets, yet the basement was just behind her, its damp air etched into her bones, her exposure stuck to her skin. It had been waiting for her, she supposed, like the vultures who sat on the roofs around the market, stretching their wide, leathery wings. Her father had known to dread something like it; he'd looked at her with that dread ever since her mother left and now Minna had fulfilled it. She'd allowed them to inspect her like a horse.

But I can explain myself, she would say. Couldn't she? Couldn't she say that today was simply a means to an end, which would dissolve the means? For marriage, she thought, a lasting marriage, would erase disgrace. She even had a secret idea—secret enough she barely admitted it to herself—that marriage might be more like girlhood than her girlhood had ever been.

She could explain herself, yes. Her father—bewildered, looking at his hands—would consider her explanation. But, see? she would say. Look. She had been given her Look and now just look at her, running toward her duty, the east side of the street turning orange as she ran, the orange light on the limestone making laughter of the sober lamps and wrought gates. She was almost there, at her mistress's gate. She had not run since she was a girl, and already—see?—she was running, like a girl, her feet pounding, her ears ringing. The perfection of it, the ease, the hysterical grace through her bones, astonished her.

THREE

SHE threw open the door and immediately regretted it. Her hands, at least—she should have washed her hands. She must smell of that room, the woman's hands, the doctor's moth-eaten beard. There would be soot in her hair, weakness in her eyes, rank remainders of nakedness all about her.

But no one looked at her. The younger girl, Rebeka, was serving in her place, legs stuttering, small shoulders at her ears, trying with all her might to balance the tray in her left hand while pouring gravy with her right. The gravy spoon was old, soft silver, bent to an impracticable angle; she dropped it once, twice. Minna stood still and let her drop it a third time. The girl had to learn, now that Minna was leaving: first, how to do it right; then, how to fail and not fall apart. She would always be failing, even when she did everything right. When Minna took the tray from her shaking hand, Rebeka smiled gratefully, then ran from the room.

Galina and tonight's suitor had noticed nothing, of course. The decanter was already empty. They laughed heavily, gusting the candles with their breath. Minna ladled gravy over roast, then ladled more abundantly when she saw how it soaked in—Rebeka must have panicked and undercooked the meat. Only when Minna coughed, the rust air coming back up in her chest, did they look up.

"Ah!" Galina pounded the table. "Our heroine is back!"

The man pushed himself back from the table, but did not rise—as if briefly forgetting then recalling his own eminence. His nose was red, his jowls so low and swollen they looked stuffed with doorknobs.

"So this is the American bride!" he said, his eyes roaming Minna, up down, breast to breast. Normally she flinched at such attention, but tonight she found it amateur, laughable.

"You've passed," Galina said.

"I won't know until next week."

Galina flapped her eyelashes slowly. She'd layered on too much rouge, and not enough lip paint, and looked slightly confused—like a fruit that's started to rot on one end without even ripening on the other.

"You'll pass," she said.

"How couldn't she?" asked the man. He chewed laboriously as he spoke, his teeth packed with meat. "Look at those eyes!"

"She'll pass," said Galina.

"She'll go to America."

Galina paused for a second, as if she'd forgotten. As if Minna's going away hadn't been her idea in the first place. Then the look of surprise fell from her face, and she leaned in toward the man, raising her glass—

"To America!" she cried.

"America!" he called back. "The American bride!" And Galina and her suitor swayed toward each other and away, toward and away, like the music-box men who walked in pairs along the Bazarnaya and sang along to their cranking.

To call the men "suitors" was a charade, of course. They were no more looking to marry than Galina was young. She wasn't even rich anymore. Everything in the house had been acquired decades ago, by ancestors who were all dead—and much of that had been stripped away when the Russians came two years ago. Anything that shone, they'd taken. The glass they threw out the windows. They left only what was wood or dull metal and a collection of random objects, like the gravy spoon and the decanter. Galina might have begun to possess her remaining possessions then, to treat these candlesticks, for instance, as her own; instead she ordered Minna to stop polishing them—to stop wrapping them, between uses, in squares of felt wool. Leave be, she said, let the trinkets rot. She sank deeply, indulgently, into living among remains, cursing her grandparents for not warning her, refusing to go to their old box at the Opera House. She didn't care, she said, what anyone thought. She was cruel one day, punishing the house like a storm; the next she was frail, cowering. Once Minna had found her rocking on her knees, grabbing at her hair, her combs broken on the floor. "I can't do it," she cried in a high, small voice. "I don't know how." But when Minna touched a comb to her scalp, Galina wailed. She couldn't even bear Minna's hand on her arm. It was as if she'd been turned inside out, her nerves laid on top of her skin. All Minna could do was wait until she slept. Then she cut the largest knot from the back of Galina's head, and Galina, when she woke, looked refreshed, and never seemed to notice her missing hair.

"America!"

A woman like that could not marry.

"America!"

Or maybe, Minna thought—hopefully, righteously—it was the other way around. Maybe, once she'd married, a woman could not be like that.

"America!"

Galina and her man were hysterical now, nuzzling each other, howling. *America, America, America*. The word barreled through the room and Minna remembered another chorus, repeating itself, a tune her father used to sing to her on summer nights like this one. She would have cooked his dinner, then turned into his child. He'd stopped sending her to school by then—she must have been nine, maybe ten. Still he swept the kitchen floor and brought her milk in bed and she would lie there while he sang. He faced away, toward the window, his voice made fuller and warmer by the glass. La dada, la dada, la dada. There might have been words—she didn't remember. But she remembered the reason behind his song: to coax her to sleep even with the sky still bright. And she remembered, as the drunken revelers flooded the room in their serenade: the night she crept back out and saw her father in his rocking chair on the porch, moths beating around his head, holding a book to his face as the light thinned: the instant she realized there was a trick in his singing, that he wanted her to do what he couldn't do himself.

FOUR

"Can I help you?"

If the old woman guarding the door was looking for a secret word or signal, Minna didn't know it. She generally avoided the waterfront's narrow, stinking streets, where the paving stones fell away to rock and sand and men played dice in doorways. The docks left a smell in your hair, of mussels and beer. They were no place for an upright young woman about to start her real, upright life. But Minna had been called back to the municipal building yesterday, where she was given a photograph of her husband-to-be, an itinerary, kopecks for her travel, and this address. *For your papers,* the man said. *They'll take care of you.* Then, when she'd stared at him a second too long: *Run along now.* He gave a little wave of his wrist. As if Brody, Hamburg, New York, were just around the corner. *Run along.*

"Can I help you? *Devochka maya?*"

The hag's endearment made Minna suspicious, until she looked more closely: through her wrinkles, the woman was smiling. Minna glanced behind her, at the street, where a Chinese woman wobbled past on shoes made of stumps. Down a little alley, a sailor hawked stolen necklaces; down another, a painted lady beckoned a passerby. Usually the whores in their costumes made Minna's stomach drop out. She'd feel panic, shame, a shameful fascination—the set of a jaw, the curve of a nose, would make her start. But now she felt the photograph pressing into her waist, the fog-damp square of her husband-to-be, folded in two and tucked inside her bodice. Just as she'd left him.

"I'm here about papers," she said, suddenly bold, and this was all that was required. The door swung open. The old woman disappeared behind it.

Minna felt her way down a dark hallway of doors, all closed but one, at the end, where a yellow haze of kerosene and smoke trickled out into the hall. She stepped gently across the threshold, and squinted. Three men were playing cards around a table so small it looked like a board balanced upon their knees. When she coughed, the fattest one looked up.

"Let me guess," he said. "America."

And when, she wondered, would she stop introducing herself, excusing herself, delivering herself, with a cough?

"I was sent by Rosenfeld's Bridal—"

"Yes. Like all the Jewish girls. Going off to be brides. Well. Better than you're sold as a lady of the night, no? That is a worse fate, you agree?" The man's cheeks lifted to his eyebrows—a forced, pitying smile—then it was gone. His eyes hung open, the whites large and tired. His Russian was thick with Greek, it lifted in all the wrong places. "You know," he said. "You could pass for better than a Jew."

The other men looked up. One nodded. "Blue eyes," he said.

"Thin lips," said the other.

"Almost like there's no blood in there."

The first man chuckled. "Is that right?" he asked Minna. "You've got a frozen set of lips?" He tapped the table, considering. "So you want to be a nice German girl instead? I got the papers right here. No one ever picked 'em up. They're more legal than the ones I'd make you."

Minna looked at the man. He was being straight with her, she guessed, in his crooked way. She could be a nice German girl, with a nice new name. German was close enough to Yiddish— she would get by. The girl's passport would be her yellow ticket: it would let her drop out of her own life and into another. She couldn't pretend she'd never dreamed of doing just that. And what better place to begin than in this yellow room so thick with smoke it felt like a jar of honey, on this street of nobodies and everyones. Minna giggled; she couldn't help it; and as soon as she giggled she started to laugh: her mouth mawed open, saliva rose off her tongue. She couldn't remember the last time she'd laughed without faking. It tasted sweet, almost amorous. Then the men began cackling with her, showing their brown and gold teeth, pleased and jittery as hens. Minna shut her mouth. Her tongue felt suddenly filthy; she'd let in too much smoke. What kind of woman laughed in front of men like these? And what kind of man would be waiting for a German girl named whatever name they would give her? No one. Or the wrong someone. Whereas the man in the photograph in her bodice was waiting for Minna. Of course, she didn't know his name yet, and the picture was too grainy to clearly make out his features, but she could see that he looked down at the camera slightly, and that he stood in front of nothing but sky, as though he'd chosen to be photographed on a city rooftop. Which showed, it seemed to Minna, a certain confidence. Men like Galina's would pose themselves in armchairs, surrounded by whatever trinkets they'd managed to hold on to, samovars and candlesticks and oil paintings bunched together as on a stage set, suggesting they went on forever. Minna would not mind marrying rich, of course. But she imagined herself preferring a quieter, more self-assured kind of wealth. If a man stood on a roof, it was likely to be his roof. Which meant that now it would be Minna's. A roof and the house beneath it. A sink and running water. And beyond these comforts, beyond these dignities, the man was waiting for her as a man waited for a woman.

When she shook her head, the men let their laughter die. Their faces melted back into a collective fatigue. They looked disappointed, but not surprised—as if they'd known all along that she didn't have it in her to escape herself.

FIVE

ODESSA fog arrived like a street cat woke: suddenly; ominously. This time, it flew up from the docks, bringing rumors of violence. Osip Pirigov, who ran the shop below, came up the stairs to tell them. Osip was a small man with a habit of importantly, nervously, checking his pocket watch every few seconds—as if he was still allowed to practice law, as if someone might still be waiting for him at the Fankoni for a lunch of Italian pastry and wicked confidences. His nervousness was heightened by the news. His tongue seemed to shiver. "All Moldavanka is shuttered, the defense is on high alert, what you need from me buy now I'm closing I'm taking the family we'll be gone within the hour."

Galina laughed as Osip's watch came out and he slinked back downstairs. "And where will they go?" she said, stretching out on the tattered divan. "And when nothing happens? When nothing.

Happens. How stupid we'll be. Like every time. Like mice running from our tails."

It was true that since the last pogrom two years ago, none of
the warnings had materialized. Everyone hid and prayed, then
they came out a few hours later looking stunned and pleased and
also somehow guilty, and they went about their lives. And the
"defense forces," the *yeshiva* students with their wooden sticks,
looked vaguely embarrassed: a team of boys without a sport,
boys who'd never climbed a tree let alone beat anything.

Yet what could one do but prepare?

Minna locked the gate. She stood in the fog for a minute,
breathing, then hurried inside. She snuffed out the lights, closed
the shutters, drew the drapes. A queer, involuntary thrill gripped
her limbs, the same charge she used to feel just before a storm
in her father's house. He would always sense it, and chastise
her—there was wood to cut, and lightning to fear!—but Galina
snored on the divan and Minna indulged the moment. It was
ridiculous, arrogant, but she felt as if the rumors were for her,
to make her departure a necessity, a flight, instead of the unremarkable exit she'd been making for days now: a long, wobbly
slide through the city, off the continent, into the sea. She swept
the house, then mopped. She dusted what remained to dust. She
cleaned with the puerile joy of someone who did not have to
clean.

It was nighttime before she remembered Rebeka, in the cellar. She found her sobbing in the dark, draped in a washing she'd
abandoned, sheets and towels twisted round her arms and head
as if to make herself a ghost. Everything was soaking wet. The
girl shivered wildly. Minna dried her off, brought her up to the

attic, and tried to distract her from her fears: this is where you'll
sleep when Minna is gone; watch your head, yes, the ceiling's
too low to stand, even for a girl, it was the same for Minna when
she first came, you'll get used to it, your back will grow strong.
She talked like this, in a brothy, falsetto voice. She lay with Rebeka on the narrow cot, the girl's face mashed against her shoulder and thought, I am comforting her, I am giving her something
like kinship. But as Rebeka's sniveling slowed, it grew ugly and
deep and knocked like pebbles in her chest. She sounded like an
animal.

"Don't cry," Minna said. And now her voice had a sudden,
iron rod down its middle. "Shush shush. All the *children* will be
fine." Then, though it was a lie in every way that mattered: "You
live in a very beautiful house."

A̲LL night, nothing happened. But the next day, the streets
stayed empty, the rumors persisted, Osip Pirigov did not
return to his shop, all through Odessa and beyond, in the cellars
and barns and attics of the southern Pale, Jews waited. The second night passed the same way, the only sounds Rebeka's weeping. By afternoon, Galina was practicing old dance steps in the
dining room, stomping to her own needle-throated, tuneless
music, her fat arms embracing the air. The noise was making Rebeka cry again, which made Galina sing louder. Minna walked the
girl back up to the attic, twisted a rag around stockings for her
to hold as a doll, and half rocked, half shook her to sleep. Then
slowly, clandestinely, deliciously, she took out her photograph.
Tilted toward the window, he could almost be smiling; tilted

away, he seemed to frown. His age was indeterminable. The picture was too poor to make out much more than that he wore a beard—she couldn't even tell in what style—but he looked sincere, she thought, in any case. A little anxious, maybe, but that was probably being up on the roof.

Or maybe it wasn't anxiety, Minna thought, but impatience. Maybe her fiancé had been interrupted for the picture.

She liked this last idea. The man she would marry was a busy man. He would not bluster into the house like the suitors, as if they'd been standing outside all their lives, waiting for Galina to let them in. Minna did not think she could bear such demands. She imagined a good husband being a little bit like a good dog, the ones the wealthiest Russian girls walked on Nikolaev Boulevard: they walked alongside but not too close; they told everyone you were respectable without saying a thing. When Galina first urged her to sign up for Rosenfeld's—an idea that stunned Minna by becoming more than one of Galina's passing fancies—she'd said, *being married is like you can breathe for the first time.* Granted, Galina had never been married. But knowing the opposite of a thing often seemed to Minna to be the same as knowing a thing itself. Hunger, after all, was made of food, and thirst of water. On corners, she'd heard the beardless *maskilim* arguing about whether people had once been apes, yet their excitement seemed to her unwarranted—was it so difficult to imagine hair when you were covered in skin?

She named her husband Ilya, after the dairy boy. Ilya was older than Minna but not by much. He wasn't rich, but he was industrious; he pushed his cart with an ease that masked its weight. It was an ease Minna associated with his being a gentile. Ilya was so fearless, so certain of his place, that he didn't even bother trying to hide his fondness for a maidservant: no matter how busy he was, no matter how raggedly Minna was dressed, when he arrived and when he left, he always called her *fraylin* and blushed slightly as she dropped kopecks into his palm.

She was sorry for having stolen that bottle from him, for the doctor's visit. He would never think to suspect her. His toes turned inward as he walked.

D OWNSTAIRS, Galina was sulking. She wanted to play backgammon. "Please?" she asked, a dreary pleading in her eyes—which was only ritual, of course, the ritual of pretending Minna had a choice. As if they were friends, or sisters. When Minna first came, she'd fallen for it. She'd smiled and felt flattered and made a fool of herself being kind.

But Galina didn't want kindness. She sat at the head of the long table and directed Minna to sit at the other end—so far away Minna would have to lay out across the table to make her moves. Minna climbed onto the chair, set up the pieces, and commenced the fine art of letting Galina win. The board's felt was faded a pale, splotched green. Its edges were frayed. It had once belonged to Galina's mother's father's father—or at least this was what Galina said half the time. The other half, she said she couldn't remember.

A long time ago, Minna had hated Galina for not remembering. She'd hated the indulgence of it, the waste. She'd thought memories were something you could and should choose to keep, that they would not forsake or smother you like real people or things, that if you cared for them, they would be immortal and fixed.

Then she'd begun to lose her own faces. Smells. Songs. What did her father's morning voice sound like? Who was the owner of the hand that gently stroked her head once, along the main street, and what had Minna done that she'd expected to be hit instead? Who had taught her, patiently, how to write? Had there been a building on the square that was made of brick? Why had she started collecting pebbles when she was very young, polishing them with her skirt, one by one, and putting them to bed in an old tobacco tin?

She felt sometimes as though she were walking blindfolded through a room, using only her fingers to see, and someone kept moving the furniture.

Galina threw the dice, made a face, threw again. She captured two of Minna's pieces and hooted. If the mobs were coming, Minna thought, they would know which house to attack first. Yet she couldn't, somehow, summon fear.

Galina laid one of Minna's pieces on her tongue, stuck it out, and shouted, *Ahhhhhhh!*

The memories came back sometimes. She saw her mother's face, pale and unsmiling, a rift in her eyes, which looked away. Once, Minna remembered a woman in her father's house, a faceless, peasant-seeming Christian woman, her skirts wide, her hands coarse, and with those coarse hands the woman plucked every one of Minna's pebbles off the floor—they had been spread out in clumps, singing and laughing—and threw them in the river.

Minna didn't trust recollections like these. She suspected she jumbled things, connected the wrong events, dredged up what was convenient. Maybe she made things worse or better than they were. And then there were the episodes which disappeared again—though how could she be sure, of course, if she didn't remember them? She only sensed their missing, like one sensed a hair caught in one's mouth.

Galina won once, twice. The third time, unsatisfied by Minna's silent, shrugging concession, she shouted, "Victory!" and shoved the board off the table. "Whoops," she said drily as the pieces rolled and bounced across the room. Minna's muscles twitched, as if to action—*pick them up!* Yet her bones stayed heavy. Early afternoon was turning into late afternoon. Violence suddenly seemed an impossibility. The game pieces settled into the floor cracks. The day after tomorrow, she would board the train, lockdown or not.

Galina watched her across the table. "I couldn't help myself," she said.

"Of course."

"I'm sorry."

Minna didn't answer. The seconds made her feel brazen.

"You'll leave," Galina said.

"Yes."

"You'll hate me."

One of the black pieces stopped at the wall, on its edge. It blended almost perfectly into the sooted wainscoting; Minna squinted and it was gone.

"You'll tell people I was a witch. You'll go flouncing off to America telling your stories and I'll be the witch. You never talk now but you'll start to talk and you won't stop. You'll be one of those women. I'll be worse than I ever was. You'll say I made you leave. That's true, I'm making you leave. But you won't tell them I did it to protect you."

Minna's eyes snapped into focus. The black piece reappeared.

Galina slapped the table. "Look at me."

Her eyes were red like she'd been drinking, though she hadn't; the vodka had run out yesterday. She looked as she'd always looked, Minna supposed: inflamed, mean, ill with longing. But at her temples was a strange yellow hue, as if she'd smeared herself there with buttercups—and above it, wisps of frizzy gray hair. Galina, she realized, had tried and failed to dye her own hair. And with what? Minna felt a sudden, dangerous pity; she found herself wishing that Galina had asked for her help; she heard herself cough in apology. She wondered if this was how people felt when they saw their mothers grow old: sorry but repelled, repelled and sorry.

"I never let them touch you," Galina said.

Minna swallowed. This was true. Galina's men had tried to touch her. They started for the attic steps. They groped her at the table. And Galina had always stopped them. She had her own reasons, of course, her slippery pride, her need to prevail. Still, Minna lowered herself now to the floor.

"I've guarded your purity."

Minna started sweeping the pieces toward her. Part of her wanted to laugh, though nothing was funny, though it was becoming less funny by the second. She knew what Galina was referring to. They had never talked about the night of the pogrom: Minna hiding in the attic, balled up under her cot, listening to the men fall upon Galina; and Galina's growling screams, the disgusting noises she made, so disgusting Minna hated her more than she hated the men. She'd pretended, she'd told herself, that Galina didn't really mind. Galina had been giving up her body for years, as freely as the old women on the Gigantskaya Steps gave advice. What was left to defend? And she'd told herself there was nothing she could do. If she went downstairs, they would not leave Galina alone, their appetites would simply widen. She thought of them like that, like stomachs instead of men: it was easier to let them go on if they were headless, helpless; it was easier to stay in the attic.

Minna wasn't proud of these thoughts. She wasn't proud that she'd used them again in the years since, when the noises haunted her. She wished that night would leave her like other memories, lose its way and be gone. Then she wouldn't have to feel Galina's gaze on her now and know what she was seeing. Minna's humility had been her one weapon, her mask. To admit that she contained cruelty, bottomless seas of cruelty, was to give up her advantage.

"See?" Galina said. "Look at you. You're too old now, too slow. How can I keep you? It's not dignified anymore." She picked up a game piece from the floor near her chair and pretended to toss it to Minna—but too hard and too high, so that it landed on Minna's back. So that Minna was a horse all over again.

"For whom?" Minna asked impulsively. She saw, suddenly, that to leave here, she would have to do more than walk out the door. The Russian mobs were not coming. Her debt was not shrinking. She was on her knees again, on the floor. The game piece felt impossibly heavy through her dress. The truth was, the whole truth, if anyone should want to know the truth: after the men raped Galina and broke all the china and stole all the silver, after they had gone and Minna had stopped her ruse of having been asleep, after she crept downstairs and found Galina's door locked and went around surveying the damage, this was what she'd thought: Why didn't they take the brooms? Or the pots or pans or buckets or spatulas, or anything at all of use? Why should everything, always, stay the same for Minna? She had lived as her father's daughter and then she'd lived as Galina's servant, and none of her tools had changed, or her perpetual missing. She missed her father, yes, but when she'd lived with him, she had missed her mother, or at least the idea of her. And before her mother left, she must have missed something else, whatever infants missed when they were slapped through with air.

"For whom is it not dignified?" she asked, and now she did not bother hiding her disgust. She would not, she would never, miss Galina. She made her voice louder. "For whom?"

Galina stared at her. She was not sure, Minna could see, whether she was meant to answer the question, or skip straight to punishment. And there was no one to tell her. All the people who might have told her were dead. She looked, as she often did, as if she wanted to ask Minna's advice. Outside, there was the long silence. Something like mourning passed through Galina's eyes. She stood. She lifted her skirts slightly, as if to curtsy. Then she kicked, and the game pieces flew, but her boot barely grazed Minna's leg.

O NE memory Minna had never lost: the sound of her brother's cries, like chickens being chased by a fox. They changed his name three times, trying to trick Death. These were her father's sisters; her mother had already disappeared. They rubbed the baby's back with rye bread. They poured salt and pepper into their palms and lifted him over the stove, into the chimney. But he never stopped crying until he stopped breathing. And then they would not speak of him, and they would not let Minna speak of him. She had not been so blessed, they said, that she could afford to tempt misfortune. She was not so good that she could complain. She was not so smart that she would remember, anyway.

SIX

THE fog lifted. Minna tried not to be disappointed, though she'd begun to nurture an image of herself departing the next day in its silent shroud. She tried not to be annoyed that the talk of an attack had passed, too; that the glitter in the streets wasn't broken glass but the fog's residue, lit with sun; that she had not been anointed a refugee.

She made herself dress and join the procession of fellow Jews toward the market. They walked slowly, heavily, for there had been no declaration of peace this time, only a gradual, collective fatigue with the situation, a calling off of waiting.

Minna meant to plod accordingly, yet she felt her steps quicken. She tried to keep her head down, like the others, but in the aftermath of the fog the city looked radiant, every window gleaming, the limestone columns and steeples and arches so white they appeared weightless. She reached the edge of the market square and here was radiance, too: apricots and cherries pouring into bins, breads throwing their powder, the song of carts coming to a stop.

She wasn't prepared to feel anything but relief at leaving Odessa. When she first arrived, the limestone buildings had reminded her of the mines, and of her father's death, but they'd also looked beautiful, which made her ashamed. She didn't know then—she didn't know yet—that pleasure was its own necessity, as grimly serious as mourning. So she'd buried it, training herself to see the stone as her father might have, creating her own system: white, strong as marble; green, prone to crumbling; yellow, easiest to work. And don't forget, he told her. All holes were the same hole, once you'd been down below. Odessa, *pearl by the sea*, was only earth turned inside out.

It had been easy, this way, to think the city poor and temporary as herself. Yet there were the curved balconies adorned with half-naked statues. The gargoyles brooding at the roofs. The polished horse hitches and heavy railings and ornate gates. Here were the old, established cats, sunning themselves underfoot.

She rested her fingers in Galina's coin purse and counted the money by touch.

She was at the fish stall now, facing the fish girl with her long, curved knife, her admonishing *What?* Minna felt a sudden urge to tell her about Rosenfeld's: to boast—to beg—to ask her to come with her. She paused, imagining the girl smiling, saying yes. She imagined them boarding the boat together.

But the girl had already gone back to cutting heads for broth; she swatted a fly at her ear. It was nonsense, Minna told herself. This city. This tired, dry square, which she'd traversed countless times only to leave, every time, with nothing of her own. This girl. They'd spent years exchanging fish for money and never bothered to introduce themselves, or even to say thank you, or good-bye. And the girl's hands stank, Minna guessed, in a way that lemons could not solve.

What? the girl asked again, when she looked up to find Minna still there.

Usually Minna asked for mackerel or halibut or perch, but she found herself pointing at a cheap, bearded bullhead. The girl sniffed and obliged. Minna took her parcel of fish and headed for the vegetables. Radishes, she thought, Galina would want radishes tonight, for no suitor was coming, always radishes when she was morose. And chocolate. And vodka. But Minna didn't move to the vegetables. And she didn't walk toward the chocolate man, worrying his tarp against the sun. Instead she was leaving the square. She took thirty kopecks from the purse for a bottle of vodka—that, Galina could not do without. Then she hid one ruble in her left stocking, and one in her right, and she used what was left to buy herself a pour of sunflower seeds into her apron and a hair comb from a peddler on Komitetskaya whose wares she'd never let herself look at. A small comb, but not the smallest.

S HE was almost home when she saw the *zogerke*. She averted her eyes quickly, but too late—the woman was broad-shouldered, her wig elaborate, her perfumes vast: as she swayed toward Minna, she resembled a fat hen. The *zogerke* was the one at the Old Synagogue who prayed for the women who didn't know how, and showed them when to make their faces sad, or hopeful, or ashamed, and who, when she was off duty, waddled through the streets admonishing girls like Minna who never showed up at *shul* anymore to let her admonish them. For a time, when she'd first arrived, Minna had attended. She'd gone every third week, the arbitrary interval Galina permitted her, and tried, vaguely, to follow the *zogerke*'s directions, her famously agile nose. But Minna wasn't looking for prayer, or obedience. All she wanted was to hear the sounds she'd heard in Beltsy. Yet the songs, it turned out, were different here. Their tunes were altered, their moods heightened; they sounded foreign to her ears. And the long weeks away made Minna feel like a stranger. Which she was. So she'd stopped going. And now every so often the *zogerke* would spot her in the street and grab her arm and lecture her on the dangers of faithlessness. Minna would nod, and cower, and placate, and nod, and wait until the *zogerke* was satisfied. But today she looked straight at the woman, and saw that her jeweled hairpin was missing most of its jewels.

"We do not see you anymore," the woman said.

"It's true," Minna said.

"Have you been to another *shul*?" The woman frowned. It was a drastic frown, the corners of her mouth seeming to drop to her neck, one of her many expressions that were meant to be seen from a distance. Yet she stood close enough she might have taken a bite out of Minna's ear.

"Well? *Have* you?"

"No."

The *zogerke* raised her thick eyebrows, lowered them, pushed her lips together as if sucking on something. "No?"

"No," Minna said again. She pointed with her free arm as if at something just around the corner. "I'm going to America now," she said. Then she twisted her other arm out of the *zogerke*'s grip and watched the woman's face make its expression of shock.

T HAT night, Minna showed Rebeka the hidden shelf in the attic where she could store her "personal items." She knew the words were unkind as she said them. The girl had nothing. Minna could have made up for it by saying she had almost nothing herself. Yet she didn't. She felt as if she were already living her new life, as if this moment with Rebeka was already a story she was telling and Rebeka was Minna and if Minna was not careful, the Minna who was telling the story would never be able to leave the Minna in the story behind.

She walked Rebeka down the stairs, showing her the middle-of-the-night route. Step here, not there. Not here, there.

She showed her the spoon in the cupboard. A baby spoon Galina must have forgotten, too small to fill the mouth but still. This was the way to eat their leftovers—scooping, silent, never touching the plate.

She showed her an old pillowcase, a scissors, how to cut a strip from the edge, no wider than a quarter inch. This way it will last. Now wrap it around your pinky finger. Now clean out your ears.

Outside, the air was cold, the sky dense with stars. The houses across the street steamed lightly, still breathing out the fog. The night smelled of moss and wheat and fish. Always fish. She thought of the girl's hands, and of the woman's hands. Later, she would miss the fish, but now it sickened her. She felt superior, civilized. The stolen rubles were hot in her stockings. She turned to Rebeka.

Never believe her. Don't believe that she loves you, don't believe that she hates you. Don't believe that she is rich, don't believe that she is poor. Don't believe that you are safe, or that you will die. Believe in your own flesh. Guard it, even if the way seems wrong.

Minna's voice had started to shake. She sounded like the *zogerke*, she thought.

She stopped talking and showed Rebeka how to lock the gate.

M INNA was half asleep when she felt footfall. Hands grabbing her shoulder, her neck, her arms. She screamed, once, before she recognized the smell: vodka, perfume, salt.

Galina hauled her down the stairs, through the dark of the kitchen. Minna's hip hit the wall, the large cast-iron pot. She shielded her face with her free hand. Then she was being dragged down the hallway; she knew they'd reached the end when she tripped on the threshold. She caught herself with one hand. Galina yanked her back up and pushed her onto the bed. In the light from the street, Minna saw through Galina's nightgown: purple and white, hair and ducts and fat. Galina pounced. She grabbed Minna's hair, pulled her by the scalp down onto her back. Minna fought to get free, but Galina was twice her size; she set a knee between Minna's legs and pressed upward. Minna wondered if this was vengeance, or envy, or some intimacy she didn't know the name for. She shouted, but Galina's fist filled her mouth, tasting of alcohol, then Galina paused, as if considering—her knee pressed harder, like the stone wall Minna used to straddle in secret—until at last, the fist withdrew, and Galina fell onto Minna. She lay there for a while, limp as a victorious wrestler, her nose digging into Minna's collarbone, her hair covering Minna's face. Then she lifted her head, and looked at Minna, her face bewildered. She kissed Minna's cheek, moved off her slightly, and said, "Shh. Sleep. There's still time."

I N the morning, in the kitchen, Rebeka had made Galina's breakfast by herself. She stood facing it, nodding her small head, moving her lips. She was counting, Minna realized, devising a system for getting the tray right. She would have felt the banging last night, from the cellar, through the walls. She might have heard Minna's shouts.

"Tea," the girl whispered. "Tea. Cream." Her head bobbed frantically. Her hair was so thin it barely disguised the outline of her skull. The girl loved her, Minna realized. But she knew better than to take it personally. "Boo!" she cried, to give Rebeka the fright of a child, so that she gasped, and turned, and laughed—and could be left.

G ALINA gave Minna one ruble, a coin purse, and a parcel wound in a sheet.

"It's yours," she said, her voice smooth, her eyes innocent. Minna's right wrist hurt from her fall; she took the sheet in her left hand. Inside was a pillow, she could tell, and something else, a bit heavier.

"It's yours," Galina said again, and it was difficult to tell if she thought she was bestowing a gift upon Minna, or simply making a statement of fact. This was the pillow Minna had brought with her when she came. She had made it herself, in a room full of goose feathers and women who were trying to make her a better girl. The Charity Women had sent her, just before she left for Odessa—as if a last chance at something, though she was committed by then to Galina—and because she knew it was the end, Minna did as she was told. She'd stripped the feathers from their stems and stuffed the pillow and sewed it, though not so well that it kept its down, not so well that the Russians bothered splitting it open. It was the pillow Galina used between her knees when they ached.

Minna said nothing. She concentrated on Galina's neck: on the fat folds, the age folds, the drink folds.

"Please," Galina said. She snatched the pillow and sheet back, then shoved them at Minna again—into her chest this time, so that Minna had to use both her arms, so that she looked like she was carrying something dear to her. "Come. Take it. Go. It's yours."

THE name Ilya was in her mind before Minna realized she was staring at him. To think the name was not odd—she had been thinking *Ilya* every time she looked at the picture—the oddness was his actual presence, here on Staroryeznichnaya: Ilya the dairy boy next to his cart, staring back at her. Minna was halfway to the train station, her parcel white and damning in her good hand. He wouldn't deliver to Galina's for another two days;

she hadn't expected to see him again, especially not like this, he making his daily rounds, she making her exit. She had let her foolish fantasy grow more elaborate and far-fetched. And it was foolish, she saw now. Ilya was not the man in the picture. He did not stand tall. His shoulders—not broad—pressed forward even when he wasn't pushing his cart. His eyes were so round even a poor photograph could not miss them, round in the way children draw eyes, like notions of eyes, unprotected and lit. He didn't even wear a beard. And he was not impatient, nor particularly industrious, he was simply kind: the kindness with which he looked at Minna made her face fill with blood.

"*Fraylin!*"

He was still two yards away. She could still turn around, backtrack, take the next street over. With his cart, he wouldn't catch her.

"*Fraylin!*"

Yet she was walking toward him, holding her parcel slightly behind her. And she was smiling—a frightful, aggressive smile that made her cheeks shake.

"Ilya." And all over again, saying the name drew her back into daydream: a new one: here: she was exactly here, greeting her husband-to-be. There was no journey to make, no unknown man standing on an unknown roof in an unknown city. He was here, smiling back at her. They would not live on an upper floor, but neither in a cellar. He would sell his milk; she would learn to sew properly at last; she would fashion a burlap mannequin, place it in the window, and start a business. Their existence would be remarkably normal—the kind of normal Minna had never even bothered to hope for.

"You're going on a trip?"

Yes. But Minna couldn't nod. Her capacity for delusion amazed her: that she could go on thinking these thoughts not an arm's length away from him, that she could so clearly see a world that would never exist. She was like the women they let out at the asylum in the afternoons, who weaved their way around the grounds in gowns as blank as their minds. Only Minna was worse, because she wasn't crazy. Yes, was the answer. Yes, Minna was going on a trip. She could not escape her escape, which seemed absurd suddenly, the dangers exaggerated, the solution drastic.

"You don't feel well?"

His eyes raked the parcel, which felt suddenly heavy in Minna's hand, heavy enough to pull her sideways and down. She had the urge to follow it, to sit in the street and cry. It was too late, of course. She could not go back to the municipal building now and correct herself, admit that she had lied, say yes, yes I work on my knees, no my "events" do not come every month, they are mysteries, I've gone ill-fed for too long, no I do not keep kosher or take the *mikvah* bath or perform charity. I do none of it. I don't even fear punishment for doing none of it.

"You're pale."

"Oh," said Minna. "I feel fine." She reached into her new coin purse and extracted one kopeck: the price of the milk bottle she'd stolen.

Ilya did not look at her. He seemed to sense that she did not want to be looked at. He seemed to know what she was doing, and to have forgiven her long before, which only made her fingers on the coin sweat more viciously. She held it out, and when he didn't move to receive it, she grabbed his wrist and pushed the coin into his palm. "I'm late," she said, with force.

Ilya looked up. He knew everything, she saw—the milk, her fantasy, the fact that she wasn't actually late. Yet miraculously, awfully, he forgave her all this, too. His wrist was still in her grasp, his fingers resisting the coin by doing nothing. They were clean fingers—and smelled, she guessed, of his cart's wooden handle—and knew how not to break hundreds and thousands of glass bottles—and she hated them, suddenly, for allowing her to do what she was doing, for thinking she knew anything at all of what she wanted.

"You mustn't be late," he said. And there was no condescension or even amusement in his round eyes, which left Minna with no choice but to pull away, pretend not to hear the coin fall to the ground, and walk toward the train, as she'd promised she would.

SEVEN

"On a ship this large," the man shouted, "the sickness is worse! The mind cannot perceive the sea, only the body knows its swells. The body knows the swells like a child knows its desires. But the adult forgets! The mind feels tricked, the mind is stubborn, the mind refuses to believe. It is this resistance, this denial, that leads the body into sickness!"

The man went on, his rant sweeping across Minna like a foghorn. She didn't know what he meant to say exactly, and she didn't particularly care: anything to distract from the terrible thunder of the engine. She stood in front of his bunk, holding on to her own up above, the wood trembling in her hands, the floor trembling under her feet, everything trembling as if the ship was about to split apart, and yet the man went on, dancing his fingers through the dank air. He claimed to have been a fisherman once, to have worked on boats no bigger than this bunk, but Minna didn't believe either was possible: the platforms were so narrow you had to lie perfectly straight, and so short you couldn't lie straight without kicking the next passenger's head; and the man's fingers were thin, too delicate to do rough work. She admired this about him. She admired, too, that he wore a vest, a scarf, a cuffed shirt, and a handkerchief, all of it layered and buttoned and tucked with great care. He was a small, compact man. His beard was trim. Next to him stood a cage holding two white doves. He claimed he was a magician now, but Minna didn't believe this either—or if it was true she decided it must be a hobby, a gentleman's diversion. He looked like he could afford better than steerage. Minna had had plans to do the same herself; with all her kopecks combined she'd been ready to pay second class, an indulgence but why not: she would ride in style, as Galina liked to say, and land in style; she would make a clean, ladylike first impression. But at the German border there had been a string of outbuildings in the forest, a fence made of wire, teenage boys shouldering rifles—the kind of station only the Germans could make look official. Payment was optional, the guards grinned. You could pay or you could strip.

Minna considered stripping. She had already done it once, after all, in front of strangers whose own legitimacy was doubtful. There must be, she thought, a law of firsts in such circumstances, a limit to humiliation. Then she saw a group of naked women. She saw the boys with the guns peeing on sticks and shoving the sticks into the women's faces.

She paid the toll. And what she had left she spent at the docks in Hamburg, on oranges and apricots and long, heavy, powdery grapes, then on chocolate and walnut brittle, then at the last minute, reprimanding herself for her frivolity, on dehydrated biscuits. Then she ate all of it except the biscuits before the boat even boarded. And so here she was, in steerage, with nothing but biscuits and the sunflower seeds she'd bought her last day in Odessa. She hadn't expected it to be so foul. She hadn't expected to long for the hard cot in Galina's attic.

"You must teach your mind humility!"

Minna had been warned, like all the single girls, against talking to strangers. She'd been warned on the train and on the roads and at the checkpoints and on the docks, by mothers and rabbi's wives and women who had nothing better to do than shake their fingers at her. *Talk to strangers, you'll become a slave. You'll wind up in places you never meant to be. Brazil. Texas. Evil places. You'll do things you'd never do in your worst nightmares.* But Minna knew the kinds of girls who'd get themselves caught in such a mess. Girls who were taught suspicion, but only of evil spirits; doubt, but only that they would reach heaven. Even before she left the village, Minna hadn't been one of these girls. Her father would say, as their fathers said, "This is done, this is not done," but then, unlike their fathers, he would promptly do the opposite himself. He'd lost his willpower; he swung between drink and abstinence, cleanliness and filth. And so Minna learned that it was *this* world you couldn't trust. She developed instincts. And this man, her instincts told her, was not out to enslave her. Through the cage, with a thin wrist, he stroked his doves; his hands were absentminded, languorous, another sign that he'd known leisure. Galina would call him a *feygele* and Minna thought it could be true.

"The humbled mind lets go, and is released!"

That the man spewed nonsense didn't bother Minna. Just the

opposite, in fact; it made him seem wholly indifferent to the dim squalor around him. The engine roared, the people were poor, an accordion wobbled, a baby screamed—yet the magician was somehow insulated. Exempt. Respectable. Which was how Minna intended to be.

B Y the second day, the floor was slick with vomit. People argued: it was something in the water; no, it was a storm; it was always like this; no, it wasn't usually this bad. The ones who spoke in Yiddish or Russian, Minna understood, but she couldn't see how their debates would be of any use. Each time the boat tilted, the sick passengers groaned with the engine. By the fourth morning, they'd started to cry. They muttered unintelligibly, or in foreign languages. The air was too warm—it smelled of rye and urine. A baby died. From light to dark to light, the hold was the same, a vibrating, steamy swamp. A small band of passengers ferried the sick out to the fresh air of the deck and threw buckets of seawater across the floor. Out they would go, in they would come again, led by a man with a bandage wrapped around his head who seemed to think that such ministrations made a difference. They didn't. People kept vomiting. The air vibrated and steamed. Minna's head felt like a child's toy being cranked, its springs about to explode. She waited for the nausea to find her. She swung her head left and right, pursuing vertigo. Only the well, she thought, would go mad.

Yet each morning, she was well. She began to feel as she had in the village, surrounded by other children yet unable to play their games, to follow the rules. There were hundreds of rules.

Always count each other like this—"Not-one, not-two, not-three . . ."—
so as not to entice the Angel of Death. Don't walk backward; for every
step you take backward, your parents will burn in hell for as many
years. Playing with fire will make you a bed wetter. Eating the first crust
of bread will make you stupid. Minna knew—knowing was her
problem—that it was all laughable. She told Galina once about
the counting and Galina nearly fell over cackling. "The backward
Yids!" she cried, and Minna ended the story there. She never
told her how strongly she'd wanted to join the other children. If
she believed in the rules, she'd thought, if she believed in God,
obedience would come easily. If she feared, like the others, she
would be free of choice, and therefore of sin, and she would no
longer have to fear. Yet something in Minna had resisted. There
was her sense that the other children sneered at her behind her
back. There was her stubbornness—her pride—her father's
pride. There was her tendency to stand apart: what her aunts
called her dim-wittedness.

She sat hunched in her bunk, facing the wall, cracking sunflower seeds between her teeth. She couldn't hear the crack; she
only knew it had occurred when she felt a stabbing in her gums,
and tasted the hull fall away from the bitter seed, and smelled, or
imagined she smelled, over the bile, something of land. She spit
the hulls into her palm and tossed them over her shoulder. The
ship bucked, the bunk bruised her bottom. Minna continued to
feel immoderately, noxiously sober. She thought of the "doctor"
recommending she put on weight "en route" and wanted to cry.
She wondered if there were other Rosenfeld girls on the ship.
She'd looked for them on the docks; she felt she would recognize
them, somehow, and that they would recognize her. But most of

the girls on the docks had been huddled together, in packs. Other Rosenfeld girls would probably ride second class. They would not have succumbed, like Minna, to grapes and chocolate.

She pulled out her photograph.

In the dark of her bunk, the picture held new possibilities. She covered his hands with her thumbs and liked the way he kept them in his pockets: he was a man with his own secrets, his own vices, a man who wanted but did not need a woman. She pressed two fingers, vertically, to the edge of the picture: a house, tall and lean and white; her longer finger the chimney. She hid the man's feet and liked that he was not so tall that he could afford to slouch. She took out her new comb and, as he watched, tugged the snarls out of her hair.

Yet sometimes she couldn't help but glimpse the photograph unembellished. She saw details she'd missed, or chosen to miss, when he was first handed to her. The hands were empty and nervous, hanging awkwardly at his sides. The pants were too short. The toes pointed outward. The knees were locked.

She folded him back up, slid him away again, gone.

But on the fifth day, the problems worsened in front of her eyes. The pants seemed up to his knees now. His neck was goose-like, shrivelly, to match his toes. He was fearful and ugly.

In desperation she set Galina's parcel in her lap. She had saved this pleasure as long as she could, and she unwrapped the sheet gravely, methodically, pretending her fingers belonged to someone more delicate, taking time, at each unfolding, to smooth any wrinkles. She had nothing but time. But Galina's work was hasty, nothing more than a rough winding of cloth, and the contents spilled out before Minna was prepared: stuffed in with the pillow was a fall of silk, the color of . . . she held it up, then brought it down, trying to see without drawing attention to herself. Lilac. She was almost certain. She found a neckline, trimmed with lace. A hem, more lace. A white satin belt. Attached to the belt was a note, in Galina's surprisingly graceful handwriting, the product of private tutors: *When my mother wore this, it was very modern, very up-to-date.*

"Help."

The man stood in front of Minna's bunk, the right side of his head and jaw wrapped in a bandage—which was simply a rag, she saw, blackened with filth. He was the one who led the "bearers," as Minna had come to think of them. In and out they went, carrying the sick, though it never helped: the patients didn't revive; the babies didn't stop dying. In his arms was a girl, Minna's age perhaps, or younger, or older—it was impossible to tell anymore how old anyone was.

Minna stuffed the wedding dress into the pillowcase and hid the bundle behind her. "I don't feel well," she said. "And my hand hurts." Which was true, but barely—her sprain from her final night at Galina's was almost healed.

"I can't hear you," called the man, "and I don't care what you're saying. Get down from there and help. The only person who's done less is your downstairs neighbor, and he's got his filthy pigeons for an excuse."

The man was not large. He didn't look particularly strong. He was working hard, it was clear, to hold up the girl. Yet Minna felt an odd immobility, a heady delight at staring down at him. His Yiddish was the old kind that sounded like a song, the kind spoken by the oldest men in the smallest villages, yet he was young, so it only made him seem more self-righteous. Minna couldn't help herself. She leaned down and shouted: "What happened to your face?"

He narrowed his eyes. "You would like to know?"

"Yes!"

"Come down and I'll tell you."

"I'd rather not."

"I can't hold her up forever."

Minna shrugged. Where she'd come up with this game, what she wanted from it, she didn't know. All she knew was that she didn't want to work on the man's useless assembly line. She didn't want to work for anyone but herself, in her own house; and even then, not carrying work. Certainly not carrying other people. She willed herself to throw up, but her stomach was calm as a stone. Then the man had suddenly handed off his burden and jumped halfway up the bunk to face her. He yanked off his rag and glared. Minna flinched. But there was no blood, no deformity. There was only the man's forehead, pouring sweat, and a vague imbalance to his face, so vague she could not at first locate it, until he shook his head roughly and she saw: one earlock swung at his cheek, but the other was missing. Only a few uneven hairs were left, ugly as chewed thread, sprouting from a patch of raw, red skin.

"There you are. Your Majesty. The Russians had no shears. They used rocks to shred it off." Then, to himself, "Forgive me, God, I use my wounds as money." He gripped the bunk and pulled himself closer. He might be crazy, she thought, the kind of crazy that compulsively shared the most personal business, like the drunk who used to roam through Beltsy, stooping into people's faces and listing off his sins. "Say what you think," he commanded Minna through clenched teeth. "Say you think it was our fault. You think we did not resist. We asked for it. We are weak. We are men of air. Say it."

Minna had heard of synagogues where the men had gone on praying even as the windows were smashed. In Balta, two towns over from Beltsy, there had been a pregnant woman who volunteered herself to be shot, as long as her other children were spared. But Minna's thought, right now, was that she hadn't thought about these events—she hadn't thought about anything—as thoroughly as the man accused her of thinking about him. Who could bear to? She thought, despite herself, that she liked being called *Your Majesty*.

Then she saw the man anew, as if she were looking down on a forest; she saw how in the midst of his thick hair and thick beard, his clearing of flesh was perverse. Like a cat's asshole suddenly exposed.

"Or would you rather not, Your Majesty? Would you rather come down from there and be what you are?"

"Stop," she said. "Please stop."

What she did next, she knew, would look like charity to a bystander. Even she would look back one day and think she'd acted out of a sudden, selfless grace. But in truth she did it out of desperation: she simply couldn't stand to look at his repulsive wound.

Galina's sheet, between her teeth, tasted of lavender and vodka; it tasted, compared to the air in the hold, almost appetizing. She tore a strip from end to end, wrapped it quickly around the man's head, and tied it off tight.

He didn't thank her, but neither did he protest. He looked less crazy, more ashamed.

So she had ruined her trousseau. It had been pitiful anyway.

As Minna carried the sick, she did not look at the bandaged man. He was the bearers' Moses, but Minna refused to be one of his followers. She was determined not to look apologetic, or poor, or contented with her lot. She adopted a birdlike way of carrying so that her underarms would stay dry, and tried for a face like Galina's grandmother, who'd stared coolly out from the gilded portrait above the mantel, whose lips looked as if they'd never been apart. Minna's partner in carrying was a Belarusian laundress named Faga, a large woman who talked about the mother she'd left behind, the cousins who awaited her in Chicago, the spoons she carried in her dress, the candlesticks she kept lashed in her bootlaces. Faga belched and laughed and cried as she talked, as though it was always the first time she was hearing about her own life. A useful skill, Minna supposed, to be entertained by oneself, yet also embarrassing and unbecoming. And Faga's seeming familiarity with everyone they encountered, her easy smile, her lack of apology for her wide hips and shelf of a bosom, all this produced in Minna a discomfort she could bear only by turning it to judgment. Faga's calves were thick with fat and candlesticks. She carried a rag at all times, not a handkerchief but a rag, to wipe her nose and hands, to soak up the sweat from her brow. Her arms were thick as a man's, as if she intended to keep doing this kind of work.

"Watch you don't trip!" Faga called gaily as Minna backed out through the hatch, her fingers slipping in the wet armpits of a girl whose skin had begun to resemble the ship's drinking water.

The sickest girls were the quiet ones, the ones Minna was not—girls whose husbands or brothers or fathers had gone ahead and sent for them. Their main fear when they'd boarded the ship was enslavement in a strange, tropical land. Now they mumbled that they wanted to die. They wanted a cup of tea. Milk. Slivovitz. Every so often, they gained focus and became aware of the hands on them. Their heads flew up. Their limbs stiffened. They speared Minna and Faga with their eyes.

"There," Faga would say. "There there, we're almost there." Though they were never almost anywhere but the place they'd been half an hour ago. Each group was allowed only a set amount of time in the fresh air. Then they were carried in again, and another group brought out. These were the rules, dictated by Moses.

The work made Minna hungry. Her biscuits had molded, but she ate them anyway, until Faga saw and threw them overboard. Then Faga brought out her own biscuits, a special recipe, she said, that her mother had made before Faga left. Faga broke every one in two and gave Minna halves and a pocket to store them in and they went on working, like that, the biscuits divided precisely between them. It seemed to Minna the kindest thing anyone had done for her in a long time. And though Faga's mother's biscuits were heavy as mallets, and made as much noise when they broke between the teeth, they never turned moldy.

In she and Faga went, out they went. Minna learned how many steps it took to cross from the deck's railing to the hatch. She knew, heading back out into the gray glare, how thinly to squint her eyes to prevent blindness. She could balance on one leg, hold up half a body, and kick a latch closed all at once. In, she held her breath. Out, she inhaled deeply. She would forget to keep her lips closed and catch herself slack-jawed, then shut her mouth until she forgot again.

A woman was found, her skirts soaked in blood. At first the bearers thought it was a miscarriage, and tried to stanch it with straw, but when they brought the woman outside they saw that the blood was brown, sometimes black, and fell away in clumps like wet paper. Three men fought over who would summon the ship's doctor—each one wanted to see cabin class, each one must have dreamed he might be adopted and never have to return—until Faga swatted them apart and went herself.

The doctor was mustached, his cheeks and collar clean. His Russian was pure. He looked tired but in a temporary way, as if he'd been playing whist in his cabin for too long. He knelt next to the woman's head, his lips near her ear—an intimate gesture, Minna thought, until she saw his nostrils convulse and realized he was simply avoiding the woman's lower half, from which an unspeakable stench was rising. The woman could not make words. No one knew her, or where she was from. As the doctor asked her questions, she nodded her head or shook it, or nodded and shook it at once, her mouth open so wide, baring so many teeth, that her pain began to look like hilarity.

The diagnosis: the woman had been so appalled at the lack of privacy on the ship, she hadn't emptied herself since they left Hamburg. She hadn't even urinated until last night, when her bladder began to tear. By now it was too late. Her bowels had ruptured.

The other burials had been infants. Their parents had carried them to the rail, swaddled in the cleanest available linens. Falling, they could have been bundles like any other. Feather beds packed with rolling pins. China. A mortar and pestle.

But this woman could only be handled from the waist up. The men lifted her by the arms, dragged her to the edge, and heaved her up until she was performing a backbend over the rail. The dark, clotting stench trailed after her. The men rocked her slowly, pushing her farther out each time, and when they could no longer reach her arms, or chest, or waist, someone grabbed an oar.

She was unconscious, Faga assured Minna, though she did not look certain; her hand, on Minna's shoulder, began to shake.

She must have had a weak bowel to begin with, the doctor said. But no one was listening to him anymore.

A woman, falling, was unmistakably a woman. Her boots pointed like a ballerina's slippers. Her dress flew up around her stained thighs. It might have been better, Minna thought, if they could have undressed her. If they'd made her naked, as she so hated to be, she might have been spared from recognizing the falling woman as herself.

I N they went, out they went. Minna felt a growing gratitude for the sick passengers' abundance, and for their permissiveness. They never felt any better, yet they let the bearers go on, lifting, struggling, bearing. So that the bearers, at least, could feel better. For this, Minna was beginning to suspect, was the true purpose of their work. It might be dull, and repetitive, and irrational, but the act of carrying afforded those who carried a certain pride, even a pleasure. Even Minna experienced this. She let herself indulge it. She found herself itching, during breaks, to get back to work, to go in and out at the prescribed times and pick up the prescribed people and set them down again and start all over. Only in the moments before her break, when she felt the toll of the lifting on her arms and back, did Minna see the cruelty in the system. She would find herself, in a moment of exhaustion, slapping a girl's cheek to wake her. Or she would glimpse another bearer wiping a forehead roughly, or using a not quite necessary force to heave a sick passenger onto a bunk. She wondered if maybe she and Faga and the other bearers weren't all that different from the basement doctor and his assistants, or from the German boys in the woods, sustaining themselves on others' weakness. Maybe the more irrational a system was, the crueler it had to be.

She avoided the eyes of the magician, who still looked the part of a gentleman, who did not leave his bunk except to fetch water and relieve himself. He hoarded the same loaf of bread he'd been eating the whole time, singing, "Magic bread!" He broke off a piece for each bird, then one for himself. "Seawater and oatmeal!" he cried, to anyone who would listen. "Wash yourself with seawater and oatmeal!"

But if there were oatmeal on the boat it would have been eaten already. Faga's biscuits were running out. Minna shared her sunflower seeds, then these ran out, too. The ship's soup grew thinner each day, until it was only broth. Even the sick complained of hunger. At first, Minna had dreamed of the simplest food: butter on warm bread. Then it was potato soup, thick with cream, flecked with parsley. Now she dreamed of oranges from Messina, raspberry preserves, a frosted cake like a castle. Someone licked the smell of schmaltz off the mess table. Others snapped splinters off the bunks and chewed. A boy was found dead, in a trunk, curled in his own fluids. No one claimed him. When the bearers came for him, someone had taken the bread from his hand. Minna wondered if dignity was not as formidable as she'd imagined it, neither as elusive nor as profound. If it was merely the ability to keep what belonged inside in, and outside out.

O NE morning a cry went up from the bunks nearby: two men warning the magician: they were going to eat his doves.

"What right have you?" they shouted.

The magician called back, "I'll eat your children!"

"But you have your loaf, you braggart!"

"What if I'm hungry for taste?"

"What could be tastier than a dove?"

"Perform us a trick, Mr. Magician. Make us *all* something tasty!"

"Give us something to love!"

"Let me alone."

"He can't do it."

"He's a fraud."

"He's got contraband in those birdies."

"When we cook 'em, we'll be rich!"

"Cook the birds!"

A pounding began, a chorus of hands and feet spreading through the bunks, overwhelming even the engine. The magician, emerging from his bunk, took his time. He tucked his rumpled shirt into his trousers, then buttoned his vest. He winked up at Minna, on her bunk. "A regular humanitarian you've become."

Minna said nothing. Before, she'd stayed away out of vanity, afraid he'd judge her. Now talking to him seemed dangerous.

"You won't assist me, then?"

But he didn't wait for her reply. He reached into a bag and spun around to face the crowd.

"No! A trick with the birds!"

His hand emerged, flourishing a set of metal rings.

"Birds, birds, birds, birds!"

The magician began to move. He turned, in a circle, dropping the rings from one hand into the other, showing that they were unattached. He rocked from side to side, on tiptoes, his thin fingers handling the rings with a lithe, shocking tenderness. The calls began to subside. When the magician held the rings aloft— "Eight!"—his voice had filled with a tremulous bass. He held up two rings, one in each hand, then began, slowly, to cross them above his face. He drew them apart, crossed them, drew them apart again, so that they looked like boys in slow motion, teasing for a fight. One of the bearers opened the hatch, letting in more light. A stillness overcame the bunks.

The magician crossed the rings. He brought them close to his face, took a deep breath, and bowed. He let go of one ring, but instead of dropping, it swung from the other ring, linked.

The cheer wavered at first, then grew more solid—a heat off the bunks.

"He's not done yet!" shouted one of the men. "Don't let him off!"

The magician held up a third ring. He tossed it in the air, snapped his wrist once, and watched his chain of rings grow into three, then he gathered them into his hand, blew, and placed them, one by one, over his neck. He removed two, held them up, and passed one through the other, followed by his arm. He made a farcical strongman face, his cheeks shaking with effort, then pulled his arm, and the ring, back through. He took more rings off his arms. He made stars. He made diamonds. He linked five rings with one blow, unlinked them with another. People were clapping now, not waiting between tricks.

"So prove it! Show us you're not a fraud."

The magician lowered his arms. He closed his eyes. He knit his brow, bit his lips, crouched as if concentrating with his entire being—though Minna was close enough to see a quiver in his lips, a private joy. His arms were fluid as he presented three separate rings, then rigid as he pretended to struggle, banging metal against metal. He grimaced. He seemed to stop trying. Then, suddenly, the rings were linked.

"Hurrah!"

"It's the same trick! We've already seen it!"

The magician bowed in all directions, then faced the man who'd been yelling. He walked up to the man's bunk, bowed again, and held out three linked rings to the man's largest child, a boy who looked to be eight or nine. "There! My tools. See for yourself!"

People gathered around the bunk to watch. The boy pulled at each ring in turn, then at two at a time, then went through the process again. He closed his eyes. He gnashed his teeth. The magician stood with his back to the boy, perfectly still, his face full of mockery and triumph. The boy shook the rings. He knocked them against the bunk. His father danced around him, snarling directions, his nostrils glowing with impending humiliation. Finally the boy, exasperated, hurled the rings into the air.

It was then that one fell off, rolled in a circle, and returned to the boy.

All fussing, all encouragement, all jeering, stopped. Minna saw the magician dip his head discreetly, eyeing the remaining rings in his hands. The boy picked up the fallen ring and brought it close to his face. He smiled, though in his smile was a kind of dread. "There's a hole," he said—or at least this was what he must have said, he wasn't loud enough to be heard. It was his father who grabbed the ring and cried, "There's a hole!"

The magician had drained of color so entirely Minna thought he might fall over. He did not look at her. His eyes were on his bunk. The boy's father was displaying the ring to the crowd, slipping it onto another ring, showing how they linked, slipping it off again. "It's simple! A gimmick! Any child could do it!"

He faced the magician, holding a ring in each of his hands, which he'd flung out to either side of his ears as far as they would go so that he bore a certain resemblance to the gentile God.

Still the magician did not turn toward him. "Those are not the right . . . you took the wrong . . ."

"Speak up!" the man growled.

"Those are the wrong . . ."

"Wrong? Right? What is wrong and right in magic? Magic must be magic! How else do you expect us to believe? How else do you expect us to restrain ourselves? Your birds are so plump! And if the rings are not magic, what are the birds?"

"Please . . ."

"It is simple to eat a real bird."

But the man had taken too long with his gloating. A flash of white streaked past Minna. Galina's sheet. Moses' bandage. He was running the birdcage toward the hatch. The man went after him for a few strides, quickly lost the chase, stopped. He turned back, and ran at the magician.

When the cage was returned empty, the magician had been beaten, but he wasn't dead. *If I wasn't so fucking hungry*, the man kept saying as he shook and punched and kneed, *if I wasn't hungry, I'd finish this right*. Then he took the magician's bread, and left him alone.

I F the passengers had known that the next day the sea would fall flat, that the gray sky would come undone with sun, perhaps events would have unfolded differently. Perhaps no one would have behaved so poorly if they'd known how close they were to the end: when the hatches were thrown open to the light, there was relief, yes, but also a woozy agony: people moved timidly, guarding faces with elbows, as if remembering a shameful dream that was dreamed too close to the surface of sleep. There was confusion. Minna and Faga felt it, too—they looked at each other shyly. This was the moment everyone had been waiting for. This was the whole point, to come out on the other side, this was what their friends or fathers or sons had done before them, and yet it suddenly seemed as if it would be easier to go back. One forgot that the ship was not the world, in part because of its rocking or your nausea or your need for bread, and in part because you had to guard yourself: if you thought of other people on other ships, making the same crossing a hundred miles to the north or to the south, or if you thought of a house you'd left behind, a particular corner, a doorknob, the scent of a particular drawer, or of the places you had yet to live in, the dish pattern you had yet to eat from, it would seem as though you supposed that you might disembark the ship one day. And if you imagined such an invention as a roller coaster, awaiting you on the far shore; or the game of baseball, awaiting your sons; if you imagined future people, on future ships, with ballrooms, say, and swimming pools, ships people would board for pleasure, for a notion of daring minus any real dare, if you imagined one day being one of these people—it would be as if you aimed to do more than not die.

Land looked at first like a storm. A piling on of clouds at the horizon, a confession of anger, which suddenly revealed itself to be solid. Trees, rocks, city.

The magician became abruptly penitent, and sociable. In the new light, Minna saw that he looked like anyone else. His cuffs were yellow, his scarf and vest stained with bird droppings. His right eye was black from his beating. His beard was crusted around his mouth. He walked around, finding the Jews and handing them razor blades.

"I've heard it from relatives, I've heard it from on high! With a beard it will take twice as long to get through. With *peyes*, four times! Do it now. God will forgive. You can grow it back later if you must."

He demonstrated his courage and technique by shaving

himself in front of a group of men—"Magic, now, *this* is real magic!"—then moved about from bunk to bunk, showing everyone the results.

Moses stopped at Minna's bunk. She was combing her hair; she'd been combing it for so long it had started to crackle. Moses didn't seem to notice. He was watching the magician, and shaking his head. "You know?" he said. "I tried to free his birds. But they wouldn't fly. They fell straight into the water. And now I am barely sorry."

M INNA found Faga on the other side of the inspection line. She was waiting just outside the door, for Minna clearly, yet when Minna approached to say good-bye, Faga nodded cordially and said, "Good luck, dear." There was nothing of the embrace Minna had expected, and wanted, just a little.

"Thank you," Minna answered. She started to wish Faga good luck, too, then stopped; she worried Faga might be insulted. They hadn't been peers exactly. Faga had been older and stronger. And now Minna was going off to start a new life while Faga continued her old one, washing clothes, albeit in a new place. Faga had heard all about Minna's house, with its running water and comfortable bed and even—possibly! Minna had added, for accuracy's sake, because Faga seemed to trust her—possibly even a servant. So it seemed natural that Faga might be a little jealous.

"I'm going this way," Faga said, pointing toward the city.

"I'm waiting here. He's supposed to meet me here."

Faga touched a finger to Minna's cheek. She smiled. It was a gentle smile for such a large woman. And Minna understood.

Faga wasn't jealous. She simply wanted for Minna what Minna wanted for herself, and didn't want to get in the way.

"Don't worry," Faga said. "You're worried, don't worry. Just keep your eyes up, that you'll see the handsome man." Then she walked away, her chin high, her dress jangling with spoons.

EIGHT

M INNA Losk."

Hearing her name, whole, confused her. It sounded like
a cousin's name might—related to her, but distantly. She stood
still, in the spot where she'd been instructed to stand, waiting to
hear it again.

"Minna?"

The voice was deep. The man who appeared before her was
short and thick. His nose was broad and bulbous. He wore a
strange hat, perfectly round, and a collar without a collar: it simply ended, like a ledge, at his neck.

"I'm not Max," he said, and smiled as if to reassure her.

"Who's Max?"

"Max Getreuer. Your husband. Husband-to-be."

Minna was indeed reassured. Though the name Max struck

her as a bit small—gone as soon as it was said, leaving an itch in the back of the mouth. "Then who are you?" she asked.

"Jacob." He held out a plump hand. "I was sent by Max to *fetch* you. *Fetch*. An English word, do you know any English? No? We'll stick to Yiddish, then—for now. They said you were fair—and here you are. Shake hands, shake hands. Don't make me look a fool."

Minna gave him her hand, which Jacob proceeded to pump up and down. His voice, she heard, was growing higher, and up close she saw that his beardlessness was not a result of having shaved. His skin was nearly as smooth as hers, with a faint smudge above his lip as though he'd been rubbed with coal. He was a boy, probably younger than she.

"Where is Max?" she asked.

"Oh, he's not such a *keen* traveler. Do you know that one, *keen*—no, of course not. And he's busy, Max. Very busy."

Jacob grinned as if he'd made a joke. Behind him, Minna saw the quiet girls whose fathers or brothers or husbands had not yet come for them being gathered together by a woman in a feathered hat, who was calling, "Clean rooms! Clean rooms!" The woman's boots were pointed, and polished; her dress was wide with petti-coats; she held a parasol against the sun. Minna guessed the woman was either entirely legitimate, or else a kidnapper. "Come, girls!" she trilled. "Come with me, clean rooms! Do not be led astray!"

"How far are we traveling?" she asked.

"Not far." Jacob grinned again. "Far. Four days—maybe five." He saw Minna's alarm. "It's not so bad, you'll see, if you like that sort of thing."

"What sort of thing?"

"Oh. The world, I guess. You look uncertain. Well. No one except me is ever certain about anything. The train leaves in an hour. Are you hungry?"

Minna laughed—at the boy, at the absurdity of his question. Her legs felt suddenly weak. The stones beneath her swelled and rocked. She looked out beyond the arrival station—Castle Garden, they called it, as if here one could be processed and stamped into nobility—and saw New York City. It was dark, compared to Odessa, and tall. The mouths of the streets looked like tunnels.

"There's anything you could want, all sold off carts. Sausages, rolls, nuts, coffee. Every street a market. Anything you could dream of. This morning I bought this hat! You like? None's kosher, of course, but until we're back on Max land that's all right with me. Of course I shouldn't presume. The lady may feel differently." Jacob did a little jump, lifting his round hat. "Does the lady feel differently?"

Minna giggled and shook her head. If she had the energy, she thought, if she were not stuck with him, she would probably avoid a boy as overeager as Jacob. At the very least she'd be embarrassed for him. He was like a boy actor playing a man actor playing a boy. She followed him into the narrow streets, stumbling as she learned to walk on land again, her feet slamming it unexpectedly. Jacob bought her meat on a stick, then meat in a roll—"Compliments of Max," he said. "Thank Max!"—then a cup of coffee which scalded her throat. She asked for another cup, to see if Max could afford it, and because she wanted to be awake to see the city.

But no matter how hard she tried to pay attention, Minna would not remember many details. Less than a mile to the east, a great bridge rose above a river, shining in its newness, but they didn't know to go look. She would remember the streets: the hard, dark stone, America's granite; the smell of grease and smoke. Brick and marble and carriages and cripples. The whole way to the rail yards one long stumble, her ears vibrating with the ghost of the ship's engine. New York, she would think—New York, she would say, years later, once she'd found the right words, and then honed her delivery, once she'd begun attending the sorts of evening gatherings where one said such things—New York is like being in the middle of a parade where everyone has been called home, all at once, in all different directions.

Then she was on a train again, and Jacob had enough money to buy them a bench—"praise be to Max"—and before they left the platform, she fell asleep.

I T felt like days, her sleep. She woke only when the train stopped, and even then she woke in sleep, her head flopping against the window. She dreamed the kind of dreams that seem to be dreams of other dreams. She dreamed of Galina curled up in a trunk, and in the trunk a hole leading to the sea. She dreamed of Galina, afraid, not knowing how to swim. Faga holding Galina in her arms, rocking her, cooing. She dreamed she was on a train across America, dreaming. She dreamed of the men who'd shaved, per the magician's instructions, and of the stark white outlines left by their beards, so that as they stood at Castle Garden awaiting inspection, they looked more bearded than they ever had when they actually were.

Minna felt something touching her face. This went on for

years, the fingers traveling her features, again and again, as if the toucher did not trust that Minna was still Minna from one moment to the next. When she finally woke, she was gazing through her own fingers. The train was passing through a woods so thick with ferns it looked bottomless. For a long moment she couldn't say what continent she was on, then she turned to see Jacob, smiling.

"You're alive!" He handed her a roll and a square of cheese. "We're past Pittsburgh. You missed it. Gorgeous, filthy place."

"Where are we going?"

"Sodokota. That way." He pointed ahead. "It's not the most cosmopolitan place, but there's plenty of land. Well. Plenty of grass and rocks. Yes. I can see you know all about it." He bent over his lap, removed a long blade of grass he'd tucked into one boot, as if to demonstrate—Grass!—then straightened back up. "Didn't they tell you anything?"

"They?"

"I don't know. Whoever Max wrote off to—he's not a detail man. Or at least he didn't tell us any details. Where you're coming from, for instance."

"Odessa."

Jacob let out a whistle. "City of Thieves?" He set the grass between his teeth and let it bounce as he talked. "Well. I won't lie. Where we're going, in a word, it's not Odessa. You could call it a farm, but it's not really that yet either. We've got chickens, one horse, one cow. A mule who may or may not be alive by our return. A tool approximating a plow."

Minna couldn't tell if he was joking. She couldn't imagine

him a farmhand, though she could imagine him pretending to be. "How long have you worked for Max?" she asked.

"Oh . . ." Again that slippery grin. "As long as I can remember."

"And still the farm is not a farm?"

"We've only been there one year."

"And before that?"

"Well. In a word. We were just like you. Sailed into New York two years ago, hungry as dogs, then got sent to Cincinnati, where the rich old Jews liked us plenty. They housed us and fed us and gave us English lessons and jobs in a furniture factory. Very kind, the rich old Jews. But then people like us kept coming, and they weren't so happy anymore. Imagine. Their dilemma!" Jacob drew in his chin and spoke in a booming voice. "'How will we teach so many, all at once, how to dress properly, and clip their beards to a hygienic length, and walk without their feet flopping and their heads in the sky, and talk without their hands flailing, and tell their women to stop looking, every one, like a widow?!' You can imagine. They'd worked so hard to prove that they weren't dirty Jews, and then here we were, thousands of dirty Jews! They sent us out into the towns, in a word. But some, who were willing, they sent further." Jacob raised a finger. "As a farmer," he mimicked, "even a Jew can be free! He can build a new Palestine!" He laughed. "*Am Olam*, they called us. Eternal People. As if the name would be enough to sell us on the scheme. Well. It was. The rich old boys . . . well, the rich old boys backed by the richest of them all, the Baron de Vintovich himself, the man who's concocted the whole mess, they gave us money for tools, and food for the first year—though Max only took half of what they offered."

"He's proud?" It was the only question Minna could think to ask, though the answer, she understood, was beside the point. Jacob wasn't joking. They were headed for a farm. Or a not-even-a-farm.

"Proud. Yes. And suspicious. Most of us who joined were sent to colonies like Bethlehem Yehuda. New Jerusalem. There's even a New Odessa! But good old Max thought it couldn't be a good idea—so many Jews crammed together all over again. So he decided to go it alone."

"Did you want to go to a colony?" Minna asked.

"Of course!"

"Then why stay with him?"

A look of despair crossed Jacob's face. "Well. In a word. Actually." He winced. "Max is my father. I'm sorry. I didn't mean to trick you. Oh, it's not funny anymore, I know. Maybe it wasn't ever funny. Samuel says I'm never funny actually."

"Who's Samuel?"

"My brother. He might have come for you, he's older and most say smarter—and better-looking, too, nose like a Roman—but he's also the only one of us with half a wit about the farm."

Minna said nothing. It was hard to tell if the train had sped up or her blood had slowed down.

"I guess they didn't tell you about the stepmother part. You don't look pleased, I must say. You look downright *Indian*, in fact—now there's a good one for you. You'll understand soon enough. But I can assure you, we're good boys. Samuel's not half the ass I am. At least not so plainly."

Minna refused to look at him.

"Don't worry," Jacob said. "We'll survive."

"I didn't come here to survive." This was said before Minna could stop herself from saying it, her voice one she hadn't heard in years, sharp and stubborn—*thick as clay*, her aunts used to say. The passing trees seemed to be watching her, instead of the other way around. Behind her, Jacob laughed.

"What. You'd rather die?"

"Ha," Minna said to the window. She didn't want to be a stepmother any more than she'd wanted to have one. When the rabbis came knocking, encouraging her father to find another wife—*Bavegn!* Move on!—Minna would stand in the corner and glare. The only stepmothers she'd known—or not known, no, stepmothers one only saw—were odd, quickly aging women with an acute jumpiness about them. They'd been divorced for not bearing children, or driven from their own villages for unknown but easily imagined reasons, or they were simply too dumb or poor or ugly to have married on the first round. Stepmothers communed with other women, but as inferiors. From what Minna could gather, the stepmother was expected to love another woman's children as if they were her own, but not so intimately that she was—like a real mother—also allowed to hate or punish them.

"Where are you even from?" she asked Jacob. "Or will you make that up, too."

"Kotelnia. South of Kiev. It was a town, like the others. Our mother sold wood." He paused. "That's the truth."

"Have you heard of Beltsy? Near Kishinev?"

"No."

Minna frowned.

"Have you heard of Kotelnia?" he asked.

"No."

Jacob shrugged. "Well then."

THE train drove through another night. When Minna woke, the forest had fallen away to clumps and lines of trees. The land was pale and dry. There were fields, and houses, and every so often a dirt street lined with wooden buildings that could almost count as a town. Minna felt blank, almost fine, watching all this. There were yards to go with the houses, and in some cases fences. Everything looked dusty but new, as if the whole country was a woodshop.

"For you."

Jacob's voice cracked. She woke more fully. Her circumstances returned to her. She tried to ignore them by making her eyelids heavy, narrowing her frame of sight. Even the people, she thought, looked dusty. Later, she would learn to distinguish them—Swedes or Danes or Germans or Finns—but for now she noted their pale, strangely simple clothes, and the mild way they held their faces, as if without great expectation. She could get off at the next station, she thought, and drop herself down among them.

"Minna."

Jacob handed her coffee in one of the tins he carried looped around his belt. A couple days ago, she had thought this habit charming, but now it struck her as a cumbersome, impractical thing to do, an American affectation though she suspected he got it wrong, just like the grass between his teeth which he often wound up chewing, absentmindedly, until he'd swallowed it. The tin was too thin for hot coffee, the kind she associated with street people. Minna set it down on the bench untasted, forcing Jacob, when he sat, not to spread his legs as wide as usual. She wondered if his father and brother took up as much unnecessary space; if, at the next station, she could in fact work up the courage to step off the train and be gone. She imagined herself standing on the platform. She imagined herself walking down one of the pale, dusty streets. But she couldn't fill in any of the details—where she would go, what she would eat, who she would meet and how she would understand them, or they her. It was fantasy, all over again—Minna Losk, lost in fantasy. Which had got her, thus far, where? On a train hurtling past towns that were not hers, heading for a not-farm with not-sons and a lame mule.

"Aren't you going to eat?"

She had avoided, so far, looking at the rolls Jacob brought for breakfast. She had principles. She had anger to attend to. But now she was defeated, and hungry, and she peeked: the rolls were frosted in white, like little cakes. Saliva sat on her tongue. She turned toward the window as she took the first bite, which left an addictive sting on her tongue—the frosting stiff and perfect, the inner roll flaky, a luxurious waft of vanilla bean filling the roof of her mouth—and when she'd eaten the whole thing, her fingers and lips were sticky. There was nothing to do but wash it down with the coffee, then take the handkerchief that Jacob held out and wipe her hands.

"You could be my sister," he said.

Minna threw the handkerchief back at him. But he wasn't

joking, she realized. His face was humble, like Ilya's, a round boy face wanting nothing but to be liked. He didn't mean it as she'd taken it, as a comment on her age. He meant *can*. You can be my sister.

"Why don't you shush for once," she told him. The roll had gone to her head, all sugar and a longing to give in. "Shush." *Sister*. It was an indulgent thing for him to say. Not like a fine piece of jewelry might be indulgent, solidly, tolerably, but in the lazy, shapeless way people talked about places they'd never been to.

AT some point when Minna wasn't looking, the houses had grown less frequent. The trees were lonesome now, scattered in ones and twos. The fields had the parched look of late summer, the rows overgrown but crisp, as if you could reach a hand in and effortlessly lift the plants out by the roots. Even more of them looked like they'd never been planted at all. They weren't fields, she realized; just rolling, empty land.

They were getting close, Jacob said—close, at least, to where the rail ended.

Late in the day, the sky began to look bruised. The falling sun followed them, crimson bleeding into plum. Far off, Minna saw smoke, but there was nothing between her and it except the desolate, purpling hills, and she couldn't tell how far off it really was. It could be a warm house, or a factory, or a whole village burning.

But if there was fire, she thought, there had to be a woods somewhere. There had to be something apart from grass and grass.

"How old is he?" she asked.

"Max?"

"Who else?"

"He won't tell you. He's—suspicious."

"I'm not asking him to tell me." But already Minna wasn't sure she wanted to know. "How old are you?"

"Fifteen."

"And Samuel?"

"Eighteen."

She thought of skin as old as her father's and felt an illness in her throat.

"Your mother," she said. "How old was she when she died?"

"Oh, she didn't die."

Minna was silent.

"She came to see the land, then said she was going back to Cincinnati. I have my suspicions. I think she would have gone somewhere bigger, like Chicago. She likes crowds. 'Soh-ciety.' There's a word for you. But Samuel says she wouldn't have gone that far from us. In any case, she only stayed two days."

"It must be quite a place," Minna said bitterly. "This 'farm.'"

"She isn't a rough sort of woman."

"Unlike me, you mean?"

Jacob pulled a fresh piece of grass from his boot.

"He didn't have to send away for a complete stranger," Minna said. "He could have picked a wife the way most people do. Don't you have any family left in Kotelnia? Friends, at least? Someone who knows someone?"

"A few."

"Why not ask them to find him a nice wife who looked just like your mother?"

Jacob hesitated. "I don't know, I guess. Maybe he didn't want them to know she'd left."

"So on top of being proud, he's a coward?"

But Jacob's eyes had taken on a forlorn glaze she didn't want to look at, and Minna dropped the conversation. She understood. Max had hired Rosenfeld's for the same reason that her father had gone to the mines. She turned her face back to the window. Night fell quick and dark between the hills, like rain filling puddles. She wished they weren't almost at the end. She wanted to ride through to morning and wake in another land again. Farther on, according to Jacob, farther than they would go, there were real hills, even mountains, called Black like Odessa's sea. Here, though, it was barren. Here was a place like the Russian steppes, where she'd heard wolves sniffed in packs and turned children into meat. She shivered at the idea of walking off the train into the dark. Jacob meant well, but he was not a man you'd trust to protect you. He wasn't even a man.

He'd fallen asleep.

Or perhaps he hadn't. It was hard to tell, when he started to talk suddenly, whether he was really asleep or just pretending to be. Minna guessed the latter when she saw his thumbs searching each other in his lap. "Forty to one hundred and twenty," he said.

It took Minna a moment to understand what this meant. Then she recalled: in the Torah, Moses had lived to be one hundred and twenty. The men in Beltsy had used this number the same way, saying it after their own age so as to obscure their years and throw off the Angel of Death.

Which was another way to say: Max was forty. Which meant

nothing, of course. Which should not cause this burn in Minna's stomach. It was only years, piled up.

MINNA's dismay subsided a little as the train drew into the platform. There was a firebox raging, and lanterns swinging, and a reassuring commotion in the air. It was as if they had arrived backstage in the night's theater—as if all the blackness had only been an illusion, manufactured here. She felt a surge of hope.

"Welcome to Mitchell," Jacob said.

"Mishel."

"MiTCHell."

She tried, quietly; the word made her lips flop out. The air was warm but lacked any dampness. Her face felt taut in the way that made one remember it as a skin, a way she hoped would make her look older when Max first glimpsed her.

But Jacob, standing on tiptoe, was looking for a man called Otto. A neighbor, he explained, who'd offered to drive them back.

"Don't you have a wagon? At least?" What sort of man missed—twice!—his new wife's arrival? Minna wanted him to see her now, with her face taut. She had combed her hair—again. She was travel-worn, depleted, yet even this felt somehow womanly—her cheekbones, she imagined, looked high and indifferent. Minna's cheekbones, Galina always said, were her one stroke of elegance.

"Of a sort," Jacob said. "But only the one horse. The mule's not much good for distance. We're still most of the night from home. Besides, Otto's picking up supplies off this run."

Minna huffed. "Otto."

"A German fellow! This tall." He lifted an arm as high as it would go. "This broad." He cupped his hands around vast shoulders of air. "A real American kind of German."

They found Otto's wagon, then Otto himself. He greeted Jacob with a handshake—briefer, Minna saw, than Jacob would have liked—then turned to Minna. He took her hand in his and spoke to Jacob in English.

"'The little bride,' he calls you," Jacob said.

Otto's face was warm and frank, so bare of artifice or beard Minna felt slightly embarrassed, and sorry for having thought of the German boys at the border waving urine-soaked sticks in women's faces. Otto didn't linger with her hand, and his ears stuck out, an awkwardness which tempered his height and struck her as further proof of his virtue. He took her bundle and lifted it into the back of his wagon, then Jacob helped him load two barrels of kerosene and a tall coil of rope. Otto nodded toward Minna and again said something to Jacob in English.

"You can speak to me in German," Minna said to him slowly, in Yiddish. "I'll understand you."

Otto smiled and looked to Jacob.

"I've asked him to talk to me in English," Jacob said. "For practice. He says you can use that rope, for a pillow."

It was almost like a nest, once Minna settled in. She found a skin of some kind, and covered herself with it. Buffalo, she learned later. The wagon dipped and jounced, but the rope buffered her from the hardest blows. Her head fell back. She drifted through a haze of tobacco smoke and English, listening to the kerosene shift in the barrels.

Only much later, when she woke, did Minna remember her fear. How long they'd been driving, she was uncertain; she knew only that an utter, saturated darkness surrounded her. The men did not speak. There were stars, and a quarter moon, but these seemed more distant than Minna had ever known them to be. Her eyelids were heavy. She longed to sink into the rope again. But what of wolves? And what else might be watching from the unseeable stillness surrounding the wagon? She pushed herself upright. She rubbed her eyes, pulled on her eyelids, stared alertly into the red-black air.

Later, she would look back and think fear was like that for her, when she was young, and truly had things to fear: a thing to be remembered, like an item on a list. And so often she'd focused on the wrong ones: she'd feared the dark night, for instance, instead of her future. She would feel sorry for herself, that she'd missed certain wonders, and bit her fingers so often. She bit them now, guarding against sleep, but her fingertips were still callused from the yarn and the tactic wasn't effective. She scuffed her boots against the wood floor, only half aware that she was also trying to rouse the men from their silence.

"We're almost there," Jacob said. "See?"

Minna climbed out of the rope and leaned out the wagon's side. Up ahead was a light—a single, dim orb the color of sap. She couldn't see the outlines of a house, just the light, which looked so odd, so out of place in the rest of the night, she felt a pity for it——as if it were the traveler and not she.

"Don't worry." Jacob spoke in Russian now, as if to keep something from Otto. "Think of it as an adventure," he said. "That's what I do. Every day. I just pretend I'm on one big adventure."

Beside, the light, a figure rose. Otto called, "Hunh!"

NINE

I T was hard to tell, at first, whether Max was unnaturally tall or the doorway was unnaturally short. He stood as he did in the picture—the real picture, that was, undistorted by Minna's more optimistic contrivances: hands empty by his sides, feet pointed out, knees locked. His beard was not trimmed in any style; it was simply hair, covering much of his face.

Minna didn't move. This had been her last chance—her arrival. She'd come so far. Now she was here. And that was him.

Otto swung down with the lantern and helped her out. Minna teetered slightly with the shock of firm earth, then she began what felt like a mile-long walk toward Max. For a man standing in front of his own house, he looked nervous; he wore a caught, wincing smile, as if he would like to somehow re-arrange himself but feared seeming indecisive. When he spoke, his voice was passably deep but crumbly, like a dough rolled too thin.

"Minna." He looked at her hand, which she had forgotten to hold out. Then, shyly, he took it in his own, and said, to her horror, "My love."

Minna almost jerked away, before she remembered that Otto and Jacob were watching. She was embarrassed for Max even more than for herself. He was not young enough to be naive—where had he learned to expose himself in such a way? He could not love her, of course. He'd just met her. And besides, who used that word out loud? Only poor people could marry for love. Minna tasted the salt of rising tears. She was determined, she was desperate, not to fall apart. She thought, *At least his fingers are soft—at least they're not a poor man's fingers.* She ignored the fact that his grip was like wet paper. She ignored what soft hands might say about a farmer. Maybe, she thought, he meant "love" simply as an indicator of fact—the fact of the situation between a husband and his wife-to-be. Like one might look at a bolt of cloth at market and say, out loud, *muslin*, just to have said it.

She took a deep breath. "Hello, Max," she said.

"Please. Call me Motke."

Otto cleared his throat. "Safe and sound, then," he said, enunciating his German carefully. "I will be going. Tell Samuel I said hello."

"Wait!" Max dropped Minna's hand. "I must pay you . . ."

"Nein."

"But I must."

"Nein." Otto held up his palms, turned to Jacob, and said something else. If he was aggravated, he hid it well inside his clipped,

clean voice. He stood, as Minna's father had, with his legs set a bit farther apart than necessary, as if he might be called upon at any moment to hold up a falling rock. Her father, Minna realized, had been younger than Max was now.

"Here, please . . ." Max reached into his pockets, stammering.

"Don't be stupid," Jacob said, climbing down at last. He let out a sigh of resignation. "That's what he's saying, in a word. Don't be stupid. He doesn't want your money."

Max continued to protest, but Otto had already leaped back into the wagon. He called good night, the wheels creaked into motion. Minna looked up at the house, straining her eyes to see it more clearly, but there were only stars, dim with their own crowding, and the bouncing glow of the wagon. She felt a wretched envy.

Suddenly Max called again. "Wait! Her trunk!" But he didn't run anywhere. He turned to Jacob. "He left her with nothing."

"It's right here," Jacob said, holding up Minna's bundle.

Max eyed it suspiciously. "I thought you'd bought flour."

Jacob smiled. "That would have been smart."

Max stiffened. "Yes. That would have been smart."

The night blared its excruciating silence. Then a groan broke through: Minna's stomach, announcing hunger. She waited for her face to burn, for her mouth to say *zayt moykhl*—yet neither happened. She couldn't locate any desire to impress Max. Instead a belligerence welled up in her. She took the bundle from Jacob and turned to Max. "They told you I would arrive with luggage? You thought I was rich?"

"No. If you were rich, you wouldn't come here."

"What did they tell you?"

"Almost nothing."

Minna was suddenly sorry. But this wasn't remorse, or even pity. It was closer, perhaps, to sorrow. She wondered if Max was as disappointed by her youth as she was by his age. She wondered with what money he'd paid for her crossing. And the Rosenfeld's examination? Did he have any idea what he'd paid for? She tried to find his eyes in the dark, then thought it better that she couldn't.

"Then we are even," she said.

Max's outline seemed to melt slightly. He turned. She could see his lips now: thick for a man, and alarmingly pink. "This is a discussion for another time," he said. "You are hungry. My love."

INSIDE, the house—the room—felt even smaller than it looked, the scale almost miniature, as if built for dwarves. There was a short table. Three shipping crates for chairs. One bed, a small stove, a bench lined with buckets. The floor was dirt, the walls were dirt. In one corner, a hole had been dug out: here she saw, emerging from a blanket, curly black hair. The other one, Samuel, asleep. Or pretending to sleep, she thought. More likely he just didn't want to meet her. Which was fine. Minna did not particularly want to meet him. It was enough, for one night, to meet a husband. Better to leave something still unknown—though she wished, instead of a stepson, that it might be a second room. The air smelled of breath and smoke, and something richer, ranker— a pile of horse dung, she saw, by the stove. Their fuel, she realized.

"Please," said Max, and handed her a steaming plate.

What kind of meat she'd been served, Minna couldn't tell, but it tasted sweet and was warm. When she offered some to

Jacob, he looked to his father, then shook his head. She didn't offer again. She felt greedy and light, and though the baseness of her hunger disturbed her, along with the baser baseness of how simple it was to ease, she had a sense that her future called for a certain hoarding, and ate the rest without stopping even to say thank you.

TEN

THE men were gone. Minna felt it before she saw. An earthen stillness in the room. She rolled over. The only window looked like it might have been a mistake: a snag of light near the door, white as a rag. If she faced away she could almost be in her attic in Odessa. If not for the smell of dung. If not for the uncovered straw beneath her, or the knowledge that in this room, this plank bed was the trophy. Last night, before laying himself down in the hole with his sons, Max had lowered his eyes and said, "You'll have the bed."

She'd been full with meat, and sleepy, and glad to be left alone. She was glad for it now. Still, there was a flatness in her chest, as if she were trapped beneath a pane of storefront glass. She thought of the eggbeater in Galina's kitchen. She thought: I should have taken it. I should have taken the eggbeater and the good spatula and the good knife. Like Faga. I should have taken as much as I could carry.

The door was lighter than her hand expected, made of broken-down crates, and opened too quickly: the sky was fierce in its light. She stumbled out squinting; seeing no one, hearing nothing, she squatted to pee. Then haltingly, warily, she blinked her way to vision. She couldn't believe, at first, that her eyes were working properly, for there was nothing to see but grass, the same infinite monotony they'd ridden through on the train. Minna turned to face the house and saw that it was built into the side of a short hill. It was, she realized, more of a cave than a house. She circled around to the other side, where there was no wall or door; if it weren't for the little tin chimney poking out, the hill would look like nothing more than a hill. So that must have been where Max had stood for the photograph. He'd appeared to be standing in front of nothing but sky because he was. There might be nothing for miles as tall as this meager hill they called a house. She thought of the brick house on Beltsy's square, and remembered its secret: there wasn't a single brick. It was a wood house, like all the others, glued over with tin plate and painted to look like brick. A trick—empty as the magician's rings. And everyone had gone around adoring it.

She stepped carefully up the side of the hill, stopping before she got to the place where she estimated the hollow began underneath. If she fell through, she guessed, she would land on the stove. It would make a fine cartoon.

She raised an arm to shade her eyes. Behind the hill stood a tree, and tied to the tree, like a horse, stood a cow. Near the cow was a small kitchen garden, a few feet across, and a little roof, under which six or so chickens dozed on their nests. The cow was thin, her udders like raindrops about to split from an eave. The tree itself was barely twice the size of a man, and hunched and tangled—stunted, not young. Twenty feet away, a structure of some kind had collapsed into a pile of boards.

This was the yard, then. Minna lifted her eyes slowly, uncertain she wanted to see beyond. But there was a field, a small field yet real, a real field plowed and planted with a respectable crop of wheat. It was something, she thought. Next year—she dared think it, Next Year, and was proud, for she'd made a promise of her own accord, or as close as she'd ever come to her own accord— Next Year there would be more. More rows, more crops, more food, more money. Minna could picture the order of it, the bounty. She could see fields running to the horizon.

Then she saw more clearly through the sun's glare: the wheat wasn't right. The seeds had fallen off; the stems were bent and tangled; in some patches they were lying down, all in one direction, as if they'd been flattened by an impossibly massive wheel. Minna was conscious, suddenly, of the air at her back. She was alone, not as she'd been in her father's house, or in Galina's attic, but an alone that made her afraid to move in case she'd find herself gone.

At the edges of the ruined field, there were rocks, piled into little mountains. Past these, a long, lopsided swath of dark soil had been turned up but not yet planted. It was nearly September. Hardly time to break new ground. Even Minna, who'd done little more than weed her father's vegetable patch, knew this. Yet there, at the far boundary of the plowed earth, Minna spotted the horse and mule, and three figures, digging up more rocks.

Minna shuddered, a chill through her bones of too much sun too fast. Her ears buzzed, but she could see no insects. Her eyes watered. She closed them, opened them again. And there, way off, so sudden in her vision that they seemed to have grown just for her, was a line of tall, broad-limbed trees, their branches heavy with leaves, following the path of a small creek. She felt a dazzling relief. An exaggerated dazzle, perhaps; even so, she let it wash over her. She thought: I grew up among trees, in the forest. And maybe that, too, wasn't fully honest, since Minna had grown up on the edge of the forest, or more accurately at the edge of the town. But she was desperate for the story to cohere. It depended, she decided, on which way you faced, and Minna's father had preferred to face away from the town and toward the forest and Minna had been his daughter and son and done the same. Yes. Minna and her father would eat their supper facing the forest, sitting in silence, side by side, watching until the birds disappeared into the trees and the trees disappeared into the night.

Minna remembered thinking of their watching as a form of guardianship, a supervision of the most natural and necessary sort—as if without her and her father, the trees would never rest. But now she realized she'd been wrong. Standing in the dry air under the hot sun on the hill that was the cave that was now her house, she thought it hadn't been the trees that needed protecting, but her and her father who'd needed the trees. To see everything all at once, sky whole, horizon whole, sun whole, was punishing. It seemed to suggest that there was nothing else to know.

A bird circled overhead, high and silent, as still as if stuffed. Minna wanted to run toward the trees and creek, but she wanted to save them, too; some part of her feared that if she was too eager in her attentions, the trees would reveal themselves as mirages by the time she reached them. She shifted her gaze back to the figures of the men—or of two boys and a man—from here, they looked all the same. They worked at a distance from each other, shoveling their rocks into small piles, which were then loaded onto a flat of wood attached to the mule. Every so often, the mule was pulled off a little farther, and the flat dumped, making a larger pile of rocks. Meanwhile the horse was hitched to the plow, but no one was plowing.

The method, Minna thought, was not all that it could be. There was a link missing somewhere, a faulty assumption, a confusion of priority. The horse and mule barely worked. They stood at the edge of the dirt, looking smug, facing all the grass that hadn't been turned over. There was so much grass, growing so brazenly to the horizon, that the farm—the yard and the field and the newly turned soil, even the trees—appeared to be little more than a blemish. Beyond the grass, apparently, was a country, but it couldn't be seen from where Minna stood. Up and down the men went, stones spitting out their sides, the sunlight bleaching them so thoroughly that their movements became negligible, as if they were simply larger rocks, tending the smaller ones.

B ACK in the dark of the cave, she could barely see. She sipped from the smallest bucket, hoping it was the clean one, and when the water tasted of nothing worse than wood, she gulped it down. She sat on one of the boxes until her vision returned, then covered her eyes with her hands. Her hands smelled familiar. Blood pounded in her neck. *Breathe.* She calmed herself in the urgent, giddy way one does when the only other choice is panic. Then she spread one finger at a time, revealing the room in stripes so narrow she could almost pretend that it wasn't real. Line of board. Slice of blackened iron. There was a clean edge of light. Half a candlestick, curves like knuckles. A scrap of white—

Minna was up, moving toward it, her fingers on the fringe before she realized that it was just the corner of a folded prayer shawl. She stepped back, embarrassed. What had she imagined it might be? A note from her predecessor, offering advice? A piece of lace? Proof, simply, that another woman had existed here? Ridiculous, the very thought—Max's wife had lasted only two days, barely long enough to see the "house" dug let alone to leave behind a souvenir—yet Minna couldn't stop herself. She looked under the pillow on the bed, lifted up the blankets in the hole. She peered behind the stove. In one corner was a box with a few shirts, all men's, all threadbare, the pockets ripping loose. She felt the edge of the table, the undersides—there was no drawer. She opened a sack and found potatoes, opened another and found an inch of flour. In a small tin there were coffee beans; next to the coffee beans was a small stack of magazines which looked to be primers on farming. Under the shawl were two stacks of dishes and tins, a prayer book, a pair of leather boxes—Max's *tefillin*—and a possibly dead cricket. Minna laid a finger on its back, easily crushed it, then pulled down the prayer book, which she gripped by the cover and shook. When nothing came loose, she shook harder. Finally a sheaf of paper dropped out and she knelt down to look. But it was only a section of the book, broken off by her assault. She tried to shove it back into place, then realized she was grinding the whole book into the dirt. She yanked it up and the pages fell out again. In the synagogue, she remembered, when a book so much as touched a bench, the women cradled and kissed it. But in Minna's rush to pick up the pages, she tore one, and in the seconds that followed, which felt like hours, as the letters grew blacker and more accusing, she decided it would be easier to bury the page than fix it. She started to dig. That the floor was dirt suddenly seemed a blessing.

If you were careful, her father said, *you could make a decent seamstress. That would keep you. That would be a decent way to live.*

But no. Never careful. Worse than your mother.

Minna grew aware of herself, scratching like a rat. A shadow had tilted into the room: tall, but not Max. Taller than Max, and with longer arms. But these arms weren't skinny, and they ended in fists. Minna squinted, trying to make out his eyes, then realized she must look mad. She grabbed the prayer book off the ground and opened it as if to read. He might leave, she thought, and pretend he hadn't seen her. He might laugh, like Jacob would. But he did neither. He stepped closer and squatted down, and now his face came into view: long and sharp-jawed and rough with black stubble. He was better-looking than Jacob, yes, even handsome, yet somehow difficult to look at. Hard. Or maybe Minna couldn't look at him because he was looking at her as through a nearly gone piece of soap—as if he was seeing fear and sin and bone all splayed out, and this confusion that he'd caused in her fingers and toes, a tingling close to pain.

She closed the book. "Don't just watch me, then."

His hand reached toward her—warm from its fist. "Samuel," he said.

"Yes." She slipped free. "I deduced that."

"Are you all right?"

Minna stood. She felt dangerously tempted to answer him honestly. A sudden longing to talk and talk. But the grass, she would say, but the light, but this was not what I expected. But what did she expect?

She dusted off the book with her skirt, turning so he couldn't see her face. "You won't . . ." She stopped.

"No." Samuel rose from his squat. Again he reached his hand toward her. Minna mistrusted him suddenly—not that he wouldn't keep her secret but that he would keep it out of kindness. His curls stood in jagged chunks around his head, yet somehow they didn't look silly; they seemed to be watching her, like his eyes, for another misstep. Which might include, she thought, her taking his hand again. Then he was saying, "What? You want to keep it?" and Minna realized that he was looking at the book. He only wanted her to give him the book. She felt relief as she handed it back, then a stab of injury as she watched him place it on the shelf. His movements were efficient, his back straight. She couldn't tell if he cared about the book itself, and the words within, or just the fact that she'd been desecrating it. When he turned again, his expression was as illegible as at first.

"Is there anything you need?" he asked.

She wanted to cry.

"To prepare dinner I mean." He spoke gently. "Is there anything you need. I've been the cook, up until now."

Minna straightened. It was simple, she told herself. A simple question. All he wanted was a simple answer. She brushed her dirty hands against each other, set them on her hips, and swallowed. "What do I cook?"

"That's easy," Samuel said. "There are few options. A pancake out of potatoes, a pancake out of flour. There's butter made last week, in the well"—he pointed at a board on the floor—"and milk from this morning. If there are extra eggs, eggs."

"And meat?" she asked.

"We're waiting a shipment. The nearest kosher butcher is at Sioux Falls. He'll come through in a couple weeks. Maybe."

"What I ate last night, that was the last?"

"Only the best, for the bride."

Minna inspected his face carefully, trying to find a hint of venom, but he had nothing of Jacob's soft cheeks or Max's nervous eyes, only a self-sufficiency that was beginning to anger her. And the word *bride* from that perfectly symmetrical mouth. She no longer wanted to cry, she wanted to hit him, this older boy who would be her stepson, who seemed decent, almost gracious, yet also calculating, who made her feel nervous as a hare. She was not used to wanting a person to like her.

She worked to keep her voice steady. "When do you eat?"

"When there's food ready."

"I'll call for you, then."

"You might try shouting." For an instant Samuel looked possibly, vaguely, amused. Then he turned to go.

"I can shout," Minna blurted.

Samuel grabbed the top of the door frame and stopped. He kept his back to her—an affected pose, she thought, meant to make him look like a man. She chose to ignore the fact that it succeeded. "Is there a rake?" she asked.

"A species of one. What for?"

"The ruined wheat. I thought I'd use it to make a fire that didn't stink of shit."

"Ah. You're blunt. And you can shout. Yet you haven't asked what happened to the field."

"I didn't think it mattered. It's done."

Samuel released the door frame, let his arms fall to his sides, and breathed out a long, weary sigh—the kind of man's sigh Minna couldn't help but feel she'd caused.

"I'm sorry," she said.

Samuel stepped out into the sun. "The rake's behind the chicken house. But remember," he said, turning to face her, and she saw a crack now in his facade, the way the deepest cracks appear only in the brightest light. She saw, for an instant, how utterly unhappy he was. Then he smiled—her first glimpse of his strong, white teeth—and said brightly, "When the wheat won't make fire, it's not your fault."

ELEVEN

For a week, Minna devoted herself to finding a technique for burning the wheat. The stems were bent or broken but not snapped, so before she could rake, she had to cut. She found an ax behind the chicken coop, a dull single-bit but sufficient (*like this!* she heard her father say, his arms raised: *chop!*), and after milking—which was more difficult than she remembered it ever being with her father's goat—and washing and mending and pressing and weeding and a quick pull of potatoes from the garden, she spent the better part of the mornings hacking away on her knees.

If Samuel hadn't predicted her failure, she might have given up on the whole idea. But he'd been so sure of himself, almost snide: *When the wheat won't make fire . . .* and so in the afternoons, after serving dinner, she started up again, trying to make bundles of the cut wheat. The key was tightness, for which she needed twine, and the closest thing to twine was grass. But the grass was insistent on being grass. It snapped, mocking her, lying in her lap half the length it was before, then half again, then again, until only shards remained. It was sharp, and cut through her calluses. Her neck went stiff from looking down.

She imagined what she must look like from the outer fields, all morning beating the earth, all afternoon bent like an old woman over her lap.

But if the men noticed, they said nothing. Just like they said nothing to her about anything else, really, apart from the weather (the sky went on cloudless) and the food (her latkes, in particular, they praised). When Samuel and Max walked out into the field, Jacob would hang back and toss English words at her—*rock, sun, water, grass*—then make her say them back, and laugh. He let her hold a glittering, rainbow-colored, crescent-shaped rock that reminded her of a mollusk, or snail, and a sharpened piece of flint he claimed to have been given by an Indian when he was wandering he wouldn't say where. But around his father and brother he was newly shy with her. Max spoke to Minna softly but said little, his softness not a symptom of warmth so much as distraction, the same distraction that seemed to overtake him in the fields. Max, she observed, didn't dig with his sons so much as he traveled along with them, his shovel often nothing but a place for his hands to rest as he stared at the sky, until the boys moved on and he followed, more docile than the horse. Samuel viewed her out the corners of his eyes, except when they had to exchange necessary information, in which case he looked at her for the shortest possible time. Once, finding her in the yard on the verge of tears, the cow having just kicked over the measly two or three cups of milk it had taken Minna twenty minutes to pull, he gave her a curt glance, tied the animal's hind legs with a strap of leather, said, "Better to hobble her," and walked away again.

Minna wanted to shout at his back, *I know! I know!* But she didn't know much of anything, she realized. She'd sold her father's goat as soon as she could. She'd only half listened to her aunts' housekeeping advice. She'd never even completed her numbers lessons in school, which meant that she probably would have made a lousy bookkeeper, too. Even her father's ax—as soon as she could chop a log in two swings, he'd taken it away.

I know!

But Samuel had disappeared around the house.

It was as if there had been a collective decision to pretend that Minna had always been here. Or maybe it was Max's decision: maybe he'd directed his sons not to ask too many questions, thinking questions impolite. Max was exceptionally concerned with politeness, a concern which struck Minna as farcical, given its context. The men washed themselves in the same bucket she used to wash the dishes. The outhouse was made of crates, and stood only a few feet from the cave. There was little, within a few days, that Minna didn't know of their habits and smells and noises. And yet no one had asked where she was born, or whether she had siblings or parents or any family at all, or what she had done with her life up until now.

These weren't questions Minna ever thought she wanted to be asked. Yet it seemed possible, here, that her forgetting would finally overwhelm her remembering, that her past would evaporate into the gaping sky and leave her only with the present. Which was the gaping sky. Which were these strangers who refused introductions, as if they refused the notion that they were strangers. As if that might make them less strange.

Most frustrating, there was no talk of a wedding. Jacob had said *stepmother*, Samuel had said *bride*, but Minna had not been informed of any plan. She knew that engagement was not marriage. She had endured a brief engagement once before, soon after her father died, when her aunts betrothed her to a tailor's son, a short boy with eyes that were always moist. But when her aunts left, the boy's family sent the *shadkhen* to tell Minna that there would be no wedding. They had agreed to it only to please the indomitable aunts, but Minna was unsuitable, the orphan of a harlot and of the miner who couldn't make her stay.

She had been glad not to be getting married, but troubled, too, for she'd been rejected by a boy who looked like he was always crying. It was not as simple, she discovered, as wanting or not wanting. There were things you wanted only because they would mean that you were wanted. And now with Max, it was the same. That she didn't care for him, that she could barely imagine caring for him, that she caught herself, frequently, staring at his older son, barely mattered. She had brought herself here, across an ocean, for the purpose of marrying Max; if he decided she wasn't what he wanted, she couldn't claim indifference. She couldn't return. There was nowhere to return to.

LATE one morning, she was cooking dinner and, as an indulgence, a way of rewarding herself, letting her mind drift to Ilya, when Jacob ran in, grabbed the spoon from her hand, and dragged her outside.

"*Stone boat*," he said, pointing toward the field where Samuel was leading the mule as it pulled another load of rocks. "That sled is called a *stone boat*. You know *stone*, you know *boat*—you understand? It's funny, no? *Stone boat?* It sounds like a boat made of stones, but really it's a boat to carry stones!"

"Like *wood stove*," Minna said. "It's not that funny."

"Oh, come on." Jacob elbowed her softly. "Not even a little bit?"

She narrowed her eyes at him. "Why did you bring me out here?"

Jacob smiled. "Well. Since you asked. I was—I am—I worry you've forgotten what I said—about having an adventure."

"But this *isn't* an adventure."

"You could pretend it is. If you were happier. You're too unhappy."

Minna stood silent.

"I'm afraid you'll run away," Jacob said.

This was true—Minna could see it in his lower lip. She might have found it touching, if she wasn't so irritated. "Where would I even go?" she asked. "How would I get there?"

"Exactly! You can't leave."

"I don't get the sense that your father or brother would mind."

He shook his head. "He's going to marry you—I promise."

"He barely seems to know I'm here."

"He's just waiting."

"For what?"

Jacob gave her a desperate look, his lips twisted into his teeth.

"They're not divorced," she said, realizing.

"She dropped a Get at the Mitchell post office. No stamp, no postmark—not a clue where she was heading. Now he just has to sign it. He's going to! He's just waiting."

"For what?"

"I don't know exactly."

"He doesn't want me."

"No! He—I'll talk to him."

"Please don't."

"I will!"

"Jacob."

He pumped his arms, as if to run.

"What about Samuel?"

"What about him?"

Minna dragged a foot in the dirt. She wished she could take her question back. "What makes you think he wants me to stay."

Jacob studied her for a minute. "He hasn't said anything about wanting you to leave," he said. Then he smiled brightly, wiggled his fingers—ta ta!—and took off for the fields.

I N the days that followed, Max must have signed the Get, for he began to show Minna signs of affection. A pat of her hand, a poke at her hair. At first Minna thought the gestures merely polite. He'd been terrified, she realized, the night of her arrival, the first time he'd taken her hand. And yet he kept on reaching, trying to prove something, she supposed, to his sons, to her, to himself. That he was young enough? American enough? He was trying too hard. She hated watching him tremble as he pinched her arm before bed, hated watching his mouth move silently—praying, perhaps, that he wouldn't be struck down for contact with a woman who was not yet his wife. There were men, she knew, who feared that sort of thing. Moses had probably been one, before he'd found himself trapped on a boat with women and girls in need of carrying. In Beltsy, once, Minna had followed her father into the men's section of the synagogue and found herself promptly hauled out by the elbow, led into the dingy, lace-curtained women's room in back, and ordered to pray to God to forgive her. Minna had forgotten how to pray—they only went to *shul* twice a year, once on Yom Kippur and once, as today, on the anniversary of her mother's leaving—and so she cried instead. She couldn't see through the holes in the lace to find her father. She was angry at him for not having stopped her from following him, and sorry for him, too, that he was so lost in his misery he couldn't remember the rules, like other adults, and that he had a child who could not pray. Minna cried until the woman next to her grabbed her hand, and leaned down to explain, in a friendly hush: *The man's body? Contains his mind. The woman's? Only a body. We are body bodies. Yes? Understand?*

Minna had not understood. But she remembered. And over the years she'd seen how her body became a body body. Each swell of flesh, each darkening, each sudden hair that appeared full-blown, like a black moth from a chrysalis, made her more powerful and doomed. This was what made Max shake, she knew. To him, Minna was dangerous simply because she was she, and he was he. One day, apparently, he would take off his clothes. He was already doing it, in his mind. He would take off his clothes and reach for her and so on and so forth—and here was where Minna's mind left her, just like the woman at *shul* said, because to think clearly about the so on and so forth would be enough to make her gag.

A T night, while Minna washed the dishes, the men studied and prayed. Or Max studied and prayed. Samuel appeared to study but looked conflicted about the praying; one minute his eyes would be closed, his lips moving, then suddenly he'd be staring at the door, as if the mule and rocks and ruined wheat had gripped his thoughts. Jacob usually propped his chin in his hand and tried to pretend that he wasn't dozing.

There was only one lamp, which Minna insisted they use. She didn't mind scrubbing in the half dark of her own shadow, listening to her hands slip in and out of the bucket. There was no running water, as she'd imagined, nor a sink—not even a stone one, as she'd allowed in her worst version of her future life. But one had to adapt—Minna knew how to adapt. The bucket was strong, at least, and had no holes, and held water. If the air outside defied her existence, the water reaffirmed it: a finger plunged; a noise was made; water moved aside. Her grass cuts stung.

Only when she got into bed and pretended to sleep did the men begin to talk.

"The flour is almost gone." Max, in his offhanded way, as if commenting on the taste of the coffee. Which was also almost gone.

"We ought to make hay." Samuel. "Put up feed for the winter then sell the rest and buy flour."

"Mm." Max.

"It may be time to stop clearing rocks."

"We can't stop. Where will we plant, in the spring?"

"Where we planted last spring. It would have been enough . . ." An edge of exasperation in Samuel's voice. A quieting. A sharp inhale from Max.

"Why bother?" Jacob yawned. "Why bother repeating your-selves?"

Over the course of a few nights, Minna put together the story of the ruined field: while Jacob had been off "fetching" her, the wheat came ready for harvest, followed by a perfect day, hot and dry. But it was the Sabbath, and Max refused to work or to let Samuel work, and that night a hailstorm came and crushed the wheat.

Which surprised Minna—not the hail, but Max's refusal. She could have guessed that he would be observant, based on the questions they'd asked at the Look—but she'd assumed those were formalities, asked to every girl. In New York, when Jacob said *kosher*, Minna had made the word small, a token sort of *kashrus*, like how her mother had kept house, separating meat and dairy but halfheartedly, as one might separate quarreling children. She hadn't imagined that they would have to forgo eat-ing any meat until a *shoykhet* arrived with his special knives, or that the two stacks of plates—one *milkhik*, one *fleyshik*—would not be allowed to touch each other. She hadn't expected Max to don the *tefillin* every morning. She'd assumed, she realized, that Max's observance would be like her father's—full of desertion and guilt, not of diligence and prayer. She'd never known any-one, not closely, who so strictly followed the laws.

No one told the story of the Shabbos hail directly, of course.

Jacob hadn't been there. Max was ashamed, and also unrepentant. Samuel tried to hide his frustration by approaching the issue sideways:

"It may be that we've cleared all we can handle for the time being."

"It may be worth considering that we've saved no seeds for spring."

"It may be time to start putting up hay."

Samuel spoke to his father like people spoke to the old: trying to correct and redirect him without his knowing. Which wound up being more insulting, it seemed to Minna, than Jacob's flagrant disobedience. Jacob was honest, at least. One night, Max was delivering a quiet lecture on the importance of keeping their fundamental goals in sight—freedom, self-reliance, a new Zion for a new age—and Jacob didn't even wait for him to finish before asking, "Who needs Zion? We have America."

"We are Jews," said Max.

"Ah. So we'll starve, even in America!"

"Do you imagine, in Eretz Yisrael, that they work on holy days?"

It was Samuel who answered this without pause, as if he'd rehearsed for just such a question. "Perhaps one should stop imagining Palestine and start imagining South Dakota. One hundred sixty acres in South Dakota in need of a barn. A well. A new wagon. Two oxen would be cheaper to feed than the one mule. One could even imagine what might be accomplished if one was to put aside one's pride for a moment and accept a small contribution from the Baron's Aid Society." Samuel didn't emphasize *one*; it floated, a clandestine accusation. "We're not alone, after

all. That's a false idea. And we're not original. One might want
to believe we are, but why, if one also wants to believe that we're
building a new Israel? Who ever heard of one man—"

"Sender." Max's authoritative voice, which was too despon-
dent to sound truly authoritative. "Sender, that's enough."

A loud knock against the table. Jacob. "Enough with the Yiddish! Call him Sam." He knocked again. "Sammy! Call me Jake, and
call him Sammy! And call her Willamina, while you're at it. Or
Minnie. Minnie! Yes!"

Minnie. Minna wondered sometimes if her younger brother,
if he'd lived, would have been like Jacob—a diverter, a squelcher
of all earnestness. It was as if Samuel had been born into one
colander and Jacob into one far below that, and all the lightness
that ran off Samuel landed on Jacob. Another night he announced,
"Here's a joke. We need a joke. Otto told me this one. Why
didn't Jesus want money like all the other Jews?"

Silence.

Finally Samuel, muttering: "Go on, then."

"Because his hands were nailed to the cross."

"That is meant to be funny?" Max, outraged.

"I knew you wouldn't get it."

"Otto is an anti-Semite."

A groan from Jacob. "He didn't mean it like that."

"How else can it be meant?"

"He could mean it both ways." This was Samuel, of course.
Who rarely made a statement, Minna was beginning to realize,
that could only be interpreted one way. Even performing simple
tasks, he seemed to hedge: as he patched the chickens' roof,
or sorted rocks from potatoes, his hands moved with a thick,

tempered strength, and yet his eyes seemed to watch them mistrustfully. He wanted to be everything to everyone, model yeoman to his neighbors, studious son to his father. The Jewish American who wasn't Jewish, the American Jew who wasn't American. "Otto could be joking and serious at the same time," he continued. "He could mean well and mean badly. He may not know which it is himself."

"He knows." Max sniffed. "When I stayed for supper that one night? I think he fed me pigs' feet."

"That may be all they had."

"But he said it was chicken."

"Maybe it *was* chicken."

"It wasn't chicken."

"You didn't sound so sure"—Jacob again—"a minute ago. What does it matter now anyway? You haven't grown hooves."

Minna smashed her face into her pillow, stifling a laugh, but a piece of straw went up her nose, tickling, and she couldn't hold it in. She coughed as cover. The men shifted slightly on their crates.

She wondered what kind of looks they gave each other. Surprise? Warning? Tenderness?

It often happened this way. Their sudden silence. An uneasy peace. Which might help explain, she thought, why she was brought here. So that just when a mean, true argument was imminent, they might remember her, and stop.

MINNA continued pulling up grass in big fistfuls. *Wheatgrass, Indian grass, switchgrass, big bluestem*: one day she would decide to learn the names of her torture and be disappointed when she found them nowhere near as precise as how she'd identified them then: *sharpest grass, shiniest grass, curly grass, hardest-to-pull grass.* She pulled all of it up from the roots, giving in to the slices in her palms, watching the dry soil break into dust, which reminded her of an ancient tin of cocoa powder in Galina's pantry that she had sometimes dipped a finger into, after wetting it in her mouth. Minna missed the pantry: the cool air, the cold brass latches, the knowing, as she strayed off task, exactly what her task entailed, and to whom she answered. The men did not know, or seem to care, what she was doing. There were long moments in which she barely knew herself. She lost the idea of the twine, failed to recall the wheat.

Wheatgrass, Indian grass, switchgrass, big bluestem. The roots, as they ripped, made a crack, which added a small, murderous thrill to the moment. Minna felt little guilt. She remembered, from Beltsy, longer, slower ways for plants to suffer: trees eaten by moths, or pole beans by deer; carrots and potatoes gone to flower and fungus. Her father's long, tangled ivy, which sat on a stool in the hall just outside her mother's shop. The plant had been her mother's, and so had turned for her father into her mother, and he refused to trim it, or even arrange it, so that the vines unfurled in a great sprawl across the floor. They climbed up one wall, covered the window, twisted around the legs of a chair which was never again moved. When her father remembered his watering, the leaves shone. But in its dying seasons, the plant curled and hardened; whole lengths of vine looked like they'd been fried in schmaltz; the house filled with a diseased scent. A few times, Minna had filled a pot with water and approached. But she couldn't see how to get to it without stepping on it, which would break the brittle ropes, which her father would surely notice. Which would ruin him, she thought: he needed the plant to need him, just as he needed to neglect it.

He'd called the plant Weeper. Minna had heard others call such plants Spiders. Brides.

She ripped roots and watched the earth fall open. If the grass was particularly stubborn, she squatted, tucked her skirt between her legs, and levered her elbow against her thigh. One afternoon, she pulled so hard, and the roots broke so suddenly, she hit herself in the face with her fist. Her eyes watered—she touched the bone in her nose.

"Making progress, I see."

It was Samuel, behind her.

It was as if he only noticed her when she was on the ground, on her knees, going slightly crazy.

"Leave me alone," she said.

"I'm serious." His voice was unusually cheerful. "I've never seen a human being work so efficiently as a plow."

Minna tucked a loose clump of hair behind her ear, and turned. Samuel smiled. He walked closer.

"What is it you're trying to do, exactly?"

"Make a twine—to tie the wheat."

"And let me guess. The grass keeps breaking."

"How observant," Minna said.

Samuel lowered himself into a squat next to her. "What if I told you I had a possible solution?"

"I would ask why you didn't tell me sooner."

Samuel raised a hand to his jaw. He rubbed it a few times, as if to check when he'd last shaved (two days ago—Minna knew), then he looked at Minna's pile of grass, grabbed two fistfuls, and, deftly, between his last two fingers, picked up a third, smaller bunch.

"It may be, if you tried something like this—"

"I'm not your father," Minna said. "Just show me what to do."

Samuel kept his eyes on his hands. "Don't assume you know anything about my father," he said quietly. Then he crossed two fistfuls of grass, and brought the third, from his left hand, between them. He pulled from the right, then the left again, right, then left. With his thumbs he tucked the bunches through the middle; with his forefingers he pulled them tight. His knuckles were dark from the sun. He worked fast, but not sloppily. Soon each bundle of grass behaved as a single strand, weaving around the others.

"See?" he said.

Minna had never seen a boy, or man, make a braid. She thought it an oddly delicate thing for him to do, and yet he seemed, doing it, nothing like a woman. He handled the braid less like a chore than like another person—as if he were giving it a lesson in how to dress, or stand up straight.

"It's not difficult," he said, holding the half-finished braid out to her. "You just need enough grass to cancel out the weak points." Then, as if urging a child: "You try."

Minna couldn't decide how to respond. She knew, of course, how to make a braid. It was the one thing she remembered her mother teaching her: first, how to keep her hair out of her eyes, to make herself respectable, and then later, how to braid rags into rugs, and string into fringe. Applying the idea to grass was simple, obvious. That she hadn't thought of it herself irritated her. Samuel's condescension—*you try*—irritated her more. Then there was his admonishment, still in her ears: *Don't assume you know anything about my father.* There were eighteen years of shared history she would never be let into. But she sensed that this was not the point; that what Samuel meant to tell her was that she would never know Max, that he would keep himself from her, and that his sons would protect his right to do so—that this, perhaps, was another of her purposes here: to bind the three of them together, against her. Minna thought she ought to feel indignant. But she was distracted by the sensation of Samuel's eyes on her hands. She took the braid and unraveled it and liked the surprise this caused, in his body—a slight shift in posture, a discomfort she witnessed out the corner of her eyes. She began again, careful to follow the creases he'd made, then, as she grew more confident, to choose slightly shorter distances between them, making the braid tighter and stronger than his had been.

She reached the end, and gave it back.

"That's it," Samuel said, a bit less enthusiastically than before.

Minna smiled. "Now what?"

"Now . . ." He furrowed his brow.

"Can you think of nothing?" She lowered her voice to mimic his. "It may be . . . that we ought to tie it off."

Samuel smiled ruefully. Then, looking straight at her, he grabbed a blade of grass, tore the root off with his teeth, and used the root to tie a knot at one end of the braid.

Minna held out her hands. "I surrender," she said. But Samuel's playfulness quickly vanished. He'd seen the raw, red cuts that crisscrossed her palms.

Before she could hide them, he'd caught her by the wrists.

"What happened?" he asked, running his thumbs over her skin, which had taken on, she knew, the grated aspect of a washboard. She tried to free herself, but his grip was firm.

"The grass did this to you?"

Minna swallowed. She was humiliated, not only that he'd seen her wounds, and knew what stupidity had caused them, but that she felt so grateful for his touch—the pads of his thumbs studying her palms.

"You should soak them in the creek," he said.

"Fine."

"Water will help," he said.

"Fine."

She disengaged her hands from his. Her eye felt swollen where she'd hit herself before. It would bruise, she was certain; it might be turning blue already. Samuel looked stricken.

"You know," he said, "you could forget about the grass. Give up on burning the wheat, feed it to the animals." Then, seeing her anger: "Or keep on with it. Who knows, maybe once they're dry enough the braids will burn all on their own. And if that doesn't work, there are always the trees . . ."

"Fine. You've helped enough." Minna was looking at his boots; specifically, at the holes his feet had worn into the leather, and the shapes the holes added up to. She had seen his feet, outside the boots; they were large, with high arches and a broad knuckle and squat toes, the kind of feet women like her aunts would shun. Peasant feet. Farmer feet. Well. Minna liked them. She liked them more than she thought one could, or should, like a pair of feet. She felt her tongue, dry as wool—the strange air—Samuel's

gaze. She felt regret—her distance from other feelings she'd
meant to have.

"If you have questions . . ." he began again.

"Leave me alone," she said.

And he did.

THE trees were as real as any trees. Minna sat in their shade
and floated her swollen fingers in the creek, like goyim sausages in brine. It felt fine. *Fine.* It could even have felt good, but
the water was shallow, and a little too warm, and she found herself thinking, almost wistfully, of the glasses of ice, in the room,
in the basement, in Odessa. Which was perverse, she knew—
but not quite as bad as her other thoughts, of Samuel, who, as
he'd stood to leave, had leaned forward, so close to Minna that
his hair touched her cheek. He'd paused there, breathing on her
neck. Or this is what seemed to have happened; as Minna revis-
ited the events, their nature kept shifting. He'd had to lean forward, after all—hadn't he? Based on the mechanics of standing
up, he would have had to lean forward, yes. But did he have to
draw so close? And the breath he'd left on her neck—had it been
that, a breath, left for her, like a word, or had it simply been
breath, on its way out, happening to pass by as her neck came
into range?

People had to breathe, always.

Minna worked to cleanse her mind, to concentrate on the
creek before her—but this only brought her around to another
kind of longing: to escape, like the water: to change shape, run

elsewhere, head east. It was promising, yet preposterous, to think that east still existed; that all over the world people were living in cities and towns, sleeping in real buildings and walking in real streets——Minna had seen them, from the train, not a hundred miles away!——that civilizations had been toiled over and built and perfected and yet here she was, trying to turn grass into fire. Which would burn fast, if Samuel was right. Which would provide heat, perhaps, for one-twentieth of the time it had taken to gather.

The trees, he'd said. Just before the breath, which she would no longer allow herself to think on, he'd said, *the trees*. Yes. The trees could be cut down. She had thought of this already. They could be cut, and lit, as trees were. But then there would be no more trees, and no more of this shade, which felt almost shamefully good. There would be no place to rest from the sun except for the house that stank and was really a hill and contained these men who made her feel wrong in so many different ways. And how, in such a place, to tell time's passing if not for the changing of trees? Had September already come and gone? Was it still summer? These were questions only an idiot would ask, a woman who couldn't see straight let alone run a household. Yet she had no idea what seasons did here. Jacob had told her on the train about fires and blizzards, about cyclones that lifted horses off the ground and dropped them down miles away, but he did not explain any order to these events. All Minna knew was that since she'd been here, every day had been the same. Early and late, there was the low chirring of insects, and in the heat of the day, under the sky's searing glare, a lower rumble as if thunder was coming except the rumble never built or broke, it just went on like a sound that had been going on always and would continue on long after you were gone. The only clouds came late, and these were noncommittal: long skinny wisps that dissolved by the time you looked up again, leaving only, always, the same sun. Other suns she'd known possessed some degree of mystery— they hid, then reappeared in a new place; they darkened to the color of a rose one day, and the next, went white. But here, as long as it was daytime, the sun was always visible, and the color of sun, and impossible to look at; you could barely gauge the hour without burning your eyes. Jacob had shown her the only timepiece they owned. He'd pointed to a slim bulge in Max's vest pocket and taught her: *watch*. Which was different from, and the same as, *to watch*. He said that Max didn't like anyone to use his watch, that he believed they should ignore such arbitrary measurements, that their work here was God's and that God would make His rhythms known. Minna laughed and said that sounded unlikely, and Jacob laughed with her. But he didn't offer to ask Max for the watch.

The men would go on with their digging, and their not mentioning any kind of wedding. Max wouldn't notice her eye, even if it turned the color of a plum. Samuel wouldn't speak to her again until he found her failing in some new way. No one would call her Minnie—not even Jacob. He'd tried it once and she'd protested, because she felt she had to. She'd expected him to ignore her, and say, *Yes, Minnie! Of course I won't call you Minnie, Minnie!* But he'd surprised her by taking her seriously, and ever since she'd only been Minna.

If you were a bird, she thought, say a hawk, you might notice her. You might think, there is a girl making grass into fire. Or, there is a girl whose future stepson maybe—or maybe not—almost kissed her on the neck. You might take pity on her, for being able to see so far and yet know so little of what was around her. You might answer some basic questions. Like, what would one see, in this place, if one was a bird? Where were the other people? How far was the nearest town? Was there a doctor? Where did the Indians live? Did they have scalps, like Jacob said, strung up like flags? Did they have a name for Jews? How close was the butcher with his delivery of their meat? And beyond? How far was the closest city? Where could a woman buy a hat? Where were the skyscrapers, the streetcars, the confections? Where was America?

Marriage

TWELVE

Minna's veil was cut in the yard, next to the chickens. She sat on a crate while the woman doing the cutting stood behind her. Ruth, she was called, as one of Minna's aunts had been, and perhaps still was. And it seemed to Minna that this Ruth had something of that *Rut* about her, an evasiveness so energetic as to be its own form of directness. When Ruth had said, offhandedly, that she would "cut" Minna's veil, she did not mean, as Minna assumed, the first step of an elaborate tailoring process; she'd meant that Minna's veil would be cut from a flour sack.

"Stop moving," she kept saying. And though Minna was certain that she had not moved—where would she imagine herself going with a sack over her head?—she did not protest. Ruth was the sort of well-mannered woman who longed for an excuse to argue; Minna had seen her overzealous blinking the instant she rolled up with her husband and children on a wagon nearly as tall as the hill. They'd caught Minna off guard, making bread, her hands covered in a floury paste. Ruth and Leo Friedman, they said, from five miles north. Their horses were fast, they added, as if Minna had protested their efforts; it was barely a morning's journey. Leo chewed on a pipe that looked better than corncob. Ruth wore a bonnet. The sky hurt Minna's eyes, but she resisted raising a sticky hand to shade them. Even the children looked clean, despite their journey, and suddenly the grime that had been gathering, no matter Minna's best efforts at the creek, took on a weight against her skin: behind her ears, at her nape, between her breasts, she felt as if covered in fur. Leo smiled at her in a remote, teacherly way. He'd known Max when they were children, he explained, back in Kotelnia. He was the one who'd convinced Max to marry again; he'd even found the man in Mitchell who knew the men in New York who ran the agency which had sent away for Minna. Well, he said—half yawning—it was fine to finally meet her. Then he climbed down to go find Max. The children followed, but Ruth stayed sitting, blinking down at Minna as a dressmaker might: head to toe, unapologetic. Which suited Minna, who was tired of being treated delicately. When Ruth frowned, Minna stood straighter. A confidence overtook her: the particular nerve she'd felt as a girl only when she'd done something wrong. She released her hands from hiding. They reminded her, filmed in the gelatinous paste, of the egg sacks of kitchen moths. She held them up, and smiled.

What Ruth thought was difficult to tell. She was attractive in a handsome, permanent way, with the type of robust features that made it difficult to imagine her ever having been a girl. When she stood, her waist was thick in the uneven way of early pregnancy. She held a basket in one hand and a scissors in the other and announced that it would be her honor to cut Minna's veil. Then she jumped down from the wagon, entered the house only to exit a minute later, calling it airless and foul and what had Minna been *doing* with herself since she'd arrived over a month ago? Ach. Ruth would show her how to make a proper whitewash, but first—she beamed grimly—there was a bride to be made. She marched Minna around back, carrying a crate chair in one hand, the basket and scissors and sack in the other, a damp rag between her teeth. The rag she used to wipe down Minna's hands— "Spread your fingers, dear. *Wider*."—then she slipped the sack over Minna's head.

In a civilized place, Minna thought, she would be permitted to question these people, the Friedmans, before allowing them on her property, into her house. She would have the right to tell Max that he should warn her the next time company was com- ing. Yet what good would it do here? They lived without locks or fences or any semblance of privacy. For privacy, Minna would have to crawl down between the banks of the creek, or lie in a patch of soil she'd cleared, like an animal.

So she'd let the Friedmans roll in and now here she was in her own yard with her head in her own flour sack. She'd sneezed at first, but now she was used to the thin, powdery air and only sweated, lightly, from her scalp. As of this morning, Max still hadn't made any mention of a wedding, let alone one whose preparations were under way, but this was what Minna had been waiting for. Wasn't it? And there was something restful about being inside the sack, unable to see except for the soft white light, required to do nothing but sit still. Ruth's scissors rasped softly through the cloth. Minna could sleep like this. If not for the insistent jab of Ruth's voice.

"You'll like it here."

"Mm."

"It's a wonderful life."

Minna nodded.

"Stop moving! It's wonderful. Once you have children."

A light breeze puffed the sack away from Minna's ear. *Children*. She felt under sail—as if she might lean slightly and be carried off the crate. Ruth's voice, if she let it drift, could sound like a fiddle, being plucked and massaged.

"Children of your own. You'll see. We'll have a time of it then. Sit still! That cow needs grass."

"Mm."

"It won't produce without grass."

"No."

"It needs to pasture."

"I'll tell Max."

"You'll tell Max."

"Mm."

"You do know, dear, you're not marrying much of a farmer."

Minna knew what Ruth saw as she said this: the failed field, most of it still draped in crushed wheat. The shack they called the "barn," lying in ruins from a cyclone last spring. The fields they were still clearing, though the planting season was over. She wanted to say, *I know, I know! He couldn't hammer a nail to fix a fence—if we even had a fence!* But another voice warned her off— she didn't trust Ruth not to report her disloyalty. She barely trusted her to cut her veil. Besides, who was Minna to criticize Max's uselessness? Beneath the bed was what she'd been doing for the past month: a pile of braided grass that would bewilder Ruth. Minna had gotten fast with the braids. They were a small, absurd accomplishment, but she liked to peek at them, count them, see their mass grow.

"He gets by," she said.

"No," said Ruth. "The sons get him by."

Minna's gauzy state was gone now. This was another test, perhaps. *Are you loyal, or are you smart?* She smelled the rust in the room in the basement in the municipal building. *Do you remove your clothes because you're obedient, or depraved? Are you humble, or desperate?* A girl had to choose. Ruth's scissors bit, insistent: would Minna defend Max, or did she realize that he wouldn't, couldn't, provide for her? Or maybe Ruth was asking about a more particular aspect of Minna's loyalty—maybe what she really wanted was to goad Minna into talking about "the sons."

"Sit still!"

Minna stiffened.

"I've upset you," Ruth said, loosening the string around the sack. "There, there. It's not easy, I know, coming all this way not knowing who you'll marry. Of course, I came by way of an aunt who knew a girl who'd married one of Leo's cousins. I had some idea of what I was getting into. And I didn't come straight to Sodokota. We were years in Milwaukee first." Her thumbs pressed above Minna's ears. "But it's not so bad," she added. "It could be worse. Apparently, he's leaning toward letting you keep your hair."

Minna grabbed the sack with both hands. She hadn't thought

to hope against baldness. She'd been worried about hunger and cyclones, and, when she couldn't help it, about whether Max's pale, furtive fingers on her skin would only be irritating, or unbearable. But to be shorn, like a sheep, like the women she'd always felt ashamed for? To wear a *sheytl* on her head? The wigs reminded her of stuffed rabbits, or squirrels.

She lifted the cloth until she could see her boots. "How do you know that he won't make me cut it?"

"I don't *know*. Let go of the sack, dear. Who ever knows what a man will do? The first wife wore a *sheytl*, black as ink. But Leo says Max says the boys are trying to convince him."

"Which way?"

"To let you keep it. Of course. Let go."

Minna let the sack fall. She wondered which of the boys had said what about her hair. Since his braiding lesson, Samuel had looked at her more directly than usual, which was the opposite of what she'd expected—as if to challenge, or further confuse, her memory of his breath.

(Which she was not supposed to be thinking about.)

"Their mother, you know—she was a very beautiful woman."

Minna straightened on the crate.

"I mean beautiful in the way no one disputes."

"Oh."

"Perhaps I shouldn't tell you this. Perhaps you'd rather not know?"

Minna waited.

"She had money," Ruth said. "Timber money. Lina Rozenberg was her name, as in Rozenberg Timber."

Wood, Jacob had said. *Our mother sold wood.*

"You wouldn't know it where you're from but Rozenberg's was something else. Everyone knew Rozenberg. Enough money she could have married any boy she wanted. So she chose the one destined to become a great rabbi."

"I don't understand," Minna said.

"Max, dear. That was Max. His father and grandfather and great-grandfather, they were all rabbis."

Minna started to turn around, but Ruth grabbed her shoulders and set her back in place. "I'm still working. Of course you want to know, of course you would, why Max himself didn't succeed. I'm afraid I've aroused your curiosity—though really it isn't my place. I don't have all the answers, though I do know certain things, by way of Leo. Who wouldn't like my telling you, I'm sure. But he won't have to know, will he, dear?"

Minna shook her head as slightly as she could.

"Good," Ruth said. "Now sit still. I should say, before I tell you, that Leo was younger than Max, and lived outside town—his family were farmers—so it's not as if he knows the story intimately. He knows what everyone knew—which was quite enough, as far as I'm concerned, given that people came from all over to watch the beautiful Lina Rozenberg's wedding parade, and eat from her father's feast, and dance at his dance—Lina and Max were lifted in chairs made from his trees!! Of course, that's not the point, dear. The point is what happened after. It was nothing evil, not at first—only Max, it turned out, wasn't like his father or his grandfather, he was missing some *klugshaft* or *heylikayt*, however you want to call it. Lina realized this. Everyone saw her realize it. They saw her, *bislekhvayz*, turn from him. She bore him two sons, then stopped. She was cold to his parents.

Then Max was passed over for rabbi in favor of his cousin and he fell into despair. Lina would barely look at him now. She looked at Samuel instead, she sent Samuel to *yeshiva*, said Samuel would be the next *Baal Shem Tov*. For years they lived like this. Imagine. Then the town was attacked. Leo was there, even Leo will admit he was terrified, every house emptied onto the street, chairs and mirrors and windows and cradles, everything smashed, and then the *shul* was raided, too, the Torah scrolls carried out like heads, Leo says, and the Russians herded the most pious men together and raised their crowbars and gave the men a choice, their bodies or the scrolls. And man after man chose themselves. Their knees were broken, or their arms. One was blinded. Both eyes. Then the Russians got to Max and he stood there in front of the whole town, in front of his wife and his sons and his own father, who'd already been beaten, and he chose the scroll."

Ruth paused, her scissors still. "You can tell now, can't you, how he never forgave himself."

Minna nodded. And now Ruth didn't scold her for moving and in the absence of Ruth's scolding Minna didn't know what to do or say. The whole story was awful. Minna was the only one who'd take him. She was ugly next to Lina, and poor, and desperate herself, in her own ways. Which made her, perhaps, a perfect match for Max—which made the whole business more shameful.

"Are you done?" she asked.

"Almost." Ruth tugged on the veil. "So you see when they got here, it wasn't the sod hut that ran Lina off. It wasn't the work, as the boys would have you think. And *that* is why I tell you this little story, my dear! Yes. Not as gossip, but encouragement! You shouldn't let a little hardship put you off."

The scissors made a final snap. "There. All done. I'll hem it but there."

Minna felt a breeze at the back of her head.

"Now you can see your lovely hair."

Lovvvvily, was how Ruth said it, savoring the word, and Minna understood. Ruth herself was shorn. Of course. It shouldn't surprise her, yet did: that the braided bun she'd glimpsed under Ruth's white, American bonnet was made of another woman's hair. An Indian's, maybe—or maybe it had been ordered from Sioux Falls, wherever that was, where the meat was supposed to come from, or from Milwaukee, or Chicago. Or perhaps it was a Gypsy's hair—maybe Ruth had carried it across the ocean wrapped in a shawl, like a little dog, on her own journey from Odessa, or Kiev, or Vilna, or some town Minna had never heard of. Lina Rozenberg must have had one, too, but apparently she would have worn hers beautifully. Whereas Ruth's embarrassed her; she tied it back, kept it concealed; she must have hated Lina. Ruth's scalp must be rough and gray, closer to the surface of a man's chin than a woman's head. Minna felt a rush of sorrow for her, and wondered if this was how friendship began. Then she heard again the way Ruth had said *lovvvvily*, and thought of the pleasure she'd taken in telling Minna about Max, and knew that Ruth's jealousy was the sort so minutely aimed, it was an insult: apart from her hair—which was not in fact lovely but a tangled mess, for Minna hadn't seen the point of using her comb since she'd arrived—she coveted nothing of Minna's life. She was like the noblewoman who used to roll through Beltsy on a carriage with rubber springs, who as she passed the little porches with the little people living their little lives, doled out flattery of the most condescending kind: *What a lovvvvily flower! I've never seen such a fat baby! How lucky you are to have such fine lace curtains!*

"You might have left the sack a sack," Minna heard herself say. "It will look like one anyway."

Ruth had begun raising the cloth—now she was a still, dark spot behind it. "You would rather I hadn't come?"

"I didn't say—"

"You need no company?"

Minna lifted the cloth from her face. She squinted up. Ruth's smile did not involve her eyes.

"I only meant—just—everyone will know it's a sack—"

"Everyone." Ruth laughed. "Who is this everyone you imagine attending your wedding?"

"I don't—"

"You need no company, yet you want to be seen."

Flaps of veil stung white in the corners of Minna's eyes. She wanted to pull it down again and sink back into the fog.

"Try again," Ruth said. "What is it you mean?"

Minna wiped sweat from her forehead. How old was Ruth? Forty? Twenty-five? Behind her, the children were running across the dead field, kicking up dust, cocoa powder. "I only meant, it's a flour sack. I meant, why not call it what it is."

Ruth nodded. Her smile was gone; she looked kinder. "Is that why you've done nothing about your house?"

It took Minna a minute to understand. Even then, she didn't know the answer; she'd given the house little thought except that it was despicable. Was Ruth right? Maybe. Maybe Minna wanted to leave her poverty uncovered, unmistakable. Maybe this was how she meant to punish the men. Then again, maybe not. Either way, she couldn't see how it was any business of Ruth's.

She tucked her chin. "I've done nothing about the house because I don't know *how*," she said, thinking this her best defense, forgetting that it was in fact true. She didn't expect the tears that began spilling from her eyes. They were fat tears, heavy on her cheeks; they felt almost false—like she was falsely crying. Then she realized that she couldn't stop. The swarm of children halted in the yard, and stared at Minna with a grave, brutal fascination, and she remembered the children in Beltsy, and thought these are the same as those, they can recognize an orphan. And perhaps Ruth sensed Minna's desire to snarl and stamp her feet at them, for she shooed the children away and told Minna to "Cry it out," and when Minna was done, she handed her a leftover scrap from the flour sack, told her to wipe her nose, and congratulated her. She was a real bride now. Did she know that song? *Kallehle, Little Bride, cry, cry, cry. Your bridegroom will send you a plate of horseradish. And your tears will pour all the way down to your toes.* Hadn't Minna learned that one? (She hadn't.) Didn't every child adore that song?

Ruth's basket contained one jar of jam, one of pickled beets, another of pickled cucumbers, and another of herring. In the back of the wagon were bags of potatoes, which Leo carried into the house over Max's protests. No, they wouldn't stay for dinner, no, it was all for Minna and Max, no, they had to leave now, to get home before dark. They would see them in less than a week, for the wedding, which Leo and Ruth would host.

"It will be my pleasure," Ruth told Minna. But Minna was watching Leo and Max, who'd stopped in the doorway of the house and lowered their voices. Samuel and Jacob stood nearby, obviously listening but pretending otherwise. Leo spoke with his arms folded, his pipe nodding, one hand occasionally reaching to scratch an ear. Max's hands leaped and fell. Then Leo held out an arm, offering Max the privilege of entering his own house. The boys followed. The door shut, leaving the women and children outside.

Minna tried to catch up with Ruth, who was explaining, step-by-step, the process for papering and whitewashing earthen walls. They'd had a dugout, too, Ruth said, before Leo built the two-story frame house they lived in now. Minna pictured the Friedman homestead: snow white and dustless and twice as tall as their wagon. Which still wouldn't be as tall as the house she'd imagined for herself, once upon a time. But she was adapting. Her ideas were adapting. She would be happy, she told herself, with anything taller than a cave.

"See?" Ruth said. "It's easy. You just have to make sure the paste doesn't get too thick or too thin. Moderation. As in everything." Ruth smiled, expectant. But before Minna could think to thank her, she'd turned her attention to her youngest son, who was trying to climb into the wagon by himself, using the wheel's spokes as his ladder. He kept bumping his head and falling, then starting the whole thing over again, until finally he pinched a finger and started to cry.

"Abraham!" shouted Ruth, and Minna held her breath, waiting for a tirade or slap—yet when the boy ran over, Ruth kissed his finger and let him fall into her skirts and stroked his head. "*Nakhes'l*," she purred, "*nakhes'l*," like an entirely different woman from the one Minna thought she'd met. Ruth pressed two fingers to the boy's eyes, then to his mouth, then to his nose, and he laughed now, as if it were a game between them. Then she covered his ears, and said to Minna, "When you have your own, you'll belong here." She nodded at the small bulge at her stomach. "You'll see. This life."

It's wonderful.

"It's wonderful. A blessing. Soon enough, you'll never think to want anything else."

The men emerged from the house. They might have been arguing, it was hard to tell: Leo appeared certain of something and Max just the opposite, but perhaps these were simply their standard expressions, each one amplified by the other. Samuel and Jacob followed, eyes on their feet.

"Ruth!" called Leo. "Ready? Giddyup!"

"Ach," Ruth said quietly, so that only Minna could hear. "Giddyup. This is his new favorite word."

Minna nodded. She guessed it must be its own kind of difficulty, one she'd never contemplated, to go to a new place with someone old. But she didn't look at Ruth any more than Ruth looked at her. They watched as Leo held his hand out to Max, then as Max—who was taller—stooped a little, and shook.

"It used to be Leo worked on his father's farm," Ruth said, "and Max spent all day at the the *beis medrash*, bound for greatness." She chuckled. "Now look. Here he is, trying to be a farmer."

Minna stared straight ahead. This was Ruth's victory speech, she supposed. There was a cruelty to this woman.

But Ruth put an arm around Minna's shoulders, and pulled her in close. "You know," she said. "It's better that you love him."

Minna didn't answer at first. Ruth's voice was quiet, almost placating, as though she knew the impossibility of Minna following her advice. Marry Max, yes. Love him—was that really necessary?

"I barely know him," Minna said.

Ruth took a loud, sharp breath. Then her arm was gone and she was up, pushing her son toward the wagon and walking after him, not stopping or even looking back as she called, "And you think you are original in this?"

THIRTEEN

MINNA knew about hiding. Her own as a child, under steps, begging to be found. Her father's, in his voice. There was hiding in cellars, beneath bridges, underwater with reeds for air. Hiding by cutting off a toe, or a finger, disappearing the parts they'd want when they came to take you to fight the czar's battle.

But it was one thing to hide yourself. It was another to be hidden, under a glorified sack, while near strangers and total strangers witnessed your bridegroom witnessing that it was in fact you underneath, that you had not run.

(And where would you run?)

This was her wedding, then. In Ruth and Leo's clean wooden house, with two other Jewish families, and Otto and his wife—whom Ruth invited at the last minute, to Max's annoyance—and Jacob clanging out a beat with two spoons against his knee—he wouldn't say where he'd learned to do such a thing—and a woman whose name she would never remember humming above the spoons, and Minna under the bright obliteration of her veil.

She determined, at the start, to use the veil to her advantage, to wander through the ceremony unseen—privacy, at last. But as events progressed, as Minna was led to the *chuppah* and made to sit (the poles were too short to stand under) and as an unfamiliar man's voice began to pray behind her and the dim form of Max came to occupy the stool to her side and as Minna found herself unable to weep, as she was meant to do, she discovered that her strategy was flawed, for it assumed that the face was honest, that to hide the face was to hide one's true feelings, or lack of feeling. It forgot that the face could be its own means of hiding, that without her face Minna was nothing but stubborn, unsubtle parts. Right now, for instance, she might have twisted her face into something that looked like weeping, but she could not make her body shake. It was as the magician had said: the body knew nothing but what it was: sensation: the smell of flour, the cool slime of sweat at the small of her back, the pull of Galina's mother's too-large dress across her shoulders because she'd sat without sight and couldn't adjust it and no one had helped her to adjust it and she was being pulled backward on the stool as if attached to the wall by a rope between her shoulders, as if they were reeling her in and laughing because they didn't want to focus on the fact that she wasn't weeping and that they therefore weren't weeping.

If the bride couldn't weep, who would?

A cool weight was placed in her hands. Her veil was lifted. Max nodded at the wine cup, nodded at her. His lower lip hung open, his brow showed its wrinkles; at least, Minna thought, she had her own hair. She drank—chokecherry wine, she learned later, though now she only registered it as the strangest sort of grape, a tacky grip in her tongue that caused tears to well in her eyes at last and she was momentarily grateful, but now the veil dropped again. The cool weight was taken away. A hand— Ruth's?—grabbed her wrist and pulled her to standing, or rather to crouching, to clear the *chuppah*, and began leading her in circles around Max. Seven, Minna knew, though she could not count, she grew quickly dizzy and let Ruth do the counting, Ruth do the pulling. Hunched, she felt like an ape; veiled, like the shadow of an ape, following its own wrist round and round. In her gauziness she thought of Galina laughing—oh, how she would laugh!—and from Minna's throat a panicked giggle rose up which she didn't bother to squelch. The men were beating their hands against their laps, trying and failing to keep time with Jacob's spoons, as unskilled at unison as men singing in *shul*.

Minna grew dizzier when Ruth sat her down. She closed her eyes, though it made little difference, simply black traded for white. She thought she might be able to cry now, out of sheer misery, but couldn't manage even the slightest shiver of her shoulders. Her head felt like it was still being dragged in circles. She concentrated on the one beat that kept time with Jacob, which must be Otto's, she decided, and pictured the gentile chapels down in the mine, salt-dug rooms with salt-carved icons and salt lanterns, *lickable chandeliers* her father used to call them in his good moods, he knew because he prayed in those rooms, or pretended to pray in those rooms, to those long-melting icons, so that he could rest. And Minna knew, from walking across Beltsy's Out Bridge on a Sunday morning, past where the white sides of lard hung on hooks, and from walking through Mikhailovskaya Plaza in Odessa on any morning, she knew the gentile melodies were simple ones, led by one voice and followed as one voice, like a soft, grave agreement. She felt a longing to go home with Otto and his wife. She wanted to be taken in as a child, to be sung to as if an infant.

The beating stopped. Max had her hand again. A ring, which Minna guessed Max had sold something far more necessary to buy, though she didn't yet know what. She thought of the seats on the train, the endless rolls and cups of coffee of his absent courtship, his desire to promise what he couldn't give her. The ring slid over her finger and seemed to disappear, and she itched to feel it with her thumb, this new ornament with its weightless weight, its covenants of an entire civilized race, but Max held her thumb against her hand and her fingers against her other fingers and said, Minna, you are consecrated unto me.

T HE table, shining. Globes of fat in the chicken soup. Gravy slick as rain. A silver fish, caught and gifted by one of Otto's sons. Fish! And the carrots: the shocking, flamboyant carrots rolling in butter—had carrots ever been that color? When had Minna last eaten a carrot? She had to stop herself from reaching into the bowl, grabbing, squeezing the sun into her throat—

Then she was blind again. At the back of her head was a clenching—Ruth's hands, knotting, replacing the veil with a blindfold. Minna had never heard of this custom—if that's what it was. She moved her hands to her waist, knowing what she would find: the loose dress even looser, billowing around her stomach like curtains. She twisted away. "What are you doing?"

Ruth caught her shoulders. "Hold still."

"You've taken my belt." Minna knew the point was the blinding, not the taking, but she couldn't help thinking about the white satin mashed into a knot.

"Give me back my belt."

"Don't make a scene, dear."

"I won't make a scene if you give me—"

"You're making one already."

"Give me—"

"You'll embarrass yourself. Minna. Max wants it this way."

Ruth's voice was calm—even tender. Minna had been so focused on the food, she'd forgotten about the people: now they surrounded her, unmoving as trees; now they could see her face, though she still couldn't see theirs. She felt a sudden ugliness in her mouth, spread open, all its disgust making it disgusting. She grew aware of the bones in her nose snarling.

She made her face fall flat. Even as she trembled with anger, she brought her teeth together, lips together; she willed her cheeks and nose and chin into one plane: tongueless, intractable. She didn't shrug Ruth's hands off her shoulders; she would not give her that satisfaction. She sat in the chair to which she was led, and took the fork which was handed to her. In her brief era of sight, she hadn't seen Max, but he was next to her now; she could feel the particular distance he liked to keep. Ruth's laughter circled the table as she served. Someone called for a toast, but Minna didn't dare grope for her glass for fear she'd knock it over;

she had seen Ruth's crystal, and knew that it was real. *L'chaim!*
Glasses clinked. She sat. She waited for the conversation to begin
before cutting into her food. There was the harvest. There was a
new style of plow, better for this particular soil. There was the
question of official statehood, and whether anyone cared. There
was news of a man traveling Dakota Territory, selling fraudulent
medicines, and of workers striking in Chicago, and of a strange
tower being erected in Paris. There was a story, told by Leo, about
a Norwegian woman who'd been stolen away by an Indian tribe
and taken back to live in their tepees. When the woman's people
found her, he said, she didn't want them anymore. She'd been
brainwashed. She was wearing skins and living with an Indian
man and her hair was plaited down her back.

It wasn't a true story, Minna guessed. There were likely a hundred versions—a Finnish woman stolen by outlaws; a German
woman by snakes; in Beltsy, it had been a good Jewish girl living
happily with the wolves. Here it was Indians. Always Indians. She
remembered her father telling her, *Always know where the people are
who are more despised than you*, and she supposed this was why everyone talked so much about the Indians, though no one but
Jacob—if he was to be believed—had ever met one; it was a
comfort to know they were out there hiding, living, being hunted.
Everyone loved Leo's story. The table shook. Minna picked out
different laughs: Leo's rolling, Jacob's high and staccato, Otto's
as clean and even as his clapping. The only voice she knew and
didn't hear was Samuel's, which made her self-conscious, for she
couldn't help feeling that he must be watching her not laughing,
too. She began to eat more quickly, stabbing fish, meat, a dried
sweet fruit she couldn't identify. The carrots were even better

than the sun, better than a Messina orange, better than anything food could be if it was only food and not deliverance—

"Minna. Love. We have all evening."

She stopped chewing. In Max's voice was an unusual confidence, even a command. Minna forgot, for long stretches, that Max had been married before. He'd sat at a feast like this. He'd blindfolded a bride. Or maybe the blindfolding was new, an amendment, so as to possess Minna more securely. She felt gravy dribble onto her chin. She felt a shadow rise up, a tall gloom of a gone wife. Was this their intention, she wondered, these women like Lina and her mother who left without permission or blessing? To leave themselves behind like unfinished smudges, dark enough to change the view yet faint enough to make you think you might be mad?

At Minna's neck was a pinching: the collar Ruth had made, held up by wire. Because without it, she'd said, the dress, well— how to say it—the dress was just a little bit—wanton.

B Y the time Ruth untied Minna's blindfold, the guests were saying their good-byes. The windows were black, swimming with flickers of lamplight and faces, which Minna couldn't look at directly. She felt as if she'd been somewhere shameful. Her mouth, she feared, was spattered with flecks of food. She was tired, tired as if she'd been looking into the sky for days straight, so tired that when Ruth handed her back her sash she didn't tie it around her waist but crushed it in her fist. As Max tugged her away from the window, she stared at the floor, and as Ruth began to lead them up to their room, she focused on the children's

slippers, and Leo's polished boots, and Jacob and Samuel's un-
polished boots, bandaged so thickly in cloth they had become
more cloth than leather, though for the special occasion her
what, yes, her stepsons had used fresh white rags: there were
Jacob's, haphazardly wound into shapeless blocks; and Samuel's,
so neatly wrapped she couldn't help but imagine him wrapping
them, with utter and delicate attention, like a woman might
wrap a fine scarf around her neck.

Minna's blood ran so loud she was sure everyone in the room
could hear it, and she was ashamed of this, too. She didn't want
Max and she didn't fear Max, not in the way wives were meant
to want and fear husbands, as if he were God reduced to man. She
was barely thinking of Max; she feared nothing but more shame;
she wanted nothing but sleep. On the stairs, she couldn't see her
own shoes—or rather Ruth's shoes, borrowed—beneath the
giant dress. Lifting her legs was like lifting buckets of water from
the creek. She gripped Max's hand for support. She thought how
long it had been since she'd walked up stairs, gone from one
realm to another yet still under one roof, that wooden, again,
perhaps, metamorphosis, she thought she should be grateful and
yet she wasn't, Ruth's "gift" of her bedroom felt like mockery,
pity, she and Leo and the children all stuffed into a bed in the next
one, pretending to hear nothing.

She was not grateful. And as the door to the room opened, she
was no longer afraid. It was only a room, only a square space built
to separate here from there. She had been in rooms before. She
was so tired, and there was a bed high off the floor, an iron frame
painted white with a white feather blanket and white feather pillows, too. It was just like in the story, which Minna had forgotten,

the story the women always told in the square after a wedding. Minna and her father were always there, listening, even if they hadn't attended the ceremony or watched the parade, they always went to stand among the stragglers, he with the men, Minna peering through the spaces between the women's waists. A reluctant bride, went the story . . . though the reasons for her reluctance were always changing: sometimes it was a repulsive groom who tripped over his caftan and licked his lips; or the bride's sense of duty had been damaged in the womb by her mother's infidelities; or maybe the bride had neglected to attend her *mikvah* bath and was afraid, either of soiling the groom or, less nobly, of being found out. Whatever the reasons, whatever woman was doing the telling, the story always involved the groom entering a room with a large white feather bed. He took off his clothes, all except for his *tallis* and his *yarmulke*, but when he reached the bed, he found no bride. He patted the sheets. He lifted them up. He patted again. Finally, he looked into a corner and there, sitting on a high chest of drawers, was his bride. She wore her dress still, and her veil, so that he couldn't see her eyes. The groom began to sweat. Finally, he spoke. *Well?* Or sometimes, *And?* Or, *Have you taken ill?* Once, Minna heard it: *Will you come down from there in my lifetime?*

The woman telling the story would pause here for effect. She looked around slowly, delightedly. Then, at last, she delivered the final line, which was always exactly the same: *The white bride on the dresser was nothing but a dress stuffed with pillows.*

The square would fill with laughter. Everyone laughed except for Minna, who found the story terrifying. Where had the real bride gone? But now the door closed and Max turned to face her and Minna thought, I was a little girl. She'd pitied the stuffed bride as much as she had the real one, like she'd pitied cats stuck up trees, fish stuck in grass, the village dwarf with the egg stuck in his neck. Poor bride, poor bride, poor bride. Only later did she realize that sad things were warnings: not to grow up, not to be a bride at all, not a stuffed one on a dresser or a live one who wanted to run away. But by then it was too late—she was far away and alone and knew only fools refused to be brides. And now here she was on her wedding night, and she had not wept and she didn't believe anymore that this was the end of one life and the beginning of another, or that what happened to-night would truly change her. It would mark her, for others, and her names would be lost—Losk, girl—but she wouldn't be any different until she was different and it wasn't going places or doing things that changed a person, it was something she hadn't been shown or taught and she was so tired and there was the tall white bed and she thought: the brides weren't pitiable, they were stupid. There was the cool, soft feather bed. Why not climb in?

Max was holding his own hands, smoothing one over the other, a nervous motion Minna stopped by taking them into hers. Still Max made no move, he only gazed at her as if at a small, foreign animal. But hadn't he done this before? Hadn't there been another woman, a *beautiful in the way no one disputes* woman, whose clothes he'd known how to remove? Minna's knees were about to buckle with exhaustion. She pulled toward the bed, taking Max with her, along with his cooked, woolly scent—she would bear it, she would count, the way Galina had told her—but as she pushed herself up onto the feather bed, Max pulled back. She heard him scuffing across the floor, but her eyes were already closed. She lay back. Horizontal at last. She breathed.

"Minna?"

Had hours passed?

"This is for you. To change . . ."

Minna forced her eyes open. Max stood above her, holding what looked like a white sheet. She squinted. In the light of the room's one lamp, she made out a ribbon of lace. Pearl buttons. She propped herself up to sitting. She hadn't had a true, full-length nightgown since she was a little girl. The weave was fine and soft and light across her fingers. She sat up straighter. Max had an oddly official look on his face.

"Please put it on," he said, and nodded discreetly toward the room's far corner. And somehow Minna managed to stand up and walk without laughing: women did so much changing, she thought, only to unchange, so much dressing only to undress. She thought of Galina struggling to squeeze into stockings and corsets and bones—Minna had helped her—only to be sucked out again as soon as possible by a suitor. She thought Galina must have been more ashamed of herself, in some way, than Minna had realized. She held her breath. How would she explain her giddiness? She couldn't explain it to herself except to say that she was focused on the wrong thing again. But what else should she do? Look straight at Max and begin, at last, to weep? Tell him she would put on the gown but wouldn't take it off? Tell him she suspected that it had belonged to Lina and refuse it altogether? But she wanted it. She wanted the gown and she wanted to think about Galina instead of Max and she wanted to follow Max's instructions and find sleep at the end.

From the corner, she glanced back. He was sitting on the bed now, not looking at her, of course, he wouldn't look without permission, he was a coward when it came down to it, a coward with tyranny in him, like any coward perhaps. He'd taken off his jacket. His shirt was creased as if from sweat, and though she knew he hadn't worked—did he ever really work?—she decided to pretend that he'd just come in from a hard task because his back looked stronger and broader that way. *Transform what you can*, Galina said, *then count away the rest.*

The wedding dress was big enough that after removing the wire collar, Minna shrugged the rest off her shoulders, spun the lacing around to the front, and stepped out. She wobbled slightly as she took off her drawers and undid her bodice, then she quickly pulled the nightgown over her head, buttoned the collar up to her chin—laughter again but now she felt sick, as if her stomach was filled with air—and before she could think she started to walk, and to count as she walked, one, two, three, four—and then she was standing in front of the man as his gaze ran up the white mass of her and settled on her eyes. Minna looked away. She counted one and reached for his top button, careful not to let the tops of her hands brush his beard. Two, and undid it, three, undid the next. Max didn't look up at her now but stared straight ahead, as if through her gown and through her flesh and through the wall behind her and seven she pulled his shirt from his pants, eight she reached the last button. She was surprised, sliding the cloth over his shoulders, to find his chest nearly hairless. She had imagined a jungle to match his beard but here was skin, pale, so pale it was nearly blue but skin just the same. She forgot to count she was so relieved—then Max's hands were on her waist, drawing her toward him, and she felt his beard through her gown, rough and spongy the way she'd feared, and his breath, moist, and a heat coming off the rest of him, she started to count again, one, maybe it was the same heat with all of them, a helpless fever, on the edge of deranged, nothing to do with what they wanted to be but only what they were, even the apologetic, red-bearded doctor had given off this heat, four, she ran her hands down his back, five, up, she was fully awake now though she didn't want to be, *count until the numbers are all you see*, eight and Max slid his fingers down the gown to her hips and the heat at least made his hands feel bigger, they seemed each one to hold a whole thigh, to wrap around her calves, eleven, he was at the bottom of the gown, then under it—she glanced down. He looked like he might be tying his shoes. But then his hands were on her ankles, his skin on her skin, and then thirteen they'd moved up to her knees and fourteen to her thighs again, and she waited for him to duck his head under the gown, she held her breath, she thought she could bear anything if only he didn't touch her with his beard, not there, she'd taken a bath in Ruth's kitchen this morning, her first in weeks, her *mikvah*, Ruth declared it, she'd washed her insides so carefully and now the idea of that spongy moss . . .

Abruptly, Max dropped her gown and stood. He pulled the cover back off the bed, took her by the shoulders, turned her around, and sat her down. It was even worse having to sit and do nothing but watch Max unbutton his trousers. Was she meant to lie back, to give him privacy as he'd done with her—or would that be an insult? Did he want her to watch? His trousers fell to the floor. She longed for the blindfold. It looked like a mistake, a wobbly, digitless limb, as if it had been removed from its making before it was ready. Under her chin, a finger asked her to look up. Her cheeks blazed; she'd been staring. She focused on his forehead, that clean, blameless plain, one, and let him lay her back, two, found, three, that she was thankful for his hands on her shoulders, four, even if they were damp through the gown, five, even if she didn't want them, six, they told her what to do. She lost count again and he was over her, his mouth on her stomach, but still he hadn't undressed her, still she was a white gown he was kissing, and she felt a little irritated, a little insulted— then she raised up her head and saw, grazing its way up the whiteness, Max's dark *yarmulke* flapping and flopping, and Minna couldn't stop her stomach from convulsing with laughter. Max raised his head. His face was flushed. She waited for anger. But he gave her only a sheepish grin. And in her shock, Minna grinned back. Then Max stood up from the bed again and blew out the lamp and in the after-light of the dark she saw the memory of his shape in the room and it wasn't young but it wasn't stooped, either, and it wasn't strong but it moved with a certain tiptoey grace and she thought of his grin again and saw it without his beard and as he lowered himself over her she discovered that he didn't have to be exactly Max, and she didn't have to be exactly Minna, at least not Minna encased in who knew whose nightgown. He stood onto his knees, over her, and her eyes were adjusting to the dark but not so much that she could make out details and his form up there looked impressive, a high distant object that might choose her or not. She felt him lean back and pull her gown up her calves and the air was cool and up her thighs and it was cooler and there it was again, the warm center she hadn't felt or wanted to feel since the basement yet what flustered relief to find it still there. Max's knees pushed outward and she didn't move her legs exactly, but they gave, and opened wider, then his hand was there, in her hair, stroking, as if he wanted to brush it but only the hair so that all she felt was a damp tickle and she thought he might go on a long time like that, on and on just tickling—then with the suddenness of a slap Minna was taken up inside, with the suddenness her father used to pull bandages off, Minna was filled. Pain pulsed across her hips, not stabbing like she'd imagined but an aching, glowing sort of pain, not harsh enough you could be certain that it would ever have to stop. She dug her fingers into Max's back and tried not to make a sound though in her throat her breath kept catching, a small, strangled hiccup, and she pulled him closer so they wouldn't hear her in the next room, she listened for voices but heard nothing over her own breath, over the sheets muttering between Max's thrusts, she pulled him down and buried her mouth in his skin which then hardened and rose against her lips and she realized it was his throat, swallowing, and this unintended intimacy somehow shocked her more than all the rest, she pushed him away again but he didn't seem to notice, he kept taking her up, taking her up. Then, just as suddenly as he'd begun, he collapsed. And now he made his first noise, near Minna's ear, like air being pressed out of a sack. His beard crept against her cheek. She turned her face away. His breath started to slow against her ear, then he cleared his throat and rose up slightly. His face was dimly visible. His features seemed to be nothing more than white accessories to his beard. He slid off her, pulled her gown back down, patted it into place over her legs. Minna closed her eyes and rolled away. A cool stickiness dribbled onto her thigh.

"Minna. My bride."

She wanted to vomit, then sleep.

"Did you feel pleasure, Minna? It must not be only obligation, Minna. Did you feel desire?"

A buzzing, a confusion, rooted in her head. Was it not enough to do it? Did she have to answer? Had Lina answered, and what had she said? What time was it in Beltsy? What shapes did new children see in the ceilings of her father's house? If Beltsy still existed. There had been a smell there, those nights after the weddings, a smell in the stones of something forbidden and old. She smelled it now. She heard the laughter she'd hated. She remembered how when the people were done laughing, they looked up at the sky and gasped. And Minna had always thought of that gasp as an after-shudder of their laughter, but now she wondered if it was a gasp of recognition—if they realized, in that moment, that they'd forgotten the girl who'd actually been married that night, the real bride who was in a real room in a real bed with a real groom. And had they forgotten because they were envious? Because they were prudish? Or pitying? Or had they forgotten simply because people forget? It was possible, right now, that no one in the world was thinking of Minna. Except perhaps for Max, who was behind her—who was, she realized, rubbing her back. No one had ever rubbed her back. Not her mother, unless Minna was too young to remember, in which case it might as well not have happened. Not her father. Her father, except to punish her, only ever touched her head or her hands. To be touched like this, in a place she herself could not reach, made her feel soft, and frightened. It didn't matter that Max's nails needed trimming; they grazed her through the gown with unmistakable tenderness. She wondered what happened if one grew used to such a thing. Max had asked a question. She recalled this. But she felt no need to answer it. A shudder rode up the length of her. She cried.

FOURTEEN

MINNA woke into whiteness: the billowing feather bed beneath her, the light slipping around the curtains, the curtains themselves, her gown. A light breeze stirred. She felt weightless, luxuriant. She felt as though she might call out and someone would come to see what she wanted. A girl like she had been, perhaps.

She rolled over. There was Max, on his back. There was, coming from Max's nose, the high, whistling snore she'd mistaken for the breeze.

She sat up.

This was the first morning, then. She knew better than to be disappointed. Yet her throat was as tight as if she'd swallowed a brick. Last night's tears threatened to flow again; they'd left a crust at her nostrils. She wished, at least, that there had been music, that Ruth hadn't cut the evening off with her clucking. *Weddings aren't meant for harvesttime, not a moment's sleep to spare!*

She walked to the window. There was Leo's masterful wind-break, six trees in a perfect, silent row, and beyond it his fields in their perfect rows, and beyond them the family's hay, already cut and stacked, golden piles of their labor. Minna's wish turned suddenly desperate. What wedding was ever as sober? Not a single person had danced the *kamensky*; there was no pageantry, no drunkenness, no wrestling. No noise and no stars. Not even a *chuppah* tall enough to stand under. More than cheated, she felt doomed. Even when the guests lined up to kiss her as they departed, the mood was more funereal than celebratory. Even Otto, who with his pretty blond wife looked the very picture of joy, had not looked joyous.

Or maybe Minna was exaggerating? Maybe this was only self-pity. What bride woke up hating the world? There was, as her aunts used to say, something spoiled in her. And now she was spoiled, too, in the corporeal sense.

And yet—she realized—there'd been no blood.

She twisted around, pulled up a fistful of white gown, to be certain.

What would Max make of that?

She had heard of girls pricking their fingers, drawing red smears down the sheets. But if he woke, and caught her, it would seem she had something to hide. He would question her, and what would she say? She couldn't tell him about the Look, no more than she could tell him what she'd done to make herself itch, her touching and seeking. If there was something wrong inside her, any explanation she gave would make him angry. At Rosenfeld's, perhaps—at her, certainly. In the basement, she'd felt she had no choice, but now she didn't see it that way, now it seemed she'd made a terribly wrong choice—many wrong choices—now she could not imagine Max had meant for her to submit to that. He couldn't have known. He could not know now.

She looked back at him. She'd neglected to cover him when she rose, and now she saw that at some point in the night, he'd put his shirt back on, and buttoned up his trousers, so that he looked like a man who was simply taking a nap, in his own bedroom, in the middle of the day. And she looked, she realized, like a wife. A wife standing by the window in her stainless nightgown, the collar of which was still buttoned up to her chin.

She'd been transformed, despite herself.

And this, perhaps, was the way to proceed. As if she had been this woman her whole life: a wife, married to a man. A husband's wife. Minna Getreuer. Maybe this was how Ruth had done it, once upon a time, how all women—the ones who stayed—did it: you woke up in a new place and decided to call it home. And then you had no right anymore to be homesick. Your life, suddenly, became a *wonderful* thing.

On the floor Minna spotted Max's *yarmulke* upside down, a little black saucer. She picked it up, climbed back onto the bed, and shook him gently. "Max. Max," she cooed. A deceitful cooing, perhaps—but the kind of deceit that could become honest, she guessed, if practiced long enough.

Max opened his eyes. He looked disoriented, then pleased. "Minna," he said, and reached for her face. She stopped his hand before he could say *my bride*, or *my love*. Then she shook away her annoyance, squeezed the *yarmulke* into a ball, and held out both her fists, knuckles down. "I have a gift for you," she trilled. "Guess which one."

Max shook his head.

"Please?"

Reluctantly, he sat up. When he touched her right fist, Minna was glad: she didn't like how pathetic he looked playing her silly game, or how she sounded begging him to. She turned her hand over, released the *yarmulke*, and smiled.

"You lost this," she teased.

Max raised a hand to his bare head. Minna kept smiling. She felt silly for having worried about the blood—of course he would forget to notice, or he would remember too late, tomorrow, when they were miles from the sheets. She fluttered her lashes, the coyness spilling out of her like a song she didn't know she knew. So this was how it began, she thought.

But Max wasn't watching her. He took the *yarmulke* from her hand, laid it on his knee, and smoothed out the creases. He didn't look angry exactly, and not quite ashamed, either. He looked like men looked just before they entered synagogue, arranging their collars and their shawls and their *yarmulkes* precisely so, as if they hoped, once inside, that they would all look the same.

Ruth's children had decorated the wagon with dandelion necklaces, long yellow tails that would trail along behind as Minna and the men rode off. They were meant to be cheerful, Minna knew, yet failed: they were already dusty and bedraggled and filled her with dismay. She was dismayed, too, by the abundance of food that had been given to them. Jars of beans and carrots, dried fruits, sacks of flour and corn. There, Ruth said, now you won't have to make the trip to town, you can go straight home!, even though Ruth knew "home" was nothing but a cramped cave, and Minna couldn't help feeling mocked, in the same way she now felt mocked when she thought of the man at the municipal building—*Run along!*—or of the inspectors at Castle Garden, promising so much with their officiousness and their stamps.

The day was already hot. A heat wave, Leo said, sometimes it came this late, the only thing to do was ride it out. His arm was through Ruth's, his pipe between his teeth. A real American man he made, with his beard thin enough to show his cheeks and his cheeks satisfactorily ruddy and his forearms thick and his general air of forbearance. Jacob said his family had kept their land in Russia long after it was illegal, until they'd been run off. Yet there was something of Leo that Minna did not trust. His pipe, perhaps, the way he didn't smoke it so much as he displayed it, like a handkerchief, or a watch, as if putting on airs now that he was in his element. He reminded her of Galina's suitors, she supposed. She felt a fresh wave of pity for Ruth, who was allowed an eyelet-trimmed bonnet but only over a wig, who was saying to Minna now, "For a bit of cool, you might hang wet sheets!" It seemed suddenly possible that Ruth was in fact nothing as conniving as Minna's aunts—that all she wanted was to fit in, like Leo. Yet Leo seemed to want to keep Ruth half the way she'd been before.

"Thank you for everything," Minna said.

"Just dip them in the creek," Ruth said, "and hang them across the door. Promise me you'll try?"

"If we didn't need them to sleep on."

"You can borrow!"

"You've done enough. Thank you."

"Oh. My pleasure." Ruth smiled cheerfully, then regretfully, then cheerfully again, and clutched Minna's hands. "The weather won't last," she said. "If the snow comes early, I may not see you for months." Her blinking slowed, as if she might cry. And this was the problem, Minna thought—no matter how close she came to liking Ruth, she could always find something overly dramatic about her. Now, for instance, as she stared into Minna's eyes and said, far more loudly than necessary, "You'll be with child by then. God willing."

Leo nodded. He set a hand on Max's shoulder and winked. "A little girl, maybe, for this handsome groom to spoil?"

Minna's hair burned against her scalp. Max hovered nervously beside her, aware, no doubt, of the jabs in Leo's question. The idea of a child seemed as ludicrous this morning, as impossible as the idea of snow. Ruth believed it was the answer to her unhappiness and Minna guessed it could be so, she guessed there might be a reward that she could not now fathom, but she wondered, too, what she knew of mothering. She was not patient, or soft, or particularly gentle. She had deserted Rebeka. The round of Ruth's stomach appeared to expand as she watched, and Minna felt nothing toward it but a quiet curiosity—something akin to what she'd felt as a girl when she'd once come upon a turtle laying eggs at the edge of the woods.

"God willing," Minna said. But this must not have been convincing because Ruth and Leo were silent and in their silence it seemed that they doubted Minna's suitability, too. To have them doubt her was worse.

"Well then, we're off!" Minna cried, and clapped her hands the way she'd seen Ruth do—no palms, just the flats of her fingers, sharp and stiff. She felt how such clapping could work to one's advantage, make one's whole person feel more capable. Near the wagon, Jacob was running the children in dusty, barefoot circles, holding out his Indian warhead then snatching it back. "First they'll kill you," he panted, "then they'll peel off your skin!"

"Jacob!" Minna's mouth opened automatically. "Put your boots on. We're going."

Jacob skidded to a halt and spun toward her. His mouth curled into the edge of a grin, but just the edge—it was hard to tell if he was truly stunned, or if he imagined himself to be playing along with her. The latter, most likely; still, he walked over to his boots and sat in the dirt to tie them and Minna felt a quake in her chest—vanity, terror, a new territory entered. Then she saw Samuel, standing off to the side of the wagon, hands folded behind him, watching—as though he were merely a passerby who'd found their group curious enough to warrant a stop. Minna searched his face for admonishment and found nothing. His mouth was set in a sufficiently agreeable line. His eyes, as usual, seemed made to see but not to be seen. To do nothing before them felt like defeat, so she called: "Samuel!" But once the word was out, there was nothing to add. His boots were on, wrapped as tidily in their rags as they'd been last night. It was as if he'd never taken them off, as if he'd waited awake all night for Minna and Max to finish their rites—did he imagine Minna wanted to? Did he imagine her at all? —so that they could get on already, and go home.

Yet he didn't even look impatient. He stood calm as a post, his face as neat as his rags.

T HE horse and mule, hitched together, formed a maimed, listing beast. The wagon limped along behind. The whole outfit might have appeared in one of Samuel's farming magazines, if they featured a "How Not to Travel" column. But soon enough they were out of sight of Ruth and Leo's house, and there was no one else to witness their comic struggle. The land rolled ahead. The sky pulsed with sun. Sweat pooled at the corners of Minna's mouth. She felt slightly drugged. She needed a hat. All the men had hats, and Ruth had her bonnet. Why had no one thought to give Minna a bonnet? She squinted, then heard Galina warning her, *your face will stick that way, you'll grow old young*, and shrank lower on the bench, trying to find shade between Max and Samuel. Everywhere they brushed her seethed with heat. She shrank lower. She would rather have been in back, like Jacob, stretched out among the jars and sacks.

"I wonder," Samuel said, "if we wouldn't be better off with just the horse."

"And waste the mule?" asked Max.

"And let the mule haul rocks, like it's meant to."

"That's assuming God created us with only one purpose in mind."

"He's not talking about *us*," Jacob called. "He's talking about a mule."

Minna felt a curious ease come over her—the wooze of sun through her brain, perhaps, or the familiar course of their debate.

She didn't listen to the words so much as she watched them skip across her eyes, which watered and stung. She had determined, this time, to pay attention to the route, to note every rise and dip and form a map in her mind. She should know something, she thought, of where she lived on this earth, even if it was only in relation to the Friedmans' house. But as the seconds and minutes and hours slogged on, Minna knew that she was failing. Every signless junction looked the same: two strips of dust meeting and parting again. Each lone tree was stunted and black against the sun. Even the two houses they passed were square and colorless, wood or sod. She would think them abandoned if she didn't know better—if there weren't figures in the distance, moving across the fields. These glimpses of industry seized her with panic. "Bohemians," Jacob said, pointing at the second house. "Not a word of English," he added, as if the fifty words she knew put her above them, and Minna supposed this should somehow make her feel better, but she could only think of the Bohemians shaking their heads as they watched the wagon pass with its limping animals and its dandelion tails dragging behind and its people packed together like more animals on the bench. The sun topped the sky. The horse and mule clomped each other's feet. The sun started its descent. Yet the day only seemed to grow hotter. They saw no birds, heard no insects. The dandelions broke off. Jacob sang from time to time, high wordless tunes that seemed to vaporize as they were released, so that from one second to the next Minna thought she might have dreamed the last note.

Hill like a wart, she noted fuzzily. Another landmark she would soon forget. Then she saw the tin chimney canting out from the top. Home. When Max cleared his throat, you could hear the whole day gathered in it, the heat built and erupting like a long, dry burp. "You'll call her Mother now," he said.

If it was possible, Minna's temperature rose. She felt the weight of Samuel's arm against her own. Blood rushed up her legs, into her tongue. "Max," she said.

"Understood?" he asked, and looked back at Jacob. Then he leaned heavily across Minna to gain Samuel's attention and Minna twisted around the other way, hoping Jacob might save her. Which he did, by making his voice that of a child and squeaking, "Mother? Mother, are we almost home?" And though he was teasing Max, Minna let herself laugh. She wanted Samuel to hear, to know: she had no desire to be his mother. She wouldn't be his mother if he begged her.

"Yes, *nakhes'l*," she warbled. "We're almost home, *nakhes'l*." She pretended to ignore the tension behind her on the bench, but she could feel Max gripping his knees, and Samuel gripping the reins. Had he heard her? Did he understand that it was a joke? It was a joke. She was laughing!

The wagon swung abruptly as it made the turn onto the rocky path, lurching Minna into Max. Max set her upright as one might a lamp. "Sender," he scolded.

Samuel lifted the reins to slow the animals. "My apologies," he muttered. Then he commanded the animals in English, which his father understood only insomuch as he experienced its effect: quickly, smoothly, the wagon reached the door. The horse stopped with a whinny, the mule with a grunt, and Samuel jumped down to hold the reins as Minna and Max climbed out.

FIFTEEN

T HE bed was not sized for two. One and a half, maybe—as
if Max had tried to convince himself of the promises of a
double, but only half succeeded. Minna lay on her side, face to
the wall. To make room for Max, she straightened her knees,
though Max told her not to: he told her to make herself comfortable, please, not to worry, he could sleep on a log, he could
sleep in the creek. Whispering, as if a whisper would convince
her of intimacy, though Jacob and Samuel weren't more than six
feet away in their hole. Or maybe he whispered because he was
lying. Max was a terrible sleeper. Whenever Minna woke, she
could hear him not sleeping; she could feel his shallow, uneven
thought-breaths against her neck. What his thoughts were of, she
couldn't know. Kotelnia? A synagogue? Childhood? The beautiful Lina? This last possibility would be a relief, to know that Max
allowed himself such ordinary fantasy. It might even make Minna

jealous, which—according to Galina—would help her want him more than she actually did. Max's breaths smelled like hunger, or yogurt, the only dairy she dared make in the heat. Or they simply smelled like a bottomless gust of man-made dew. In time, she thought, her neck would smell the same. Her skin would start to mush. Sometimes, when she woke to his hardness at the backs of her thighs, she thought it was already happening.

Max advanced only in the middle of the night, or later, close to dawn, when the insects outside had already begun their chirring. He must have decided that the boys slept deeply then, and Minna pretended this was true. She listened for their breath as he pulled her toward him—as he lifted himself up to make space to turn her onto her back—as he turned her onto her back. The boards creaked, reminding her of his bony knees. The cave was cooler, at least, than the air outside. She listened for inhalations, exhalations, from the hole. They were steady, she told herself, though this wasn't necessarily true, though she might have been layering the chirring over the breaths. She knew by then the particular sounds her stepsons made going in and out of sleep, which were the opposite of their daily ways: Jacob's manful groan; Samuel's fitful, almost violent tossing of limbs. But they were asleep now, she told herself, because she had to. Max tugged her gown up past her hips, spent a couple minutes tickling and brushing and fretting the hair there, then entered her. Where he learned the hair bit, she didn't know, but it embarrassed her more than anything else. It was like what girls did to dolls. She pitied him this the way she pitied his insomnia, for his sake and for hers. She counted. She held her breath. When she held her breath and counted at the same time, it was almost like a contest.

And then it was over, and that was all. The chirring softened, the sun rose, Minna made breakfast, the men went out into the world as if it was going to be new and found it exactly as they'd left it: piles of rocks on the ground, millions more rocks in the ground. The freshly tilled fields began to look like a strange, crude graveyard. Samuel and Max argued at night in their useless, agreeable way, Samuel suggesting once again that they should be haying instead of plowing, and that if they were going to continue hauling rocks they should at least haul them out to the perimeters and give them the makings of a boundary, and Max responding, there wasn't enough time, no time. Sometimes Minna thought she heard him pat his side, where he kept his watch, as if to say he knew, he knew about time. Yet he was the last to rise—she had to climb over him to start the fire—and the first to come in to supper. And during the day when she looked out she found him, without fail, in the same immobile stance, hands resting on his shovel, staring off at what she didn't know. She wondered how long it would be before he sensed her and wheeled around to catch her staring. If Max were a man to wheel around. What would he do? Stare back? Turn away? Be angry that she'd caught him doing nothing? She imagined him stomping across the broiling expanse between them. If Max were a man to stomp. And then what? Would he defend himself? Would she scold him? Sometimes she thought she would like to scold him. Or maybe she just wanted to talk, to have a "discussion," like the one he'd promised the night she arrived. What they would say, she didn't know. It was too late, perhaps, to introduce themselves, or explain. There might be nothing to explain, once you were stuck together like fish in a desert.

———

S HE gave up watching Max. Which is how it happened, one morning, when Samuel turned toward the house, that he saw her watching him, instead. She couldn't make out his eyes—at this distance she could barely tell the difference between hair and skin and cloth—but she knew they were pinned to her, under the tree in the yard, as surely as she knew that her dress was basted onto her body.

She realized that she must look as idle as Max, and as dumb-struck. He would think she spent her days staring at him, when really she spent much of her time trying to avoid exactly that. Also, of course, working. She spent her time working! She was no longer the girl on the ship hiding in her bunk. She'd given up trying to turn wheat into fire. Couldn't he *see* that?

But before she could pick up her bucket of milk, which she'd set down for a moment, or change position in some way so as to indicate that she was moving on, that her stillness was not in fact sloth, that perhaps the distance between them, and the heat— the heat!—had distorted her image, that she didn't intend to rest under the tree a second longer, that it was a rangy, water-sucking old stump barely worth its meager flecks of shade, Sam-uel had turned away, and begun his digging again, down up, filling the air with chunks of earth.

Minna felt suspicious, suspected, on guard. She felt, some-times, like a maidservant. Which was almost funny. Which was easy, in its way: to feel put upon, taken for granted, came with certain privileges. There was freedom in the lack of freedom; there was the right to dissatisfaction, and resistance. She told the

boys she'd haul the family's water herself and began a daily habit,
at the creek, of sliding down the bank, kneeling low, taking off
her clothes, and lying on her back. This was the only way not to
be seen, and to cool off, for the water was even lower now, a
series of silver rivulets in the gray sand. She craved it anyway,
craved it more; she pressed herself into the sand like a palm into
dough. She listened to her breath, amplified by the water against
her back, until it slowed to match the pace of the creek. Above
her was the sun, oppressive as ever, yet somehow from here, like
this, she could see its beauty. She could almost see how someone might choose to come to such a place, and try to make a
life. Hours passed, days, years, in the few minutes she let slip
by before she sat upright, dried herself, and dressed. Then she
tipped a bucket down to collect from the deepest pool so that
when she stood again, if someone was watching, she would appear to have done what she was supposed to be doing.

Minna's great, infinitesimal insurgencies.

Yet she had, was the truth of it. She had done what she was
supposed to do. She had fetched water. *Fetched.* Just as she had
performed all her other small uses Jacob had taught her names
for. *Walk. Milk. Feed. Wash.* The familiar motions, and the words
that went with them, brought her some comfort. She squeezed,
scrubbed, tossed, tied knots. She carried the water back to the
house. No one ever seemed to care that her hair was wet in the
back, though she must have looked as if half her head had been
dipped in ink. They were too far away, or if they were close, they
were paying attention to something else, Jacob to his archaeo-
logical finds, Samuel to the repair of tack, or tools, Max to the
sky. Later, Minna would reach up to scratch an itch and discover

sand embedded in her scalp. But Max never touched her hair. And if he did, he might not notice—or if he noticed, he might not want to know and so pretend he hadn't. It was a fine line with Max, one Minna hadn't yet deciphered, the border between abstraction and delusion. He'd also never asked about the ragged bedsheet she'd arrived with—torn to make Moses' bandage—though by morning its frayed edge had often ridden up around his neck.

O n her back in the creek, she allowed her eyes to slowly flutter. Open: the cottonwood leaves, flitting silver and green. Closed: their murmur. Open: the sky, broken by leaves. Closed: her breath, cool water along her neck, down her sides, around her heels, a slight shiver up her back. Then one afternoon, open: and there was Samuel, looking down at her, not peering or gazing or leering or measuring, but looking with such simple curiosity that for a long moment she did not think to roll over but looked back at him. He might have been observing a flower or rock he found of interest; she had never seen his face so undefended. She hadn't noticed before how strong his legs were, so that they nearly filled out his trousers above the knee, or how, when he placed his hands on his hips like a surveyor, two veins popped out at his wrists. He was far enough above her that his head appeared smaller than his waist, and this warping made her see a deviance in him. Then he seemed to recall her, as a woman, or girl, or however he would have named her naked body lying there flat and unadorned so that the thin places must have looked thinner and the hairy places hairier. He glanced away, and shoved his hands in his pockets, though the heat defied the gesture. Minna rolled over; she knelt and reached for her dress. "I'm sorry," she mumbled, but Samuel shook his head, not in the way of forgiveness but in the way of refusing her the right to apologize; in his face was a sudden ugliness. Jacob's voice came, *Sammyyyyy!!* Samuel jumped. He turned and shouted, "Wait! Wait there! I'm coming," then he looked back down at Minna, who was holding her dress up to cover her front and try-ing to sit in such a way that he couldn't see her backside. She watched him attempt to compose his face, like one might hang a rumpled cloth—she could picture him, suddenly, as a young boy at the *yeshiva*. "Don't let me see you like this again," he said, and took off running, and for a few seconds she could feel his light, fast footsteps in the sand wall of the creek, which she'd leaned into like a pillow.

THAT night he stared at her—as if daring her to imagine that she'd seen him at the creek. He complained that the bread was dry, then suggested that she try a different ratio of water to flour. "And add a little yogurt," he said.

Minna was slow to respond; she felt naked all over again. "I've never heard of that," she said.

"It's what our mother did," Jacob said. He looked at Minna, then at Samuel. "It's true," he said.

"That's not the point," Samuel said. "The point is it's better that way."

"Boys." Max held up his slice of bread. "Let your mother be."

Then, as if realizing the possible confusion, he said, "The girl's bread is fine as far as I'm concerned."

There was color in Samuel's cheeks. It was as if he'd briefly forgotten Max, as if in his forgetting he'd experienced a great relief for which he was now embarrassed. After dinner, he appeared to pray more fervently. And after prayers, and all the next day, he was kinder to his father.

SIXTEEN

THE heat broke as quickly as it had struck. A wind in the night, the door clapping on its hinges, a pungent release as if from a dream. Minna woke to a tingling in her skin and bolted upright. The air was cool. She was alone. The kettle was warm, the bread she baked yesterday gone. She touched the cutting board, groggily feeling for crumbs. They were dry; it was late.

In the closest corner of the closest field, she found Max, up to his shins in a hole, digging with a vigor strange to him. When Minna toed her boots into his vision, he swung the shovel a few more times, then looked up. His face was red, his usual lack of humor marred by a twitch in his lips, an almost-grin she might have thought flirtatious if she thought him capable of flirtation. When she asked what he was doing, he glanced around conspiratorially, then said, "I'm building you a *mikvah*."

Minna laughed. She felt light-headed, as though overnight

they'd slid across the earth into a new atmosphere. The idea of a bath in this place was divine, and bizarre.

"You'll bleed soon enough," Max said. "You'll have to bathe."

His forthrightness shocked her. At first she thought he was talking about their wedding night. Then she understood. She'd forgotten, somehow, that he would know everything she knew with regard to her menstrual "events": that they did not in fact come every month, as she'd told the doctor. I should have pretended, she thought. For a few days, I should have made him stay away, forged pain of the feminine sort. In Beltsy, a man could divorce a wife if she didn't give him a child within ten years. There was no reason to think Max wouldn't do the same, or worse. Out here, ten years would be an eternity. Here a man might wait only one. And then where would she be?

That's not polite, Minna wanted to say. But she also wanted the bath. But not for the reasons he wanted her to want one. She wanted warm water, privacy. The moment called for delicacy, she thought—a protest of the sort that leads to submission. "I don't *need* a *mikvah*," she said.

"But in Odessa, you went each week."

Yes, she'd answered at the municipal building. Yes to this, no to that.

Max's face was too trusting.

"Sometimes," she said.

"That's not your fault, Minna. Odessa is a filthy place."

Minna smiled. "Odd then," she said, "that you would search for a wife there."

Max dug the tip of his shovel into his boot. Minna wondered if Jacob had been wrong about his father's reasons for ordering her through Rosenfeld's, if it wasn't because Max had been too humiliated to tell the family and friends he'd left about Lina's running away, but for the same reason that he prayed, and made the rest of them pray—because he didn't trust people. A service, a method, a book, a God—these he trusted. She wondered if Max sensed the weakness in people—in her—more than he let on.

"Of course you're right," she said, smiling more brightly. "A filthy place. But a *mikvah*, it just seems—a bit—indulgent. To build a *mikvah* in this, well . . ."—she kept smiling—"in *this* place. Which is filthy, some might say, in its own ways."

"That's what the boys said. In so many words. That's why I'm digging it while they're gone."

Minna looked around, for the first time that day. She was filled with a sense of error. "Gone?"

"With Leo. There's work on a farm about three days north."

"You didn't think that I should know?"

"I didn't like the idea."

"You thought I might not notice?"

Max stared. He looked stunned—as if he hadn't noticed a particular feature on her face before. "It was decided weeks ago," he said.

Minna crossed her arms. She wished there were someone to guide her. Or some *thing* at least: a manual for new wives, a primer—though she doubted that such a book would even apply to her situation. What would it say of the new wife whose stepson had seen her unclothed? And not only once. Twice more Samuel had wandered over to the creek while she'd been bathing. Twice more she had caught him, looking. She'd closed her eyes quickly, pretending not to have seen, shifted her position slightly so as to look less flat, then lain there, imagining his face: curious, but also troubled; handsome, yet full of guilt. She lay perfectly still, heart thudding, until she heard his boots retreat. Then he came a third time, and barely stopped to look before he jumped down onto the creek bed. Minna startled, and sat up. "I told you," he said, through gritted teeth. He stood above her, fists clenched at his sides, his whole body taut as wire. Minna thought he might kick her. She clamped her legs together. "I told you," he said again, "not . . ." He stopped. He was staring at her breasts. On his face was a look of pain. "Not to let me . . ." Minna lifted a hand to cover herself, but her other arm was propping her up, and in a moment of witting incapacitation, she only managed to hide one breast. She wondered if the pain on his face was displeasure. She knew, even as she wondered this, that it wasn't. She had combed her hair, anticipating him. She watched him carefully. "You needn't keep coming," she said. Samuel raised his eyes from her chest. "You needn't keep being here," he said. "Where else am I meant to wash?" "You're not washing, you're . . ." He looked away. A trickle of water ran down Minna's back; she shivered. "What is it you think I am doing?" she asked, but Samuel was shaking his head. "That's not the point," he said. "Isn't it?" Minna was aware of her body as though it were new; even her knees, which she'd never thought of as anything more exciting than knees: Samuel was staring at them. Minna kept expecting herself to hide her nakedness, to reach for her dress and tell him to leave, to remind him what he was to her, and she to him. Yet she could find her shame nowhere. She picked up a pebble and threw it at his feet. "You're the one who told me to come down here," she said. "If you'll recall." Samuel chuckled strangely. His gaze traveled quickly up her legs to her hips, her stomach, breasts, armpits, throat. Then he bent, picked up a slightly larger pebble, looked her in the eye, and aimed it for her stomach. It stung; she winced; when she opened her eyes, he was scrambling up the bank. And Minna, feeling hot again, had lain back down.

What would her father say?

And Max, who was still waiting for her to respond? Who had touched, but never seen her naked?

She uncrossed her arms, crossed them again. She remembered well, when Ruth and Leo first came, the closed-door conference, the shaking of hands. That was many weeks ago now—it felt like months. She considered her choices. To berate. To nag. To beg. To forgive. None appealed. She was thinking of Samuel, how he must have known all that time that he'd be leaving, and when. And Jacob, who'd argued so stridently that she stay—hadn't he thought to warn her that he was going? Wouldn't he think, perhaps, to invite her along?

"How long will they be gone?" she asked Max.

"Two weeks. Maybe four. I don't know. It was Leo's idea." Max's voice cracked. He looked as surprised by his own ignorance as if a stranger were talking. He looked mortified. "I don't know how it works," he said, and dropped his shovel to the ground, and suddenly Minna didn't care what he had to say. They would be alone for weeks, perhaps longer. She couldn't bear him hating himself, and the work it would take. Besides, if she concentrated on it, she could feel a reprieve in the boys' departure. Samuel's pebble had left a mark to the right of her navel the size of a penny.

She crossed her arms more tightly. "So how big will this hole be?"

"It's not a hole, it's a—" Max covered his eyes. "Do you really think this place so awful?"

Minna sighed. She squatted down so that she was looking up at him—so that he, when he uncovered his eyes, could look down on her. "Of course not," she said. *Better to love him.* "No," she said. "It was a silly thing to say. Forgive me. But a bath, Motke. It would be a great help."

The boys' absence gave Max a new courage. At night, when he climbed on top of her, he muttered words near her ear. "Angel," he said, touching the place above her lip where her skin made a little valley. "You have been touched by an angel." Or, just before he entered her: "You are so good." Which seemed backward to Minna—"good" for letting him in? "good" for appearing in his bed again?—until one night as he finished she heard him whisper, as if in prayer, "My duty," and she understood that he meant, you *will* be good . . . when you give me a child. This, she realized, was what Max wanted more than anything. It was why he asked after her pleasure. It was why he was building her a *mikvah*. As if, once there was a *mikvah*, Minna would bleed, and then be fertile. As if all she'd been waiting for was a place to wash. *You will be so good.*

She expected to feel angry. That he'd been scrutinizing her bodily functions was enough, she thought, to make her angry. Yet she couldn't help feeling satisfied that he'd kept track—just as she'd begun to feel a certain satisfaction in the pains he took to touch her the exact same way every night, in the exact same order. He attended her. She was attended. "Angel," he declared in his brave not-whisper, pressing her lip a bit too hard, so that it dug into her teeth—so that in her stomach she felt a near heat, a shimmering instant of desire.

Then desire was gone. Max would make a funny sound, and stray from his purpose, and leave her oddly numb. His was not the courage, after all, of a courageous man. It was ambivalent and raw—more the courage, perhaps, of any guardian (of children, of sheep, of jewels) whose charges had suddenly disappeared and set him free. Every shovelful of earth Max removed from the *mikvah* hole was a rock he had not cleared, a necessary task he had not completed, an act of disobedience against his sons—in particular Samuel. This, she thought, was what made him nearly giddy as he dug; this he must have imagined to be his own minor rebellion. He would not think of his greater treachery, which was growing increasingly apparent to her: his need for a new child so that he might diminish his old ones, and—more to the point—the woman who'd borne them. For even his duty to God was not as strong as his need to forget Lina. He'd barely spoken of her. He kept no remnant, no souvenir. In Minna's estimation, his attempt to obliterate and replace her was so precisely the opposite of her father's hoarding that it had to come from the same affliction, a grief so shameful it could not be indulged. So the men made the women dead. If their tactics differed—worship, nullification—their end goal was the same: to be left for death, at least, was more bearable.

Minna knew—she remembered—how to be with such a

man. How to soothe and please him in his mourning. The key was discerning the shapes of the holes the women (or infant boy) left behind, then occupying them. That Minna hadn't known Lina didn't matter. She was not required to invent new habits or personalities—only to fill the void with a new body body. Which had little to do with Minna herself: she had to stay, was all, or—even simpler—not to leave, and to convince him, with every movement, that she never would. She poured Max's coffee as she'd poured her father's tea, a long lingering stream, and like her father, Max never asked her to hurry up. He had a habit, while waiting, of folding his lower lip into his mouth, biting down on his beard, then releasing it, very slowly, from his teeth, as if to draw out the crackling sound of the hairs. His cadence, when he spoke to her, was as vague as his gaze, so that anything he talked about—food, planting, rocks, weather—came out sounding inconsequential. Minna didn't mind letting him believe this, or letting him think she believed it. Standing over him, listening, she felt a familiar weight returning, the sunk, tangled comfort of needing to protect, which sometimes felt so close to wanting to protect that she did not think of being anywhere else.

She set to work on the walls, beginning—as Ruth had instructed—by making a glue from milk. Samuel's farming magazines served as paper; the thin pages tore easily and took well to the glue. She papered from the ground up, working in tall, single rows, layering the pages three deep over the sod, exactly as Ruth had said. It worked. It looked smoother and neater than anything she'd imagined herself capable of making. And the whitewash paste, once she began smearing it over the funny pictures of plows and scales and machines whose purposes she could not imagine, was so white, that the cave—if she narrowed her eyes—appeared to glow.

When Minna tired, she went out to the hole and watched Max dig. He'd made quick progress downward, then decided it wasn't wide enough and started outward again. The hole was, in fact, quite wide enough—so wide it could already fit four Minnas comfortably—but Minna did not mention this. She sat on the edge, swinging her feet, expressing quiet admiration as he laid bare dark and darker soil. She liked sitting like that, her heels thumping the earth, her only labor that of accompaniment. Max told her about a dream he'd been having—or rather suffering, *laydn*, as he put it: in this dream a rainstorm came in the night and flooded the house and Max didn't wake up and so he drowned.

Each time he told it, Minna smiled. Whether she herself appeared in the dream, she didn't ask. If she was there, if she died along with him, she guessed that Max felt guilty—and if she wasn't, if she didn't, perhaps guiltier. She smiled and said well, it didn't sound very likely, and besides, even if a rain ever did come, the door made of crates would collapse before the cave could fill with water. And Max would look at her, the skin around his eyes flushed with his work, his eyes themselves wet—with the dream, perhaps, or maybe just the cooler air, which moved more freely now, gathering itself into little frenzies and whipping the skin. He looked, she thought, mildly disappointed—as if he hoped, each time he told her the dream, that she would explain it to him. Yet he never looked offended, as she expected, at her scornful remarks about the house. The door did not concern him, just as everything else he was neglecting in order to dig the hole did not concern him. And Minna found that she didn't judge him for this. She felt similarly about her white-washing, whose purpose, after all—a lovelier cave?—was even less necessary than the *mikvah*. Together, she and Max seemed to have broken off from the question of necessity—as if, as long as the boys were gone, the coming winter was indefinitely sus-pended. In the distance, they watched cows lumbering toward the railhead at Mitchell, driven by one of Otto's sons for a ranch owner out of Texas; in the sky, they watched birds arrowing southward, shoved sideways then straight again by errant gusts of wind. Yet Minna and Max shared no compulsion to join in these preparations.

Minna and Max. Odd, to feel the names coupled in her head. Bread and butter, broom and pan. Odder still that they should come together out of mutual apathy, or defiance, or whatever one wanted to call it. Minna completed her daily chores. She swept, and gathered sad-looking squashes from the garden, and baked challah every Friday as Max asked her to do; she even threw a precious fist of dough into the fire, as he also asked her to do. "To remember the burning of the Temple," he said, when she first hesitated. There was relief, she discovered, in following the order of his order, his ongoing, forever repentance for letting the Russians tear into the Torah with their crowbars; there was a giving in that calmed her. But she didn't think more than a few hours ahead, and she did not behave practically. On the first two Friday nights, she lit a pair of Shabbos candles they'd been given at the wedding, no matter that she should save them for an emer-gency, that the lantern shed adequate light, that kerosene was easier to come by than candles. On the third Shabbos, when the candles were shrunk to thumb-sized stumps, she melted their wax together in a tin, inserted a bit of a rag for a wick, and spent an indulgent amount of time holding the rag upright until the wax hardened again. Then she burned this candle, too, and Max made no comment.

Did he think, as she did, of Samuel? Did he feel an excitement, an almost petulance, at the idea of Samuel watching them as they failed to be useful in any real way? It wasn't indolence, she would tell him. Look at the *mikvah* hole! Look at the neat, smooth wallpaper she'd made from his magazines! No, they weren't indolent. They were simply unwilling to face the truly necessary task of preparing for their survival. For that would have required more than knowledge and skills and materials they didn't possess. It would have required optimism, which required faith or else ignorance——depending on how one looked at it, depending on who one was. But Max, who was faithful and believed in God, did not seem capable of believing in the acres he stood upon. And Minna, who was talented enough at self-delusion, could not manufacture a vision of success in this vast, vastly exposed place. She couldn't see how anything they did would counter the enormity of what there was to be done.

So Minna papered with what remained of Samuel's magazines, and Max dug, and they witnessed the rest of the world move toward autumn. By late afternoons, the sky took on a crystalline pallor. Dark came early. The morning breeze grew teeth. They did not speak of these changes, or of the fact that they'd begun using the boys' blankets on top of their own. Minna didn't tell Max that two of the chickens had stopped laying, or that sometimes she thought she glimpsed Indians out the corners of her eyes, far-off shadows that disappeared before she could turn her head. She didn't tell him that she'd stopped lying naked on her back in the creek. Who knew what Max didn't tell Minna. The walls gained more paper, the hole gained more hole, but sometimes it seemed to Minna that if they'd woken up and found their work undone—the walls bare, the hole filled—if they had to start all over, neither would complain.

THE house fell in on a fine day in what must have been late September. Clouds had filled the sky that morning, splitting the sun into needles. The air was neither cold nor warm. Everything felt balanced, fair. Max had stopped digging to tell his dream. Minna was wearing her quiet smile. She liked the part where Max woke up already drowning, for the way it changed a little every time. Today he said his mouth and nose had filled with water, and the water tasted like chicken broth, so he couldn't stop swallowing it.

Minna's boots thunked against the sides of the hole. And maybe that, Max would later allege, when he blamed everyone except his God for the accident, maybe that forever thunking of Minna's boots was what kept them from hearing the cow that Otto's son was meant to be driving. But Max was wrong, because the cow, as it climbed the hill, didn't make a sound. It moved at its heavy, munching, bovine pace, hip joints sliding, sloping up toward its discovery: a private island of grass. It made no sound until its hooves fell through the earth—the roof—and even then Minna and Max didn't know what had happened, for the cow gave a cry more like a child than a half-ton beast. Minna had that thought, of a child. She recalled the sickening wails of her brother. Then the cry changed, and rose, and instead of peaking once and then descending into a moo or moan, it went on rising, its pitch tightening, growing decidedly not child, not human: it was a noise so appalling and intimate, it took Minna a few breaths before she could bring herself to look.

Only the cow's neck and head were visible atop the wreckage, writhing as it shrieked. There was no accord between its movements and its noise—it seemed to fight itself, jerking now, bellowing then. Minna looked back at Max, who stood frozen, his shock lending his eyes a certain clarity, almost a translucence, so that they looked not brown but yellow, catlike, almost lovely. Then he looked back at her, and in his forehead was that familiar wish for her to fix things. She jumped up and began running toward the cow's head, and the shrieks, and Otto's son, who was riding up so slowly from the other side, his horse stepping so lazily that they reached the collapsed house at the same time. Minna gasped for breath. The man was Otto in his straw-colored hair and big ears and in his thin, exacting mouth, but he had none of his father's warmth, or poise; he slumped in the saddle and wore the horse's laziness in his eyes, a woeful indifference that passed over Minna and moved on to the cow. He frowned at the cow with disapproval, as if to say, *There you go again.* Behind Minna, Max began to shout.

"Rope! No rope? *Cowboy* with no rope? Where is your rope? Where are your eyes? What is in your head?"

Max had stopped several paces back. He wouldn't come closer, Minna thought, unless Otto's son dismounted, and Otto's

son wouldn't dismount until Max stopped shouting. "Rope!" he
went on. *"Shtrik! Shtrik!"* until the word made nonsense, until
Minna turned and shouted back: "Motke! Stop!" And almost
embarrassingly quickly, Max's tirade came to an end. She was
sorry, for she knew that he was right. She even knew the particular rope that might have stopped the cow; she'd slept in it. But
what difference did that make now? The cow's neck twisted frantically, its head slammed the earth. Minna looked up at Otto's
son and saw behind his frown the amused despair of one accus-
tomed to being wrong. To shout at such a person was to shout at
a rock. "Can't you do something?" she asked.

He looked down at her, but his eyes had retreated. She wondered what he was seeing, whether it was the cow, or his boss in
Texas, or his father; if he was more afraid right now than he was
sorry or ashamed. Otto was the kind of man, she thought, who
faced the world with so much goodwill, so much plain, determined beneficence, that he might beat an ill-behaved son badly;
even—or perhaps especially—a grown son. That was the way of
things, people: each contained its own cure. The beating would be
violent, she thought. But then, too, tonight would be cold without a roof. The clouds were denser now, and taller, like pilings.

"Do something," she said, and pulled on the man's leg, and
though it surprised her, the rough canvas pant, the thin hot knee
within, the fact that she was touching—yanking—a strange man's
leg, she found, too, that it was remarkably easy. She thought of the
dry indifference with which the woman in the basement had
touched all those parts of Minna's body. And here Minna had one
of the man's knees in her grip and there was no peril in it, no
explosion, nothing of what she used to imagine happened when

one person touched another person—what she imagined, that was, before the basement; before Galina's knee; before Max. Perhaps the more you'd been touched, the less you suffered it. She began to shake the man's leg.

"Do something!"

He was down from his horse before she knew she'd let him go, clambering up the ruined earth, reaching into his pocket, drawing a knife. Minna winced, but couldn't look away. She felt as though she'd witnessed the cow's death before. She had seen this moment, and the moment that would follow. Later she would realize she was confusing things, that it was the bird's neck in her hands, and the woman's putrid body falling into the ocean, it was these other mercy killings she remembered. But right then, as the man's elbow swung back and the knife shot forward and the cow went silent, Minna felt no revulsion, only relief. Max cried out and she ignored him.

SEVENTEEN

OTTO's house. Otto's bed. Otto's wife, Liesl, for a bed-mate. The bed was smaller than Leo and Ruth's, but the sheets were softer. The sheets were like the house itself, full of a clean, gently frayed grace. Otto and Liesl had a way of being well off that was apparent only if you looked slightly askance at it, with an eye for use. Their house was not two stories like Leo and Ruth's; instead the rooms spread quietly out the back, each one tilting slightly off the last at a sort of knuckle, so that you could see the stages of its growth.

It would take confidence, Minna thought, to build so gradually. It would take thinking that you wouldn't be chased or have to go chasing anything for a long time.

She smoothed her hands over the sheets. A delight, a shame, sleeping beside a woman. Yet Liesl, it could be argued, if one should need to make such an argument, seemed less a woman than a form of light. Her skin was pink, her cheeks unblemished, the bones around her eyes like ivory. Her hair grew from a widow's peak unlike any Minna had seen, so low and blond and graciously pointed that it appeared as a sort of jewelry. Even Max, who'd come into the house bawling, threatening to sleep in the barn rather than endure the hospitality of *farbrekhers*, was soothed by Liesl's presence. He'd fallen into silence as she floated past; the day seemed to overtake him; he let himself be fed. Not "their" meat, but their turnips and their black bread and their sweet, cinnamon-scented pudding.

Liesl smelled of water and soap, a freshness Minna associated with clothes taken off a line but not yet ironed. Otto and Liesl, Minna thought, might be so confident that they saw no need to iron. She pushed the back of her head deep into the pillow, which was tall and plump, its seams visibly sewn and resewn countless times, and pictured Liesl, surrounded by goose feathers, her pink fingers sifting through for only the finest. A woman would have time to take such care if she didn't have to iron. And why should anyone iron in Sodokota? Max had Minna press his shirts with the kettle, but what for? The grass? The stones? God, she supposed. Max had it all wrong. And Ruth and Leo, too, with their tall house and their bought-new wagon. It was embarrassing, really, if you looked at Otto and Liesl. Real Americans tried hard at working, perhaps, but not at being. To try at that was to confess a vast, simmering doubt.

At her nape, Minna felt the after-brush of Liesl's fingers braiding her hair before bed. Liesl had said nothing, she'd simply appeared, a warmth at Minna's back, with a comb. She had a daughter, apparently, grown and gone somewhere as girls go.

Minna could still feel the loosening in her scalp, as though a great itch had been scratched. And now she couldn't help thinking of what she'd been trying all evening to ignore: her wedding wish, under the *chuppah* and the flour sack and the racket of hands clapping and spoons clanging: she'd wished that she might go home with Otto and his lovely wife.

And here she was.

Did that make it her fault?

But to believe that would be to believe that something or someone had answered her wish. Which would make her wish more like prayer. Minna did not pray. And why would this Something, this Someone, who by all evidence had never given Minna a second thought, suddenly start to answer her wishes—and in such a backward way? Who would think of such a thing as a cow falling through a house? There was danger, it seemed, in making such a wish. Punishment, perhaps, for daring to ask. Maybe you had no right to ask if you didn't believe.

She lay perfectly still, on her back. She was determined to stay like this all night, so as not to roll or kick by accident.

D AYLIGHT, and through Minna's eyelids: *My house! You destroyed my house!* She waited, holding her breath, willing her eyes shut as if to send away a bad dream, but the cries returned. *My house my house my house!*

The bedroom door was closed. Liesl had already risen. At the foot of the bed, she'd laid out a dress for Minna, plain but of a cloth finer than muslin, and with a collar Minna especially liked, dyed dark blue and printed in yellow flowers. She was glad that

Liesl had never met Lina, and could not compare Minna to her. She buttoned the dress slowly, pretending that these were her buttons, and that this was her bedroom. The voice beyond the door was only a neighbor, yes, some man who'd come in blustering about fences and trees and vegetables gone to rot and aching bones and oh, what if the world was just outside, with its gutters and feuds!

My house!

She took great pains making the bed. She drew the curtain. She folded the nightgown Liesl had lent her. In a small mirror above the dressing bureau she lifted her chin so that the collar of Liesl's dress did not sag. She hadn't seen herself since the wedding, in Ruth's mirror. What kind of wife, she thought, was not given her own mirror? Lina *beautiful-in-the-way-no-one-disputes* certainly would have had one. I would look better, she thought, with a plumper neck. Smaller ears. My nose leans to the right.

She thought of Samuel. She thought of Ilya, who was better to think on, a mirage now, safe. She thought of Max, who was best to think on, and easy enough, for his cries were on this continent; they were in this house; they were close enough Minna could feel them in her chest.

He was pacing the perimeter of the front room, too absorbed to notice Minna's entrance, throwing his arms every time he shouted, "House!" while Otto, seated at the table, punctuated the onslaught with sympathetic "mmm"s and sincere nods. His son sat nearby, saying nothing. His name was Friedrich, though Liesl called him Fritzi. Which made Minna feel a little sorry for him. Fritzi. But even when Max daggered a finger at him and shouted, *"Nar!"*—a word which enjoyed the exact same meaning in German—the boy didn't flinch. He sat backward in his chair, straddling it as he would a horse, his hands hanging loosely over the back rungs as if to show Max how little he cared. "Fool!" Max shouted again.

"Motke."

But perhaps she'd spoken too softly. She repeated herself with more force, but still he ranted and stomped, and again Minna said his name but now she was humiliatied, standing in this strange room in front of near strangers in a stranger's dress as her husband paid her no attention. Yesterday, he had listened; she had called his name and he'd stopped and she'd felt a surge of power, a rightness as a wife. But now she felt like a girl playing dress-up. That she was wearing Liesl's dress didn't help. And the yellow flowers, she decided, were all wrong; yellow made her look pasty.

"Motke!" she shouted, and grabbed his arm, and as he spun toward her, raising his other arm, Minna thought that he might strike her, and this thought was not entirely unwelcome: to be struck, at least, would demand a response; she would know what to do; when it was over, he would owe her something.

But he didn't touch her. He wrested his arm free and said, "Do not tell me to be quiet. These people—they destroy our home and they—expect us to stay in theirs, 'as long as you like!' they say—they expect us to look at their little man"—he pointed at a wooden cross by the door—"and sleep in their beds and eat their *treyf.*"

"Motke. It's only a cross." This was the only argument Minna could think to make. She was too busy wondering if what he'd said was true—could they really stay as long as they liked? Sheltered from their ignorance, and their lonesome, intimate circling, and the impending return of the boys? And why not? Maybe once they'd retrieved their few belongings, they could haul the rest of the house into the *mikvah* hole and pack it down and new grass would grow and you'd never have to know either one had existed.

"Look," she told him, pointing. "There is no little man."

"You're meant to *imagine* the man!" Max cried. "He's there, he's precisely there, as there as I am here. What kind of God hangs on a wall?"

"Motke. Please. They have shown us every kindness."

"Yes! Kindness! But to leave us a home, to let us alone. Have we bothered them in some way? Does the sight of us—"

"What? Jews? You think they care?"

"You think they don't? You don't think that's exactly what they care about?"

"Why even come here, then? Why bother moving to the middle of nowhere?"

"To be let alone!"

Minna felt a sudden recognition—as if she'd had this conversation before. It was Moses she was thinking of, with his shorn earlock and his fury, his determination, in the wake of his attack, to be more stubbornly faithful and different and offensive than ever before. She felt exhausted. Sad. Embarrassed, at Otto and Fritzi's presence. She said, "They want to help. We might stay a little while—"

"The whole winter? If we stay now, we are here the winter. As if we have nothing to do these months but thank them—"

"But, Motke—perhaps—"

"We stay until the boys return. That is all."

"But listen." The boys. Minna missed Jacob. But not Samuel. Not in the usual way of missing. Samuel she had begun to fear, as one feared sun after days of rain, the brilliant ache behind your eyeballs, the inexplicable desire to stare directly into its glare. "If we stay with Otto and Liesl, we'll have time to build a better house."

"Minna. I will not—"

"But, Motke—"

"Do not shame me."

Max had switched abruptly to Russian; his mouth looked mean and sad at once, then, as it closed, full of grief. For the first time this morning, Minna allowed herself to meet Otto's gaze. She expected pity, or disgust, but she found only his frank, kind, solid face, and in it an offer of permission, and expectation—that she console her husband now, that she defend. Which made her grateful and also angry, so that she could not apologize or thank him in the polite way she wanted. She felt for Liesl's collar, tugged it straight, stuck out her chin, then looked at each of the men in turn, including Max, with a fixed, false smile. "Excuse my interruption." She went to find Liesl in the barn.

MINNA ate one piece of bacon, two bratwurst, more chicken legs than she could count, and three bites of a pink, fleshy, frightening, delicious roast they called, simply, *ham*. She snuck these morsels as she cooked kosher meals for herself and Max, kosher meals in the koshered pan he'd made her scrape and boil and store apart from the others, shrouded in cheesecloth. Liesl cooked beside her, and must have seen Minna's fingers swiftly plucking, but she made no comment. The two women rarely spoke—not in bed, not as they milked, not as Minna helped Liesl sweep the kitchen—and yet there seemed to be no animosity to this not speaking, no ill will or competition. If anything, Minna thought, the silence expressed a certain communion: as if they agreed, without saying so, that Liesl would lie for Minna if necessary, just as they agreed on the proportion of water to vinegar for scrubbing the stove, and on the futility of their husbands' bargaining sessions in the next room.

There were in fact no bargains being made. There was Otto making offers, and Max rejecting them. No, he did not want Otto to build them a new house. No, he did not want Otto to provide the raw materials. No, he did not want flour and potatoes to last the winter. He wanted justice, he claimed, but for him the only justice seemed to be miracle: to open his eyes and be back in his sod cave. To Max, Otto's apologies were deceitful, his hospitality insulting, his efforts at reparation laughable.

Eventually Otto would excuse himself and go to work, and Max would take up his post at the windows, worrying his fingers against his thumbs, loudly chewing his beard, and speculating to anyone or no one as to the whereabouts of his sons. Something terrible had happened. They would never return. Or it was Leo's fault, Leo was keeping them too long, taking a long route back. Or there, there they were, wasn't that them? But wait, no, it wasn't even a wagon—was it just a cow?—a buffalo?—a shadow. Minna left Max alone for the most part, attending his basic needs but little more. Their argument had left her seething, but she seethed quietly, flatly. She developed a habit of nodding as he was about to speak, so as to preclude, or at least disassemble, his complaints. "No wonder Fritzi is such a *paskudnyak*, his parents should allow him to read those books," became . . . "Fritzi, *paskudnyak*, books, anh." If raising her voice had no effect, she would protest by ignoring him, and stuffing herself with *treyf* (some of which, if she was honest, made her feel a little queasy), and shrugging at Liesl's suggestion that Max and Minna take the large bed for a night.

She did not think to offer the opposite to Liesl and Otto; one day she would look back and realize that she should have, but at the time she only thought how tranquil it was without Max at her back, and the crude, defenseless stirring that was his signal.

Let the boys stay away. Then Minna could stay here, in clean, gently frayed grace, free from storm and starvation and filth and her own dangers. In polite company, one could forget one's dangers. And maybe she could manage to get her hands on one of "those books" Max so reviled, which Fritzi carried around with him during the couple days he was home from the cattle drive. He read in corners, moody and slumped. These weren't newspapers or magazines or prayer books, they were the kinds of books people read for pleasure, with soft, illustrated covers and titles Minna couldn't read because they were in English, and because, when Fritzi caught her trying, he skulked off. Which made her want to scream. Did he think her a threat? Was there disapproval on her face? Fear? Suspicion? Had she begun to resemble Max, in the way spouses sometimes did, their features meeting in subtle, irretrievable assent?

Fʀᴏᴍ the rubble they reclaimed the long wooden spoon, a blanket, Minna's bedsheet with its familiar tear, several unbroken dishes, two forks. Minna's pillow, flatter than it had ever been, even between Galina's knees. Candlesticks so swollen with soil they looked like knotted lengths of muslin. The empty coffee tin now packed with dirt. Max's *tefillin* were barely recognizable. These, Minna brushed off—she did not scrub. And she barely touched his prayer shawl, which had been separated from his prayer book and wedged into the frying pan. Whatever she did to these items, she guessed, Max would do over.

She had seen his face collapse when Otto found the prayer book, and his efforts to compose himself as Otto shook it free of dirt and held it out. Max was shy, suddenly; you could see that he wanted to kiss the book, but privately, to kiss it more lovingly, perhaps, than he'd ever kissed a woman. Minna wondered if he'd kissed the Torah before allowing it to be destroyed. She was surprised to feel a tenderness in her throat. She was sorry for Max in a true way, without pity or annoyance—as if he were a stranger she would never have to meet or touch or feed.

Then Max handed her the book, grabbed his shovel, and started digging again. But they had already stripped every layer: the grass, the roots, the sod, even the pitiful magazine wallpaper, now torn into clumps and shreds. They had reached the bottom of the pile that had been the house, that before it was a house had been a hill.

There was something almost natural about the wreckage, though Minna would never say so.

Max kept digging.

"Motke," she said gently, "you might stop. There's nothing left."

But as soon as she'd spoken his name, her sympathy shrank to a nub; in her mouth was a bitter tang: what did he think he was doing—digging another *mikvah*? Enough with his laws and superstitions and forbiddings. She thought of the old kiddush cup Galina had once used as a chamber pot, and the way her neck curved as she tilted back her head to laugh. Her profanity was more comprehensible to Minna than Max's devotion. So Max dug and Minna hated him. She wasn't meant to miss Galina. She was meant to be a wife, to stop her missings, to stop, and stay. The taste in her mouth turned acrid, all the fury she'd been stocking up fell out. She shouted at Max's back, "There's nothing left! Do you understand 'nothing'? Do you think yourself a rich man?" She shouted in Russian but still, she was shouting—let Otto hear—let Max hear him hear. "What do you think you'll find. Gold? A *Torah*?" She snorted. Her life with Max would be this way, she realized: long stretches of containment, control, followed by eruption, like a new season. "Or have you buried some relic of your wife down there?" she went on. "A lock of hair, perhaps? Her jeweled hairpin? Her prized hand mirror with the rose painted on the back?" She seized his shoulder and yanked him back. "Max!"

His calm, when he looked up, was maddening. Max, who was never calm, ignored Minna's hysterical grip and held out an object. Encased in dirt it might have been a slightly misshapen cigar.

He tapped it against his leg, spraying soil.

Minna had never shown Max her comb. It seemed an

embarrassment; a reminder of the fantasies she'd allowed herself. Now, her cheeks burning, she wanted to snatch it from his hand. But he held it up to her with a pride she couldn't concede to.

If only Otto had found it; then she could take it. Then she wouldn't have to say, as she was saying, "Oh. That. You might as well have left that buried."

T HE "prized hand mirror" had been Roza's. (Minna's mother had had several mirrors, but this one—according to her father—had been her favorite.) Its handle was gold, or gold-painted. The painted rose was pink. The "jeweled hairpin" was her mother's, too. Her father had kept them in the little table beside his bed, the mirror facedown, rose up, the hairpin just-so askance, its stones green and glittering when the sun slanted in. They couldn't have been emeralds, they must have been glass. And in another drawer—how many drawers there had been—or was that simply the way one remembered childhood, as full of drawers?—in this other drawer was a small pile of hair. Not a lock, no, whoever left a whole lock, no, these were stray hairs pretending to be a lock, hairs he must have gathered one by one, from corners and pillows and windowsills, and combed together. And sometimes Minna opened the drawer to find them holding, in a long, frightening clump. But other times he'd neglected his combing and she found them wisping around like dust.

Otto's last offer: not only flour and wood and nails and labor but the cow, the whole cow, which was bled and cleaned and hanging in his barn, which wasn't even his to give, but he would pay the rancher and he would deliver it, quartered and salted, the whole cow he would deliver to Max.

Silence.

Minna, listening from the kitchen, poised with a chunk of sausage on its way to her mouth, had to admit that it was difficult to imagine a slaughter any less kosher. She did not blame Otto for not understanding this, but she didn't blame Max, either, when he shouted, "He's a Shabbos goy! A Shabbos goy who was never invited, who doesn't even know the rules!" Another silence followed, electric with rage, then the sound of glass being smashed. A brief crackling riot led quickly to a tinkling. And it was over. Liesl had not stopped sweeping. Minna resumed the journey of the sausage to her mouth.

Then Leo's wagon was rolling up and the boys were jumping down, running thrilled into the house, they'd gone to the farm, they'd imagined a cyclone, maybe Indians—they'd thought Minna and Max dead. The accident, retold by Max in a dry, dead voice he'd obviously been practicing for the occasion, finally achieved its full inanity, and the boys laughed and laughed. Then they turned incredulous, then impertinent, demanding to know what the family would do next. They had paid good money for coal. They'd gone to Mitchell and purchased coffee and flour and all manner of other goods, they'd worked hard and brought home a bounty and now there was no home?

In their commotion, Jacob and Samuel looked like brothers; like true boys; they almost looked like stepsons. It wasn't until the next morning, when Minna sat up in Liesl's bed and saw them out the window, heading toward the barn, that their difference was clear again. There was Jacob, prancing slightly, stooping here and there to pick up a stone, all weaving and loose so that you knew he had to be smiling, and if it were only him, she might have run outside, and called. But there was Samuel, straight as a book's spine, walking without seeming to walk at all. She couldn't even see the soles of his boots lifting, though they must have, for already he was farther away, his hands in those fists he wore, his hair black in the first, pouring sun. He looked taller than Minna remembered him to be, and thinner; his shoulder blades were visible beneath his shirt.

She squinted, wishing him gone, or at least changed—at least, when she widened her eyes again, he would only be a thin young man and she would look at him and think, there is my stepson who is good at mending the chickens' roof. Instead she saw his face, though it was turned away: his jaw, sharp as his shoulders, his dark eyes locked straight ahead. She'd been waiting, she knew, to see if those eyes would still be so hard when he returned.

The backs of his knees caught the sun, one then the other. The back of his neck was brown against his white shirt.

A new shirt, if she wasn't mistaken.

They had done well, her industrious stepsons. She should be pleased.

But she wanted to kiss one of them.

She wanted to disappear.

If she walked off slowly enough, maybe no one would notice.

She could slip into the horizon, be gone; the courage to do it, a kind of poison, had to be in her.

But to disappear was to confess. To disappear was to be known as you'd never be if you stayed.

So maybe she would hide. Today, at least, she would hide under Liesl's bed, and all her poison would drain away and she would rise pure, as if from the *mikvah*.

Yet her feet, beneath the blanket, were so perfectly cool. The sheets were so soft. Her eyes were tired. Why hide under the bed when she could hide in it? She wouldn't have many more nights here, now that the boys were back. The boys were back. Boys were back. Boys back. A most casual thing to say, to think, think it enough and that will be all it is; don't look out the window; don't think of his mouth; just lie back. The boys are back. Lie back. Cover your head. Touch nothing.

EIGHTEEN

THE new house would have two rooms, a pitched roof, a wood frame. Boards would be gathered from the collapsed shed, nails and hinges and other hardware purchased in Mitchell. Minna and Liesl would turn the *mikvah* hole into a proper cellar. For a new shed, which they would call a barn, Fritzi would bring more wood in the form of railroad ties, "borrowed" from the railroad company, and the men would not question his source because they would already be raising the walls.

The house that would be. And then it was! They were raising the walls, and pitching the roof, and building a new table and new benches and beds. The ceiling was tall, the beds plenty wide. The old stove had been salvaged; Minna scrubbed it until it shone. She felt like a child who'd been given a gift, felt her chest ache with gratitude at the improvements, at the men's constant motion. How astounding to think that the purpose of all their activity was to build something for *her*. Or in large part for her. And that it took so many of them, working so hard! Otto had "helped" them buy materials, and now he and Fritzi "helped" with the work, an agreement Samuel had brokered like a puppeteer so as to make all success his father's, so that suddenly it had been Max saying thing like, *There's no sense arguing, the days are growing short, let's get to work!*

And they had—they'd gotten to work, and kept on working, and soon Minna began to feel, in their midst, wearing one of two quality dresses that Liesl had gifted her, not like a child but like the mistress of a house. She and Liesl cut into the gentle bowl of the *mikvah* with spades and she was awestruck by the ordinariness of it all. They were like people all over the country, straightening walls, filling holes, testing joints, making tight.

Then they were moving into the first room before the second had even been framed and she grew uneasy. She began to notice how many other things were not done, or half done, or perhaps not done well enough. There were *plans* to dig a well and build a washhouse, but not a single shovelful of earth had been turned over. The walls grew thick with sod but the wind grew colder just as fast. And the door latch, which Minna found exceedingly disappointing, was not a latch at all but a string, wound around a split railroad tie and set through a hole in the door, so that to open it you had to pull up, and to close it, to let the string drop back down. This was not on account of frugality, as it must have seemed to Otto and Liesl, nor of ignorance. According to Jacob, Max had carried with him to America, wrapped in felt, a crystal doorknob, left him by a wealthy cousin. For a time, this heavy, finely cut doorknob had graced the door of their cave—until, over Samuel's protests, Max had traded it for Minna's wedding ring. And now, to prove that he'd been right, and perhaps to admonish all of them, he was determined not to buy another doorknob. To do that, Minna supposed, would be to admit more than his foolishness with the ring—it would be to admit a certain foolishness with Minna. So she said nothing.

This was *fall*, Jacob said, seeing that she was troubled, trying to cheer her. Also known—he deepened his voice—as *autummmn*. And this was *fall*, he explained soberly, before throwing himself facedown into the yellowing grass.

A letter, delivered by Otto, who found her at the creek, doing the washing. She stared for a long moment at the script on the outside—*Minna*—wondering if Galina had somehow found her. Did she have regrets? Had the Russians come again? Did she simply want to know, as a person might, how her old maidservant was faring?

Otto pushed the letter closer. She dried her hands and took it. "From Ruth," he said, and smiled. He was nervous, Minna realized. She had never seen Otto nervous. Every day he showed up to work on a house whose owner either ignored or insulted him and he went politely about his business, doing much of the building himself and teaching Samuel along the way, yet now he looked like a child about to commit a small crime. He glanced back at the house, leaned in toward Minna, then pulled another object from his shirt and slid it beneath the letter in her hands.

"I am sorry for Fritzi's mistake," he said, looking emphatically at her hands, in which she was holding, she realized, one of

Fritzi's paperback books. "I can bring you one at a time. He won't notice they're gone."

Minna looked at her washing. The creek was so low now she'd had to dig a little pool and dam it with stones, but even so, the water didn't cover all the clothes: there was a dry corner of a shirt she could wrap the book in.

"It's English," said Otto, his voice cracking: apologetic and encouraging at once.

"I know. Thank you."

NINETEEN

MINNA had not received a letter since she was nine or ten, when her aunts wrote to send their regrets, they would not be coming to make Pesach that year. But that letter was not intended for her. She'd opened it though she knew it would make her father angry, then tried and failed to seal it back up, then, when he came home and saw, she'd said without thinking, *but I read better than you*—which was true but not good, or good but only if one didn't speak of it, or good if spoken about but only if they pretended she was her little brother, which was growing more difficult all the time. Just as Max had brought his sons to a place where they would grow strong, then mistrusted their strength, her father had sent her to the boys' school, then regretted it. When she said *I read better than you*, he slapped her. Then he asked her forgiveness but she was already pouring his coffee, so he punished himself by not drinking it. Though that last part, she might have wrong. It might have been that he drank his coffee, and punished himself by asking Minna to read the letter aloud.

Rᴜᴛʜ's letter was in Yiddish, thankfully. Minna would have expected her to write it in English, just to prove something, to taunt.

Tayere *Minna,*

I wish to express my condolences to you and your little family. Your recent misfortune is certainly undeserved. I understand that you will have a new house built, sturdier and of course more hygienic, and I hope that you soon come to feel misfortune turning into opportunity. Then you may truly call yourself American.

I also wish to send my regrets that we will not be able to join your little family for Rosh Hashanah. Preparations for winter must be made, and the girls and I have begun our canning.

And you? Do you expect a child?

I hope you do not think me impolite for asking. On the plains, one mustn't hide anything. It only leads to trouble.

But on to my real purpose (for does not a True Friend have a better purpose than to plaplen?*): Along with a new stove (a gift from Leo—the latest model from Sioux Falls) and an excellent tool with which to beat eggs, I have obtained a book (borrowed, I admit, but I intend to keep it all winter) CHOCK-FULL of the latest housekeeping advice. As often as I can, I will send you TIDBITS, those I think you will find most useful given your unique situation.*

(I've translated all, of course, and hope I have done the author justice.)

Therefore, I will not continue to delay:

1. *"In the city, I believe, it is better to exchange ashes and grease for soap; but in the country, I am certain, it is good economy to make one's own soap. The great difficulty in making soap 'come' originates in want of judgment about the strength of the lye. One rule may be safely trusted—if your lye will bear up an egg, or a potato, so that you can see a piece of the surface as big as a ninepence, it is just strong enough."*

2. *"Count towels, sheets, spoons, &c. occasionally; that those who use them may not become careless."*

3. *Sore Nipples*—*Put twenty grains of sugar of lead into a vial with one gill of rose water; shake it up thoroughly; wet a piece of soft linen with this preparation, and put it on; renew this as often as the linen becomes dry. Before nursing, wash this off with something soothing; rose water is very good; but the best thing is quince seed warmed in a little cold tea until the liquid becomes quite gelatinous. This application is alike healing and pleasant."*

4. *"Wash the eyes thoroughly in cold water each morning."*

5. *"When green peas have become old and yellow, they may be made tender and green by sprinkling in a pinch or two of pearlash, while they are boiling."*

6. *"Squashes should never be kept down cellar when it is possible to prevent it. Dampness injures them."*

7. *"Eggs will keep almost any length of time in limewater properly prepared. One pint of coarse salt, and one pint of unslacked lime,*

to a pailful of water. If there be too much lime, it will eat the shells from the eggs; and if there be a single egg cracked, it will spoil the whole. They should be covered with limewater and kept in a cold place. The yolk becomes slightly red; but I have seen eggs, thus kept, perfectly sweet and fresh at the end of three years."

8. "Keep a coarse broom for the cellar stairs, woodshed, yard, &c. No good housekeeper allows her carpet broom to be used for such things."

9. "Let those who love to be invalids drink strong green tea, eat pickles, preserves, and rich pastry. As far as possible, eat and sleep at regular hours."

You may be left with questions, mamele. I recall from our whitewash lesson that you are shy to admit your ignorance, but one must never, ever, be afraid to ask questions. Please consider me a fountain of knowledge wishing to shower you with experience. Particularly when your wee one arrives.

Regards to your boys,
Ruth

Minna's response was brief, her excuse for its brevity a lie:

I have only this small square of brown paper on which to write, for I was careless and squandered the wrappings from my wedding gifts, which just goes to show how truly lacking I am in any instinct for housekeeping.

And because her excuse took up half the square of paper, she only had to fill a tiny space with her note:

Not expecting——yet——any wee one. Thank you for the housekeeping tips, I will try my best to apply them to my "unique" situation, though I am, as you say, quite ignorant. Regards to your big family, Minna

WHAT Minna did not tell Ruth:
She was grateful for Ruth's instructions. She'd been grateful for almost all her advice—even her suggestion that Minna try to love Max. She was sorry that she couldn't bring herself to say this.

And there would be, she was fairly certain, no wee one. Minna still hadn't bled, even once, nor did she feel any different. A bit heavier, perhaps, but that was likely the food the boys brought back. There were walnuts and cherries and apples and beets and turnips and yams; there was yeast, and a cornmeal fine as flour. She baked bread every morning, served a full meal at midday, made the evening soup thick.

She did not tell Ruth this either, for Minna understood her own indulgence; it was clear from the way her heart leaped as she chose yet another yam, and from the way Samuel watched her hands as they chopped and mashed and kneaded. He did not approve, but wouldn't say so. Since his return, they'd had no formal greeting, no "how-dee-do," as Jacob called it, just a slide again into weather and time and meals and tools. She hadn't asked the questions that kept riding through her mind: Had they slept in a house? In tents? Had there been a woman to cook for them, and if so, what had she looked like? Nor did Samuel ask after the work Minna had done or not done. But one day she overheard him, in the yard, saying to Jacob: "A cellar? You believe they were intending a cellar with that hole? They had weeks, and accomplished nothing! And my magazines—what was she doing with them that they're torn apart and stuck to the sod?"

"Papering the walls?" Jacob suggested. "As far as I can tell."

"But why?"

"Why not?"

"She did it to anger me."

"Why would she do that?"

Minna peeked around the house now—but she was too late to catch whatever silent response Samuel gave, whatever shrug or shift in stance.

"Minna!" called Jacob gaily.

She smiled, mouth closed, and waved a hand. "Hello, Jacob."

"We were just talking about you."

"Really."

"Really!"

Samuel looked at her, but she refused to meet his eye. "You know," she said to Jacob. "If he'd asked me himself, I would have told him."

"I'll let him know that."

"Please do."

She turned, and went back into the house to cook dinner. If Samuel hadn't called her "she," she thought, she might have told him still. About the *mikvah* and the whitewashing and the general waywardness with which she and Max had behaved. Some part of her wanted to tell him, and force him to anger. But another part knew that he knew, so she went on ignoring the silent rebukes of his frugality. On Rosh Hashanah, when she opened a jar of honey, and he muttered, "That's from Iowa," his meaning was clear; she might have closed it up again and appeased him. But she was looking at how the word *Iowa* had left his mouth, open more than usual, so that she saw his top row of teeth and, behind them, the blood-pink roof of his mouth. "Iowa," she said, "How interesting," and spooned the honey out onto a thick slice of challah. Max called it a threat to his prayers and wouldn't eat it until afterward, and Samuel tried only a bite, but Minna and Jacob finished the rest quickly, then cut another slice and finished that, too, and then they stood next to Samuel, fortified and a bit loopy, as Max led them through the service. It was as repetitive as Minna remembered *shul* to be, but worse because there were no songs and no one in front of you to look at or gossip about or feel pity for. They could have gone west to the colony, where "za great von Baron de von Vintovich," as Jacob called him, would have sent a true rabbi and enough *yarmulkes* to cover every man's head, where there might be a synagogue as tall as in Cincinnati, with a separate place for the women to sit, where everyone could start the year with a new pair of shoes. Shoes, not boots—Jacob was emphatic on this point. And who knew, he said, za Baron might even be there himself. They might kiss his feet, or dance around him, like Indians. Max said—or Samuel said and Max repeated—that he didn't want to waste the time traveling, with the unfinished house and the short days and what have you. But Minna suspected the real reason Max didn't want to go to the colony—apart from his fear that she and the boys would want to stay—was some idea he had that the journey back and forth might upset Minna's chance of conceiving. Max had become more fixated on having a child now, as if to go into winter without Minna pregnant would be to admit that he'd never bring anything forth in this new world.

"Our child," he said when he woke, and after he prayed, and in the middle of the night. "Our child," he whispered, after he slid out of her, smoothed her nightgown, and—a new gesture—gave her stomach a pat. "Child of an angel."

And what would Ruth say to that? What did Minna even have to say? Nothing—it was too charitable. It made her feel every edge of her body, every place skin met air, the pulses in her neck, her wrists, the receding pulse between her legs, how utterly un-like an angel she was. It made her feel the parts of her that didn't know if they wanted a child at all—and those that wanted one, but not his. If she had Max's child, she supposed, there would be a kind of relief in it. A purpose. A knot. She might think less of other lives. Then again, she might not. She might be driven, like her mother, to go live the other lives.

She whispered back, "Good night."

But even a whisper gained force against the new wood frame, and floor. If the cave had absorbed noises, the house spat them back. When the second room was built, she and Max would sleep in there, but for now the beds lined one wall, foot to foot. She tried covering his mouth with her hand but then her palm collected his breath and Max just held her closer, as though her shushing excited him. She listened for the other bed, and some-times she heard breaths, but sometimes she didn't. She listened until her skull shook with the effort, then counted and tried to forget, or at least not to care, for the time it took to fall asleep.

But in the morning as she served breakfast, her face turned red, and her hands were clumsy, even though Jacob would be making jokes or playing spoons and Samuel rarely looked at her anymore anyway. He could go a whole day without meeting her eye, which meant that Minna barely had to try not to meet his. And yet she couldn't help trying, and hard, so that she wound up looking at him all the time, everywhere but his eyes. His general irritation was closer to the surface now, you could see it in the way he never sat entirely still, a knee or fist always jouncing, the way his jaw went rocklike at the slightest provocation. The questions they hadn't asked of each other were irretrievable now: on top of them had piled the question of the clouds, which were difficult to read suddenly, and of the cold, which you could feel in your fingernails. How long should they wait, how cold should it have to be, before they started burning coal? Minna's old grass braids were fine for cooking, but not heating, and they would run out soon anyway. And would the *shochet* ever arrive with the meat? Minna and Samuel and Max turned over every possibility, every choice, they took up sides and angles, and sometimes it seemed to her they switched just to keep debating. And what to do about the chickens? More had stopped laying; they sat haughtily upon their nests. The eggs would keep in salt, Samuel suggested, but Max said he'd never heard of such a thing.

This was on a clear, cold day, which seemed to have given everyone a headache. Jacob was out gathering the last potatoes. Max was convinced they'd been sold bad chickens, and when Samuel reminded him that they'd bought the chickens from a Jew, Max said the Jew must have been sold bad chicks. When the *shochet* showed, he said, they should have him kill the birds for meat. If the *shochet* showed, said Samuel. If, if. And the chickens weren't "bad," he added. They were cold. They would start laying again, come spring.

Minna said yes, of course, they always start again. Poor chickens. She paused. She wasn't certain if she meant poor for not laying, or poor for the fact that they would have to lay again. She explained Ruth's limewater solution to the men and offered to put the eggs up to store that way.

Samuel spun toward her as if he'd forgotten that she was in the room, cutting an old shirt for rags. "There's plenty of salt," he said.

"But the lime—"

"We don't have any lime."

Minna shrugged. "Fine."

"Where did you even get that idea?"

"Ruth. It's fine. I'll put them up in salt."

"Fine."

"Yes. There's plenty of salt."

"That's what I just said."

"Anything else, sir?" she asked.

He looked directly, sourly, at her.

"For instance," Minna said. "We could build a new chicken coop against the house. See if keeping them warmer makes a difference."

"Yes." A mild sneer passed over Samuel's face. "If we had a house."

"What is this?" asked Max.

"It's a room. Don't fool yourself."

"Such a pessimist!"

"Me? You would call me the pessimist?" Samuel turned to

face his father. From the side you could see how his hair had begun to dominate his face. It grew in front of his ears, and puffed forward from his brow. Yet this overgrowth couldn't be neglect, exactly, for every week, without fail, using the ladle's bulbous reflection to guide him, he shaved his chin and lip. *And what to make of that?* Minna would have liked to ask Ruth, if Ruth and she were friends—if Samuel were not her stepson. She would describe it: how his chin and lip were clean, bearing the sharp, mirrored angles of his face; how she couldn't help wondering if he did this for her; how he looked trapped—like a carefully composed portrait framed in fur.

"And what," he asked Max, his wilderness shaking slightly, "what would you call yourself—a realist?"

"Consider," said Max, and gave his most aggressive shrug.

Samuel folded his arms, visibly working to calm himself. "I'm sorry. It's only that I find it confusing. We pray to a God—we atone, just last month we fasted and atoned—then in the same breath we say we'll do it all again."

"Yes. What could be more realistic? One prepares for the worst."

"And then it happens."

"Not necessarily."

"But what if we were to prepare for the best? What harm could it do?"

"Pride."

"So you would suggest—is this right—I'm sorry." Samuel smiled painfully. "You would suggest that instead of working, I should pray?"

Max narrowed his eyes, in the way of his son. Samuel's voice rose. "Does praying ever work?" he asked. "Could it maybe be argued that prayer is just a fussy form of pessimism? Do you think it's possible, if you'd prayed a little less, that your wife might not have left you?"

Max touched a hand to his beard. Samuel covered his mouth. They stared at each other, full of shame, and a sorrow Minna might once have tried to mend in some sideways, upside-down way.

Instead she said, "When you two decide? About the eggs? Salt. Butchery. Tell me what you'd like done. I'll be at the shed."

On the coldest days, milking kept her warm. She'd used to hate her own sweat, to dread its scent of vinegar and work, but now she looked forward to it breaking as to a bath. She pulled fast, the cow warm against her face, hot in her hands. Just beyond the shed wall, in the spot where they had grand plans to build a privy, the ground was streaked with urine. Nothing soaked in anymore; everything ran. This seemed to be the way of *fall* here: no startling color, just a general hardening that took the soil, the grass, the sand in the creek. Most of the cottonwood leaves didn't even bother unhinging, they simply turned brown and crisp and knocked each other when the branches shook. The wind was a new thing yet again: it gained intention; it curved and dipped and homed in. You might be standing outside by the west wall of the house, watching the men pack sod and frame the second room and debate which project deserved more urgency, when a gust of wind at your back would flatten a strip of grass in front of you, then spin around and whip your eyes to tears, then bounce off the wall and head for the trees, all the while never touching the men.

LAST winter, in Galina's house, she had kept a stash of Galina's spent, soggy tea leaves and brewed a pot late each night, to make herself warm enough to sleep. She would stand in the pantry and drink it quietly, careful not to slurp, wary both of Galina, who sometimes prowled, and of her own future, in which she hoped a certain refinement would be required of her. But one night she went to retrieve her pocket of leaves and caught Rebeka there, with Minna's leaves poured out into her palm and her palm held up to her face, her eyes wide with make-believe. They grew wider when she saw Minna in the doorway. She lowered her head. "I'm telling a fortune," she whispered. Minna stood, waiting, for what she didn't know. Then she told the girl that fortune-telling was a sham, that she was stupid to believe it, and stupid to waste the leaves, and wrong not to let Minna's things alone. The girl cried. Of course. She was always crying. She was so slight, so almost-cold all the time. Minna wished now that she had been kinder to her more often. It was as if she'd thought kindness a thing like water; as if she'd only had so much and didn't want to spend it on the wrong things. (But how were you supposed to know what the right things were?) If she could go back, she thought, she would let the girl tell her fortune. She would kneel down next to her on that old splintery floor and say, "Please, mine, too." And then maybe Rebeka would tell Minna that she would cross an ocean and be wed to an old man and love his son and find herself standing in the wind, alone. And then she would have known.

Winter

TWENTY

LIESL came a final time. She was sorry, but there was still much to do, she had to finish her own canning, and hang meat, and fill the feather beds and pillows, but not to worry, Otto would keep coming, he would show Samuel all he needed and see the house through. This was the most Liesl had ever said to Minna at one time, and Minna felt a rush of confusion, and regret, for Liesl's words spilled out in a jumble and red splotches of excitement crept up her neck. Minna said, please, not to worry, she could finish leveling and tamping the cellar shelves herself.

Liesl smiled. She'd come holding a scroll, which she knelt down now to roll out. She walked on her knees to the spot where the sun hit the cellar floor, and gestured for Minna to join her.

"Here. Look."

It was a map.

Minna lived, it appeared, in a near-perfect rectangle, broken
only once in the lower-right corner where a big river jagged and
curled and made the corner hang like a sack of stones. The Missoury, Liesl said, which split the rectangle in two: this eastern
section sliced into a grid, the section to the west mostly open,
with fewer squares, and no railroads yet. The mountains were
here; Liesl pointed. Then, dragging her finger back to the right:
Pierre, Mitchell, Sioux Falls. And this is our land. And this is your
land. Liesl looked at her then, boldly. All this—she swept her hand
across the map—is Dakota Territory. Soon they'll split it here—
finger to the middle—and make it a state. South Dakota. Yes?
Minna nodded. And where is Ruth and Leo's? Liesl pointed at a
square to the north. What about Milwaukee? She pointed at a sack
of flour. And Chicago? Another sack. What about New York? Liesl
giggled. Over in the house, she said. Then she rolled the map back
up and said, "See. So now you know."

But in the days that followed, Minna wondered what she did
know. She'd already known she was somewhere. Now she had more
sense, she supposed, of where this somewhere was in relation to
other people's somewheres. But the grid was misleading—the
lines looked like roads, but weren't. And how would she travel,
and what was she even thinking, and what did Liesl mean looking
at her like that? Did she mean to say, *There are other ways to live, you
could be like me, I've known Otto since I was a girl, there are other ways to
find a husband than through the mail?* Did she expect Minna to show
up at her door one day? Did she think her so flimsy that she would
leave just because she knew the way?

Minna formed a new resolve to prefer her own house. She

would embrace the improvements, and follow Ruth's advice. She would make her own soap, and be reasonable with the food stores, and figure out how to make pearlash to sprinkle on the old beans. She would make but try not to eat preserves, and count the seven spoons twice a day. She would waste nothing, and work without complaint, and pray with more apparent feeling. Perhaps, if she washed her eyes each morning as Ruth's book commanded, she would be happier with what she saw. She would look at Max and be glad he was her husband.

It seemed a promising plan. To think of herself as an alternative, surrogate self, made up of other women, and of her house as a surrogate house, made of other women's houses—just thinking it made her feel less poisonous and clumsy. Her hands would be more gentle, her eyes more scrupulous, her appetite smaller. She'd learned as a girl how you could imitate someone's walk and know something of her arrogance, or shyness, or ugliness—now it was the same, but the effect stronger: she could become these women, possess their artistry, and eventually their satisfaction.

All this promise was enough to make Minna feel that it would be acceptable, once conditions were right, for her to keep, as her one decadence, the pleasure of Fritzi's books. Jacob would teach her the English alphabet, and how the letters went together, and at the end of the day, in the second room, when they thought she was asleep, she would read. And Samuel, if she asked nicely, Samuel, her other stepson, would build a set of drawers, one of which would be for Minna's underclothes—for she would have more, in this new life, than she could wear at one time—and hidden beneath these underclothes she would keep, one at a time, her books.

Which were only stories, in the end. And made-up stories, at that. Made-up stories she didn't even know how to read.

And so her only remaining vice would be hidden, and made up, and she would have to learn to enjoy it.

TWENTY-ONE

SUPPER was eaten, the pot clean, prayers finished. Max studied. Jacob shuffled a deck of cards he'd somehow acquired on their trip. Samuel sat with a pair of torn trousers across his knees, trying to thread a needle.

Since coming home, the boys didn't bother pretending to study with Max, but neither did they interrupt him, and so there was, each night, this time of waiting. Even the room seemed to wait—as though it sensed its counterpart, on the other side of the wall, half built. Minna was testing a broom she'd made that morning, determined as she was to have two brooms, as per the instructions in Ruth's book. She poked it into a corner and found that she'd cut the angle just right, then she aimed for a scattering of soil and was pleased with her choice of straw. Her floors were real now, wood, and the broom made a fine sound, *thrub-swish, thrub-swish*. She swept from the edges of the room inward, working around the men's feet, *swish*, knowing that she must be irritating someone, *thrub*, perhaps everyone, but not caring. They could say something, but they wouldn't, each for his own reason, and Minna liked how masterfully she knew these reasons now, and how comfortably she could ignore them. She liked how tall she felt, wielding the broom as the men sat. When all the waiting began to tire her, she asked, without stopping the broom, "What plans have we made for drawers?"

Max scratched his nose, but didn't look up from his book. Jacob stopped shuffling and smiled, as if anticipating some entertainment. Samuel squinted into the lamp, his thread trembling. "Drawers?" he repeated calmly. "For our plentiful belongings, you mean?"

He was trying to punish her, mock her. And his doggedness with the needle was starting to enrage her. His fingers were too large. He stuck out his whole tongue to wet the thread. He'd denied her early offer of help.

But she had to stay calm. Liesl and Ruth would stay calm. They would smile. They would not be spoiled. Minna smiled. "Yes," she said. "Drawers."

"A lovely aspiration," he said. "I'll be sure it raise it with the Baron at our next rendezvous."

"It's not such a luxury," she said, a bit less nicely.

"No." Samuel paused, eyes closed. He'd begun doing this, at the start of a conversation he didn't want to have, just resting there as if caught in the middle of a blink. He must have intended it as deflection, but the effect was the reverse. It caused you to observe the only strangeness in his face: the weight of his eyelids;

how many folds they contained. She stopped sweeping. She could hear the tearing of Max's beard in his teeth.

"It wouldn't be difficult. One set of drawers. A little order," she said. Then, certain that no one was listening to her, she suddenly lost Liesl and Ruth, and raised her voice so sharply it cracked: "A little dignity!"

Max looked up. His eyes were wet. He caressed his left forearm with his right hand. "You know," he said, and pointed at the trousers in Samuel's lap. "Minna could do this for you." He looked back down, turned a page, bit into his beard.

Minna caught Samuel's eye.

"I can manage," he said.

"Sender."

"I can do it."

"Son."

She waited for Samuel to falter. To throw the needle, or growl, or curse. She had the sudden idea—she liked this idea—that he feared her as much as she feared him. So that when he stood, boldly, forcing her to look up, she saw his boldness as a costume, put on, like his unruly hair and his tough walk. In his eyes she saw his knowledge of the outline of her body. When he set the needle and thread on the trousers and pushed them toward her, she was purposefully slow about putting the broom down, and slow about accepting the bundle.

"It will be my pleasure," she said. Which was, she remembered, a thing Ruth said to her once.

Samuel's face shifted; the skin around his eyes hardened; he leaned in so close she had to turn her cheek. He might have kissed her, she thought, in front of his father. But Max wasn't even watching them, and Samuel, out the corner of her eye, didn't look as if he wanted to kiss her. He looked angry enough to spit.

"Excuse me," Minna said quietly, with every intention of backing away. Her only dilemma—the only thing that stopped her—was the fact that he smelled so good to her. She nearly closed her eyes. Then she heard Jacob clear his throat. He was peering up at them, his expression one of worry, and wonder. Samuel must have noticed this, too—he leaned closer now, as if to berate Minna privately—then closer still, so that her ear filled with heat. He whispered: "I'll build you the drawers. Mother. In the meantime, why don't you keep your little book under your mattress?" Then he straightened to his full height, walked to the door, and yanked the string. A rigid stream of air. The door closed. Jacob shuffled his deck, Max turned a page, then came the hollow patter of urine hitting dirt.

A *cold snap*. Frost. The chickens stopped laying altogether. Minna had three dozen eggs packed in salt, a few more sitting in flour. One egg a day would last only forty days. Half an egg, eighty, but what was half an egg. And still the chickens ate and shat and made their chittering ruckus. She couldn't look at them without wanting to snap their necks. *Snap*, everything snapping, the air and her mind and her voice at Jacob when he snapped his fingers too loudly. Such a word, so many uses, all tending toward violence. Her challahs were flat and white and unglazed for lack of eggs, and she refused to throw a fistful into the fire, and Max asked, Why?, but she refused to placate or change her

mind and this was her first meager, awful victory. She began
rationing flour, too (Samuel said nothing, not even I told you so),
and then corn and potatoes and what vegetables they had left.
Why, Max asked, though of course he knew, though his question
was like a dog's yelp, habitual, easily stroked.

And why, he began asking, why was Minna still without child?
She had no answer.

One afternoon, he found her at the creek with the washing
and laid her down on the sand that had been the creek's shal-
lows before it became its dry banks. It was not particularly
uncomfortable—the sand was smooth, the gray walls gave privacy, Max kept her warm and was gentle with her, as always, always gentle in his insistence, his insistently gentle way—but the
cottonwoods rattled their leaves up above and Minna thought,
they were mine, and the water trickled past nearby and she
thought, it was mine. She thought of Samuel, looking down at
her. Then she thought of her mother, a terrible, shameful thought,
she thought of how many places her mother would have been laid
down. And maybe because it was not dark, or because she sensed
the beginning of a new descent, or because the bristling cottonwood demanded that she keep her eyes open, she could not
count away these thoughts of her mother, and by the time Max
breathed his finishing breath and slid off her, she half expected
him to button his trousers, pay her, and walk away. Instead he
brushed her hair back from her forehead and asked, "Is that
better? Here? Did you feel pleasure?" When she didn't answer,
he began his tickling again, in her hair. He'd never tickled her
after, only before, and Minna felt, despite herself, if not pleasure
exactly, a vague excitement. She was married, she reminded

herself, a married woman performing her duty. She might as well be Ruth, or Liesl, performing theirs. But Max was looking at her, the daylight mining his balding places, his lips too pink and full and the bottom one hanging, lazy and timid and greedy all at once. She closed her eyes and offered up a quiet moan, then a funny smile she'd never made before, a smile she hoped would convey both graciousness and finality.

Max said, "Do not worry. You mustn't think you are barren."

Minna nodded.

"It is better here. More—only us. You must relax. You must feel pleasure to bear a child."

The sky had been rough all day, clouds fuming up from the horizon yellow gray and spinning, but now they'd started to loosen and thin. A patch of clear, calm blue appeared, and Minna knew, if she wanted a child, that she would take this as a favorable sign. But she feared the child's dying. She feared its living and her leaving it. She pointed up at the blue sky and said, "It'll get cold now."

"Don't worry," Max said.

"I'm not worried."

"Good."

"But if the child, Motke—if it—shouldn't happen."

Neither looked at the other. Their embrace held—one of Max's arms digging under her neck, the other resting on her stomach. Minna thought of the ten-year rule. She'd thought it unfair, that a woman should be divorced just because she was barren, but now she wondered if the system provided an opening—if it gave you a way out without having to be a woman who left. You would be barren, but not bad. Or you would be bad, but helplessly so.

"You mustn't think it," said Max. "All will be well. You will pray more righteously."

Minna thought she'd been mouthing the words more convincingly. She thought Max didn't notice anyway.

"But if it shouldn't happen," she said again. For she knew suddenly that it would not—she knew with stunning certainty—no matter what she did, or how she prayed, no matter what she wanted, or came to want. She was defective, or else she was sinful. Which one had no bearing, she saw; Minna herself was of little consequence. Her throat filled with tears, then emptied. Up above, one of the boys shouted something and the other called back. Minna had the urge to tell Max how sometimes, standing in the yard, looking out across the plain, she would see, or think she saw, the shadows again. Thin switches of light, dim flickers through the grass. She would feel a queer longing; she had an idea of the Indians coming for her, like in Leo's story, and taking her back to their huts made of sticks and skin.

But Max was sitting up, and pulling Minna up beside him. "Shhhhhh," he hushed. "Don't think it." Then he brushed off her back, patting, like a friend.

TWENTY-TWO

No one saw the first snow begin. When had the sky gone white? Where had the wind picked up knives? The snow drove against the house in lines straight as trees. It stood toward the sky and slammed into the earth. For a time you could see the dark slash of the little barn's roof, then it was gone. They stood at the windows until the windows were white, then kept standing. Who knew how dark white could be? Minna lit the lamps and fed and fed the stove, ignoring, each time she knelt, Samuel's fists fisting tighter. Her house would be warm. She cut rags to fill the biggest gaps in the floorboards, then filled the kettle. Ruth and Liesl would have cocoa, she thought—they would make drinking chocolate, and knit. Why had Minna never learned to knit? She brewed coffee for the men, thought of milk to make it special, thought out loud: "We need a path to the cellar." The men looked stunned—they'd looked stunned since the windows went dark, like squirrels. Max nodded, but didn't move. Jacob said the shovels were in the barn. Samuel went to push the door open, but gained only a crack. Snow tumbled in like sand.

"It shouldn't hinge out," he said. "Why did we build it to hinge out?"

"Otto!" cried Max. "He knew this would happen."

Samuel kicked at the door. "*I* knew. I should have known."

"Get out of the way." Jacob held the iron poker like a pickax. "Out of the way," he said, prodding Samuel aside with the poker. He began slicing into the snow, wiggling the poker side to side, shoving the door with his shoulder. Soon the opening widened; snow blew freely into the house; Minna swatted it back with her new broom. Then Jacob managed to squeeze out and Samuel grabbed the old broom and followed him. Minna handed Max the ladle, pushed him after the boys, and shut the door.

For a long while, she heard nothing but wind. How long? She didn't know. If she had Max's pocket watch, she thought, she would keep track—if they weren't back by a certain time, she would go after them. Jacob had told her the stories: men getting lost on their way to a barn, freezing to death twenty feet from the breakfast table, eggs still steaming on a plate. In Beltsy, the trees had broken the snow, and there were other houses and the road to see your way by; here, Jacob said, people tied themselves to ropes so they could pull themselves home.

But Max's only rope was tied to the cow, and the cow was in the barn.

If Minna had the watch, it would insist that she wait the right way: tense over her lap, watching the minute hand creep, trembling as it reached the allotted time. But the watch was nowhere in the room. And Minna could not summon a suitable anxiety. Inside the spirals of the wind, the whistling and growling and purring and groaning, there was silence. Her father had taught her this, how if you listened, it was there, how the noise of the wind was not in fact wind but all the things that were not wind being touched by it, and saying WIND. During late-summer thunderstorms, when lightning swept off the steppes and took down trees and shook the house, he would rush into her room, mix air with his finger and say, *it's all right*, say, *think of the willows at the river, the house is like that, it needs to sway to stay standing, that's how it stays standing.* It was her father who was scared—she hadn't cried out—but she'd let him hold her and pretended to feel saved and this came as easily to her as the idea that the wind itself was silent. And now alone inside the dampening of snow, she heard the hole at the center of the wind and felt calm. There was coffee going cold and cracks in the floor still weeping cold and her sweater missing its top button, yet here she was standing calmly by the windows, one after another, each view the same, the world a dark, white, growling silence. Here she was moving through her thoughts as if the men had already vanished. There was a bin of coal. A sack of flour. Snow would make water. She would make do.

She was alone, and glad of it.

She was selfish. They'd always said so.

She listened for voices, heard nothing, waited for panic to properly grip her. She drank a tin of coffee, then another, until she felt a buzz at her nape, and was able, finally, to focus. On the windowsills, for instance. They were fine sills. Fine windows the men had chosen, and paid for, and put up. Three more, meant for the second room, stood against the outside wall. So much had been provided her, planned, promised. And there were dangers—yes—focus. She had to remember the dangers. The eggs, for instance—the eggs were in the cellar. And most of the canned goods, too, and more flour, and all the potatoes. So. So they had to make it to the cellar and back, and to the barn, too, and to the chickens. And she had to keep the doorway clear so that they could return, and so that when they returned they would see that she'd hoped they would. Quick. She took up her fine new broom and opened the door. New snow pushed her back. She pushed harder, until she had to squint against the snow, the lost silence, the deafening search of her ears.

Where were they?! She began to sweep.

WINTER, then. That early time was almost sweet. The snow would gain their shoulders, then the sky would break for a few days, the snow pour off the roof, there would be water to drink and wash with and the paths would stamp down almost to the ground. At midday they ate outside to feel the sun through their coats, ate with their eyes closed against the glare and got sleepy. Sometimes they napped then; even Samuel saw the limits of industry when the snow was high. Dark came early and a moon rose so close its bruises made shadows inside the house. The house felt like a house in those days, not just a room. The door string grew thick with the oil from their hands. Minna wove a small rug out of rags and laid it by the stove. She brought out her comb and a scrap of paper and hummed, through its teeth, a song she must once have been taught. Jacob instructed them in the intricacies of whist, and convinced Max to play, too, and Samuel offered up a square of felt and two dice. And because the way to the creek was never cleared, Max couldn't bother her there, and neither did he bother her in their bed. He thought she was pregnant, she realized—for the pleasures she'd pretended before the snow came, for the high mood she was in now. He wouldn't think to wonder if her mood might have something to do with his not touching her. She stopped anticipating his fingers, clenching for his approach. She forgot, almost, about Fritzi's book. Sometimes she felt during that time like the men were her brothers, all three, forsaken along with her, and she their good sister, good as a gentile Sister, her face simple as an egg. *Snow*, Jacob said, and Minna found herself nodding, as though she knew the word already. The more English she learned, the more she felt this way: the more her tongue seemed to guide the language rather than the other way around.

One day Otto and Liesl and Fritzi glided up on a sleigh, their eyes red with wind, bearing a tin of tea and the news out of Mitchell, and Minna felt proud opening her door to them. The stove was warm, but not extravagantly so. She made the tea hot but not too strong and laid the table with fresh milk. Everyone was polite. When Otto put his arm around Samuel's shoulders to give him more pointers about the house, Max didn't seem to notice that the gesture was that of a father toward a son, nor did he complain about the wrong-way door. He watched Liesl, who looked lovelier than ever and murmured admirations about the house. Minna watched Samuel. She could watch him frankly, and appear to be watching Otto. So she watched, and was happy for him, at how relaxed he looked with Otto's arm around his shoulders, and she was sad for him, too, for all the rest of the time, when he refused to let anyone relieve him of his vigilance. Otto said the snow would melt, there was always a melt around this time, and then he and Fritzi would be back to finish the house. And though Fritzi's eyes betrayed his contempt, nothing more passed between him and Max than the quick soldierly nod practiced by men who are not soldiers. The news was of weather and the recent declaration of statehood and a new dry-goods store opened by two sisters from Baltimore who'd never been west of the Potomac River and who carried, alongside their calicoes, bolts of silk from the Orient; and of an old squaw—this was what they called the Indian women—who'd heard a woman crying alone in a sod hut and delivered her baby. Everyone agreed that this was a strange but good thing, and that it might mean something, though they wouldn't presume to say what. So much politeness. Minna had made it impossible, she liked to think, for it to be any other way. Her well-swept floor. The biscuits she'd rolled as soon as they'd arrived. Even when they left, when the steam from their horses' nostrils was gone and the sleigh fell off the white horizon, she didn't feel the wretchedness she'd felt leaving their house, or (in the memories she'd revised to make them simpler, and more memorable) every other house.

TWENTY-THREE

DECEMBER 1, the kerosene turned to sludge. Minna kept the dates now, on a chart pinned to the wall, to track her use of eggs and keep a tally of their whist games. But December 1 they would have remembered anyway—it was a day people would talk about for years across America's vast middle when things were bad and they needed reminding how much worse they could be, or when things were good and they feared complacency. The day of ice. The day the air turned blue. The day your eyeballs froze. The day you had to cut the cow's tongue from its trough. Minna closed the flue, but the stove ate through more coal than it usually did in a week. She set the lamps to warm by the stove, but by midafternoon feet had crowded them out: the men, socks cracking, worked to bend their toes. She hung their boots up above. The air smelled of feet, the coffee tasted of feet. The boys wanted to bring the cow inside the house, but the path was too slick, she would break a leg. They cut into the ice, trying to gain purchase, but at dusk you could hear their axes still ringing. They gave up and came inside, joining Max and Minna at the table, which she'd drawn close to the stove, which she'd let run low to save coal through the night. They ate quickly, not speaking. Then they went to bed without undressing, short two blankets, one of which the boys had thrown over the horse, the other across the chicken coop. Minna layered both beds in every piece of clothing they had: shirts and underclothes and trousers and dresses, even her wedding dress she laid out, a lilac spirit pinned to the top. The men were already buried, burrowing. She wanted to lie down, too, but in her mind, she called up Liesl. What else would Liesl do? Minna heated bricks meant to lay the foundation for the second room in the stove, wrapped them in rags, and put them at the foot of both beds. Then she swept the room one more time, as if for extra luck. After that, her boots were the only sound. There was no wind that night. It was too cold for wind. Yet they must have slept, because in the morning on every pillow was a frozen pool of breath.

WHAT followed? It was hard to say, exactly, even if you were there. Even if you tracked the days and nights—at some point along the way, you lost track of your tracking. An easing of the cold would appear, the air suddenly soft, the windows weeping. But it didn't last long enough to melt the snow. Samuel tried to walk to Otto's for a ride to town on the sleigh, but a new snow pushed him back. They tried to plow their way out, but neither their animals nor their plow were built for snow and the horse's old tack was cracking and the mule sullenly bullied his way back to the barn. They kicked the mule, though they knew it wouldn't help, kicked it for having so many legs, and knees, and backs of knees, so many surfaces to kick, and because it would never show injury or heartbreak. Jacob kicked hollering, and Samuel grunting, and Minna kicked when she hoped no one saw. Only Max didn't kick the mule, Max with his faith, his inner minions, Max who appeared satisfied at last, now that they were truly cut off from the world. When he finished his prayers, he wore the flush of a rich man. Their food, he assured them, would see them through to the January thaw, just like last year. But last year was nothing like this, according to Jacob: the snow had never risen past their thighs; the kerosene hadn't frozen for more than a couple days in a row. He said this to Minna more than to Max, a son's appeal to one parent to set the other straight, that pitting and bribing Minna had only witnessed in other families. He wanted her to do something, but what could she do? In time, she would come to realize that he'd simply wanted her to say yes; to confirm—though she hadn't been there—that he was right. Yes, last year was nothing like this. Yes, son—as Lina might have said—you are not mistaken. But just then she was too busy being amazed, all over again, by the absurdity of their situation. What difference did it make what happened last year? You could spend a lifetime trying to call up the heights and colors and temperatures and tastes that pitched you into danger, but as far as she could tell, memory didn't save anyone. Last winter, this winter, next winter, the winter after that. Samuel offered no opinion on the matter. He'd grown sullen as the mule, obsessed with his own failures, so certain that he could have prevented their miscalculations—the poorly conceived door, the lack of a sleigh, the distance from house to cellar—that he could barely focus on anything else. He needed prompting when his turn came to milk. He threw his coat down on the stove and burned a hole in the sleeve. He forgot his gloves and came to supper with his fingertips black. Minna wished he would look at her, and find some comfort in her face. She wished he would stop punishing himself. It exposed him, finally, but in the most woeful way.

On the warmer days, you could hear the snow settling. The layers, rearranging themselves, creaked and sang and spread a vibration through the ground. Minna's muscles quivered as if anticipating a slide, a crash, a breaking open, none of which happened, for there was no steep place to slide from—yet the possibility gave her energy, an urge for order, industry. She drove nails into the men's boots for when the ice returned. She sched-uled English lessons with Jacob. She pulled the rags up from be-tween the floorboards, cleaned the house, then washed the rags and stuffed them back in. It was easy, in those milder periods, to cook and eat modestly, to feel the rationing as a form of loyalty. She kept them all on the delicate edge of hunger.

Then a snow would fall again, and the sky which had let down the snow would clear and freeze, and she would open the door and feel her eyelashes stand like the nails in the men's boots and all reason and frugality would depart. She would serve a whole jar of beans at one meal, use egg in her bread, slather the bread thick with preserves.

She understood, then, in a buried way, how Max could have chosen himself over the Torah. How, once you found yourself straying, it was easier to stay on course than to go back.

Then again, the air would warm; her sense would return.
This was the way of things, the back-and-forth, the backs always
feeling longer than the forths. Eventually, the paths cut through
snow taller than their heads. They went from the house to the
chickens to the barn to the privy hole to the cellar to the coal
bin to the house and that was all, just walls of snow and the dri-
est air you could imagine, so dry you might walk with a fistful
of snow in your mouth, breathing through your nose the ghost
scents of urine on hay and human waste in snow and coal smoke
frying the air. If you looked up, you could see the sky, often
whiter than the snow. The boys tried climbing each other's
shoulders onto the shelf above. Sometimes they made it to the
roof and dug the windows free; but the snow was fragile and
fickle and quickly collapsed, taking them with it. Minna had it in
her mind to weave a pair of snowshoes—she could see the line
in her mind on the map, a little arrow pointing toward Liesl's—
but Samuel wouldn't let her use the wood that was meant for the
second room, and she had no twine. She would have to wait for
Otto to come again. They were all waiting for that. Even Max,
who never admitted it—you could catch him searching the sky
sometimes, could tell from the way he bit his lip that he wasn't
looking for God, or even for the *shochet*, but for a German.

S OMETIMES Minna found herself thinking about the time when
the boys were gone. She thought of the candlelight and the
milk glue and the lost hours, the thumping of her heels through
the long afternoons as Max dug. She thought of it as an Era. There
was a heedlessness to those days, an almost charm, which she

may or may not have felt at the time, but which now she allowed herself to envy and miss. And because she did not berate herself for this allowance, because she didn't force herself to go back through, sifting and pinning, to determine the facts, she guessed that she must be growing older.

Two chickens died. This was after the eggs were gone and Minna had given up her tracking, after the time the boys guessed must be January, after the thaw did not come. For weeks they'd been eating flat bread for breakfast, potatoes and milk at noon, corn mush at night, so that every meal was the day before and the day after and further confused the passing of time. They only knew that it was one day and two chickens, discovered by Jacob. They heard him shout, then he came careening into the house gripping the birds by their legs. He gave a giant, lick-lipping grin before he stopped himself. Regret, recalculation: Max: he shouldn't have shouted, shouldn't have brought them in here, he should have stuffed them into the snow and come back for them at night. You could see Samuel thinking the same thing, slitting furious eyes at his brother. Minna stood over the stove, stirring cornmeal into water. She had been thinking, before Jacob burst in, whether to leave it as porridge, or if she should let it cool, slice it, fry it as cakes. Cakes would require butter, which they were running out of.

But that was the thing about the backs of the forths: on the days when the cold stood behind the door like the open bones of a jaw and her eyelashes stood like nails and she did not believe it would ever end, rationing was impossible: an act of optimism; on these worst days it seemed as frivolous as putting on jewelry, or brushing one's hair. So the butter would run out. So. So she'd use their precious milk to make more. She could smell her frugal ambitions fleeing, the other-women gone, her domestic artistry lapsing into greed. She could already taste the butter on the corn, the burned fatty crisp at the edges of the cakes. And carrots—they would eat carrots. She would open the last jar in the cellar.

And then Jacob was there, with the chickens, and she tasted leg, skin, breast. She didn't wait for Max to act or speak. She cut off the heads, hung the birds outside to bleed, packed a pot with snow and brought it to a boil, then dipped them until their feathers came loose. Liesl had lent her enough dishes so that they would have two full sets, and now Minna dusted off the *fleischig* plates. Max said nothing—not when she returned with the naked, gutted chickens, not as she made a show of cutting out the deepest, most treacherous, least kosher veins, not while she boiled them. She set his plate before him and watched his eyes take it in, his lips move through his prayers, his hand pick up his fork. The boys huddled over their food, wincing. She'd run the stove hot all afternoon, to cook the chicken, and soften Max; the room was bone-dry at the table, moist with breath up the walls.

Max began to eat his corn cakes. He finished one, started in on the other, finished that. He ate his carrots, slowly. Minna prepared to speak in defense of the chicken. Would God waste the animal's death? Would He prefer to see them suffer? And she'd bled it the best she could. There were exemptions—weren't there? For women and children, at least, there were exemptions. And for the hungry, too? That means you, she would say. Motke, God couldn't have meant for you to use your will in such a way.

Then Max finished the last of his carrots and stared at his plate and in his eyes was a look she'd known her whole life: a moroseness meant for her to see, a flagging that said, don't make me a vagrant in my own home, please, sit with me, stay. That face—she couldn't look at it anymore. She had nothing to say for herself. She began to eat. The boys ate. And when they finished, they ate what was left on Max's plate.

TWENTY-FOUR

THEY ate the second chicken quickly, unapologetically, offering none to Max. The flour was low. The last potatoes smelled of rot and snow; she cooked them, sliced thin and fried in chicken fat the way Galina had liked them, and though Max wouldn't eat these either, they were quickly gone. Minna rationed out of necessity now; she could see the bottoms of bags. She and the boys fought over who would milk the cow, with the understanding that the milker drank from the bucket before bringing it in. They fought over who had to feed the chickens. No one wanted to face the chickens: they felt guilty for having eaten them, and for wanting to eat more—and maybe, too, they each feared being the one to kill a third.

Just die, they thought—and yet they went on feeding them scraps they could not spare.

And for a time, too long a time, no more chickens died. They had enough coal to keep the house warm in the days and warmer than frozen through the nights, and yet they felt cold all the time, their stomachs barely lined with a watery paste of flour or corn-meal, or flour and cornmeal. There was always enough water to make it watery; water stood in your eyes, and fell again from the sky, deceptively light before it piled: when you drank, you could feel it slide through you: it found your emptiness, touched it everywhere, left it shivering.

They were rich only in dishes, which seemed to mock them now from their stacks.

Where was Otto? Max wanted to know. He was leaning against the east wall, head in his hands. He stood all day some-times, saying it made him warmer, then he wound up tilted and slouching like this, until he was as good as lying down. "What?" he asked. "Has the big German with his big ideas decided we aren't worth it after all?"

"Why should he help you?" Jacob asked.

"He left us. He built the door the wrong way."

"He built us a door."

"He did it on purpose."

"And what's to say it wasn't my fault?" interrupted Samuel. "Who's to say I don't know how to build a door?"

"He can't teach you everything," Max scowled. "He hasn't. He won't."

"If you wanted a benefactor," Samuel said, "you might have asked the Baron."

"O Barohhhn." Jacob clasped his knuckles beneath his chin, which was sharp now, undone of its child fat. "O Barohhhn de Vintovich, please, save us."

"He's saved others," said Samuel.

"You'd like to believe it," Jacob said.

"You might believe something."

"But I do."

"Oh?"

"I believe in Americaaaah!" Jacob laughed.

Samuel closed his eyes. "The Baron is a man, at least."

Max slapped a hand against the wall. "Enough," he said. "I'm not a fool."

WHEN the third chicken died, Jacob mmmed and ohhhed and belched. Samuel ate steadily, refusing to look at Max, who sat like a post before his plate of corn mush. Max closed his eyes and said his prayers, then he was reaching his fork for Jacob's plate, stabbing a leg, delivering it in a long, wavering arc onto his own. He cut. He brought the meat to his mouth. He chewed, not looking up, holding his fork, which trembled. He swallowed. He cut again. If he would only look up, Minna thought, for she was suddenly sorry. The boys stiffened; they must have felt it, too—Max had been their holdout, their representative in faith. For the first time since winter began, Minna thought of Moses, from the boat. She thought how disappointed he would be. She thought, though this was foolish, though it rendered the world back there as dreamlike as the world here had become, the towns merged, strangers wed, she thought that perhaps Moses and Max had known each other. They might have been friends—brothers. Moses would be so angry at Max for giving in. Now they were all four of them eating *treyf*. And it had been so easy. Beyond the walls, the snow gave off a long yelp, shrinking back slightly from the heat.

T HEY had wanted Max to eat the animal. Of course. They must have—it was only right: his eyes had gone dull like theirs; his skin was yellow. Still, his giving in was a disenchantment, the sort that occurs when you didn't know you were enchanted. It was a revelation, and over the next few days, it led to others. Jacob brought out a pistol, which he said Fritzi had loaned him for the winter, to warn off Indians. Samuel dug five bottles of vodka out of the snow, saying they might as well, he'd bought them stupidly, impulsively—*so stupid!*—he should have bought more food. Minna brought out Fritzi's book, and handed it to Jacob, who began to read.

The book was called *Old Man Jones; or, The Maiden Daughter and the Stranger*. It was a good story, the first time through. There was a wealthy ranch owner trying to save his bad son and marry off his good daughter, a poor-but-hardworking stranger who tried to help him do both, and a gang of cowboys who tried to stop him. There was town and there was country; there was a drunk and a shopkeeper and a schoolmarm and a maiden; there was drought and plague and violence and drowning and, of course, Indians. There were great adventures they were missing, apparently. Towns and countries far more story-worthy than the ones they knew. The only element missing from the book was a prairie fire, which they didn't notice until the second reading.

The third time through, they drank vodka to stay interested. Jacob performed voices for them, and sound effects. He pointed his gun at the ceiling when the characters pointed theirs. Max, in anticipation, would raise his hand and say, "Bang!" His sin with the chicken left him ashamed, but it was a broken shame that led to more. He ate more chicken, drank more vodka. Then he would pray, but silently, as far from the warmth of the stove as he could get, and Samuel would go stand next to him, and shut his eyes tight so that all the folds in his lids darkened into one, and sway. His swaying made him look pious, as his mother had meant him to be, but in fact it was simply the most visible aspect of his drunkenness. In general, the more Samuel drank, the more sober he appeared, the more troubled by his father's defections and Jacob's laughter and Minna's quiet, steady mode of filling her tin cup. She had not been drunk before. She pretended to pray, too, more earnestly than she'd pretended before, bowing her head, murmuring softly, copying as best she could, and in the simple, unthinking motions of her mouth she discovered a simple sort of comfort. Once or twice she caught Samuel staring at her with murderous disbelief, but before she could shake her vision clear, he'd walked off into a corner. Even his anger was comforting when Minna was drunk. She felt free, for a time, of want.

The corners were like other rooms some nights, set off by their distance from the lamp. They were drawn there, like cats seeking privacy. Then there were nights when the corners seemed made of solid matter, a darkness encroaching, pushing them toward the center, making them feel they might never get out. This was false—you could pull the string and the door would open, you could brace your skin against fresh air, savor the moments before the cold began to burn. Yet somehow you didn't. You sat at the table, the bones in your legs taking on the shape of the bench, and finished your share of the drink. Jacob might read again, or not. They might argue. Argument was its own intoxication; argument saved the vodka. Why do you keep that rock? Samuel might say, pointing at Jacob's iridescent crescent, which sat, curled into itself, in the center of the table. And Jacob might answer, It's from the ocean. And Samuel, Don't make things up. And Jacob, I'm not making it up. This whole country, all the grass, we're at the bottom of an old ocean. And Minna, Really? And Samuel, Don't believe his tales. Or another night, Samuel would begin, So you've got a gun. And you've got arrowheads. So whose side are you on. And Jacob would say, Both. And Samuel, That's impossible. And Jacob, Whatever you say. Samuel, You have to choose. Jacob, Why do you care so much? Samuel, Why don't you care more? And Max, head in his hands, We're not on anyone's side. Laughter from Jacob. But our own, is that right? Isn't that what you were going to say next? And Samuel, Let him be. And Jacob, Sorry. Of course. You're so good at just letting him be.

Then it would be the end of the night: and then again: so many times, they went through this end, when the beds seemed too far to reach. They'd stopped undressing weeks ago. The stove hissed, the last embers fell to ash. Then at last they found themselves under blankets, the day's fire or the gun's glint or the white snow flashing behind their eyelids. Max held Minna tenderly then, his hands cradling her belly, his toes in their thicker socks kneading the soles of her thinner stockings, working to warm her.

M INNA had thought she'd known hunger. She thought she knew it in Odessa, and on the boat, and even here, not so long ago, when the potatoes ran out. But she understood now that those hungers had been an idea—like her child idea of the forest when the town was just behind the house, or her city idea of loneliness when there were people everywhere. Real hunger required denial, a trick—you could not believe in it or it would flood you. She tried concentrating on her bones. She counted her fingers and toes. She focused on the warmth between her legs. But all this vigilance delivered her nowhere, it only led to other parts of the body, the throbbing at the back of her skull, the swelling of her tongue in her mouth. She learned to concentrate on not concentrating, to let her mind spread out, puddle-like, far enough from the body that the body was forgotten. Or at least silenced. A calm fell over her limbs. She wondered if this was prayer. If prayer was nothing more than a giving in, like sickness—if you weren't required to believe, only to stop struggling. The exercise grew familiar. The boys grew hair on their faces. And though Samuel's was a full black beard, and Jacob's a layer of fuzz like a playactor might draw on, the hair made them look alike, and like Max, and Minna gave in to their merging, their repetition, as she gave in to the repetition of hunger. She knew that she loved them, the beards, the bodies, the men themselves. She saw them out the corners of her eyes, she brushed

them as she passed. They were her furniture. You could love anyone, she thought, if you needed to. And in a curious way, not in
spite of her need but because of it, because she was hungry and
trapped, she felt safe.

ONE night she was peeing. She was listening to the snow
melt under her and smelling how her pee smelled of nothing and feeling, in her squat, the bones in her upper legs press
against the bones in her lower legs. She might not have looked
up at all. But she did, and to the north, above the wall of snow,
she saw lights filling the sky. Her first thought was lanterns—
Otto—he'd come at last. But she heard nothing. The lights grew
no closer. They shot toward the ceiling of the sky, white and pink
and almost red in places. She was hallucinating. She had to be.
That or God had come for them. He'd warmed the earth everywhere but here, and now remembered them.

She had to be hallucinating. She didn't even need vodka anymore. She went in and said, "There's a forest of light outside,"
and no one even went to see.

ANOTHER night, Minna saw Liesl's map in her mind. She saw
the mountains, the river, the squares within squares—she
saw, within the smallest within, their snow tunnels, intricate and
deep and narrow, like a new set of roads, a separate country.

The bottom of an ocean, Jacob had said, and Minna could
believe it.

SHE thought of Liesl and Ruth. The sharp runners on their sleighs. The abundance in their cellars. Then she thought: What if the snow was gone at their houses? What if the runners were put to rest, the earth thawed, the kitchen gardens planted, pole beans and peas and radishes starting to root? She could see a froth of carrot greens. She could smell the wet dirt that collects in lettuces. It seemed possible, somehow, that this, theirs, was the only forgotten place: one hundred sixty acres of snow in the middle of spring. People would gawk, then go back to their planting.

THE last chicken that would die that winter died. They ate without fanfare, their stomachs cramping. Afterward, you could smell the meat emptied out into the snow. Their revelations were commonplace now. They hated the chickens for tempting Max into sin, which seemed to have led them here: too tired to read or play cards or even to argue, the vodka bottles empty and singing out on the snow shelf. This was wrong, she knew, but it was impossible not to think that Max's weakness had led them to be forgotten. In bed one night she asked him: "Why did you eat the chicken?"

He didn't answer right away. His hands did not quite touch her stomach but hovered slightly, cupping a mound of air, waiting for the baby to fill it. She thought of her father's waiting, the shawls just so over the bedposts. She saw his bed, and then a woman beside it, the Christian woman whose face she could never see clearly, the one who'd thrown Minna's stones back in the river. The woman stood by her father's bed, spreading her arms wide to fold a sheet, and Minna wondered: What if the woman had come more frequently than Minna knew, and Minna's father had not been alone in the way she remembered him to be? What if all her loyalty was based on a misunderstanding?

"Why did you?" Max whispered back.

"What?"

"Eat the chicken."

She considered. She was wide-awake now, her empty stomach drumming beneath the dome of Max's hands. His breath was sour and hot on her ear. If you knew what I've eaten, she thought. She said, "I never promised anything."

"What do you mean?"

"I never promised."

"You must have. They said."

"I told a lie."

She could feel, at the foot of the bed, the other bed. The other eyes trained on the dark. She felt an urge to speak Samuel's name, and ask him to forgive her. She knew this was backward, knew it was Max she should apologize to, but she couldn't help herself. From the time she'd met him, Samuel had made her want to explain herself. He'd seemed to want to know her, whereas all the other men only wanted her to know them. Yet what would she ask him to forgive her for? For lying to his father, or for marrying him? For being a girl in his house? Or for her fear of spring, in the deepest, most senseless caverns of her body she pretended against yet here it was: fear of warmth, thaw, the peeling off of layers. She could not begin again the same way.

Behind her, Max said, "I don't know what to say."

Minna started to cry. She was so hungry, and it was such a peculiar, lovely thing for him to say. It was as if he'd said, do what you want. She waited for his hands to leave the place around her belly, for him to roll away. But Max didn't move.

"So why did *you* eat it?" she asked.

"I was hungry," he said.

TWENTY-FIVE

THE melt was sudden. A current of warmth came up off the horizon one morning and the snow walls started to sink and flow into the paths; by noon the slush was up to their shins. The snow was too much to go gently. If you stood still you could hear it crackle; if you stood long enough you could hear a hiss beneath the crackle. The hiss lasted for days as the snow shrank. Water poured off the roof and seeped through the windows. They dug channels around the house to keep it from flooding, then around the chicken coop, but they were weak and couldn't dig fast enough and had to bring the remaining chickens inside the house. Empty sacks floated in the cellar. The cow and horse and mule stood in water, coats dull as clay, watching the people run back and forth along their paths, which one day showed a patch of matted grass. The snow was down to their waists. They could see the unfinished frame of the second room, the new windows leaning against it, fine and swollen. They could see the cotton-woods, and snow. The snow shone like an earthly sun; they had to cover their eyes. They didn't see the sleigh until they heard runners cutting through the slush.

It was Fritzi who pulled the horses to a stop, and nodded. He looked as though he expected them to be standing there, expecting him. But of course they hadn't. Not Fritzi. His eyes were streaked with rage. Minna felt her toes, in her wet boots. She thought, Otto's dead.

Fritzi held out a sack for Samuel to take, then another. "I've brought food," he said. It was clear from the hardness in his posture that he didn't intend to climb down. Only Max didn't seem to comprehend the situation. He said, "So the man dares to come now, and sends *you* instead? He won't even show himself?"

Fritzi narrowed his eyes. You could see him trying to quiet himself, his free hand caressing his reins, his lips pressed together. You could feel his mother shushing in his ear. He said, "He was coming here. To bring you food."

Max's mouth was open. He closed it. Minna hadn't noticed how much of his beard had fallen out, or how the top of his chin was red with teeth marks. Samuel and Jacob stood silently, boys again, heads bowed.

"Where's your mother?" she asked Fritzi.

"At home."

For an instant Minna had thought Liesl dead, too. But she had only chosen not to come. She didn't want to see Minna now, or perhaps ever again.

"Please tell her we are so sorry," she said.

Fritzi smiled in a hateful way.

"Please thank her for the food."

The smile held. Fritzi seemed to wait just so he could watch them resist themselves—they would pounce on the bags, you could feel it, the moment he left. Then he left.

A WEEK later, when the road was clear enough for the boys to get to town, the stores were empty of food. They returned with a hand sack of flour a man had given them, and new tack for the horse, which the sisters from Baltimore had sold them, on credit and at a discount.

"You looked so desperate?" Max asked angrily. For a second, Minna thought he might turn the sack upside down. "They thought you were looking for charity?"

Neither of the boys answered right away. They appraised their father as if he were a foreigner, or as if to remind him that in fact he was. They'd spoken little of Otto—his death saddened them more than their father could bear—but his loss was everywhere. Samuel had shaved his beard and looked clean, and impatient. Jacob had kept his boy-fur but his thinness was not good for him; his flesh had hidden his likeness to Max, his sunken eyes and nervous mouth. His mockery held no playfulness now. He said, "We were."

Leo and Ruth, they said, had nothing to spare. They'd gone there on their way home, thinking to promise more work in exchange for food, but the children looked like little grown-ups and Ruth did not welcome them. She was upstairs sleeping, Leo said. The baby had been born dead. Leo said not to tell anyone, especially not Minna. Ruth would be so ashamed. He shouldn't have told them either, he said. But so he had.

"Poor Ruth," Minna said. And she felt this. She was sorry for Ruth, and sorry for Leo, who'd betrayed his wife's secret. Minna had misjudged him, perhaps. She'd thought him haughty, especially around Max, but now she could see that he was afraid. He was afraid of Max, just as she'd been afraid of Rebeka. Weak people made you see yourself in them.

But Max and the boys didn't seem to hear her. Or they'd stopped trusting what she said.

"We'll go to the colony," Samuel said. "They'll help us."

"What about Cincinnati?" asked Jacob. "They helped us."

"I won't go anywhere," said Max.

"You'll die," Jacob said.

"Shut it," said Samuel, and turned to Max. "You don't have to come. We'll go, then come back."

"Are you crazy?" Jacob raised his arms. "I'm not coming back here. I won't stay another week. We'll all die."

"It's spring," said Samuel.

"Yes. And then winter again. Have you noticed the way of things?"

"We'll be prepared by then."

"That's what you said last year."

"We are staying," said Max. "If we leave, Fritzi won't waste a second claiming this land."

"Let him have it."

"We are free here."

"Is that what this is?" Jacob laughed, a great hiccup.

"We have rights to this land."

"Rights to rocks, you mean? These plentiful rocks? Should we thank God for giving us so many rocks?"

"I thought you didn't believe in God."

"I was putting it in terms you'd understand."

Max stared, his eyes small. Samuel set a hand on his shoulder but Max snarled and threw him off, startling them all.

"Leave me," he said, to no one in particular.

"You'll die," Jacob said.

"Then I'll die."

H E'D gone feverish, they realized. He shook the bed with his shivering that night and would not let Minna near him. The child, he cried, don't hurt the child. When she did not correct him, his sons looked at her; then they brought their father rags she'd cooled in the creek, which ran fast now, higher and wider than its banks. Jacob sat next to him guiltily, playing spoons, but Max would not be distracted. He kept pointing at Minna and telling her to leave. She protested, but he hit her hands away. The house smelled of fever and feet and chicken shit. She left. She stood outside in the dark and breathed in the cooling of the day, the slush and mud, stars and moon, a few clouds. She had the garbled pent-up energy of the newly unhungry. She could walk to the creek. She could walk beyond it. But it was dark, and the ground was slush or mud or new streams. The barn was wet. There was nowhere to sleep, and nowhere to walk to.

Somewhere not too far from here Otto had been dug out of the snow. From the vodka bottles came the drowsy buzz of the first flies. She thought of Ruth.

She waited for the house to quiet, then entered softly, but Max woke at her weight and pushed her out of the bed. Sleep with your sons, he said. And Minna felt the fever then, or she called it fever, though she had so rarely been sick, she named the heat through her limbs *fever. Kadokhes. Goryachka.* She thought it all the ways she knew to think it, until she almost believed it, then she took a blanket Max had thrown off and lay on the floor next to the stove, waiting for her chest to stop pounding.

TWENTY-SIX

ON the second day of Max's sickness, two wagons appeared across the prairie, and behind them, a thing so unrecognizable they might all have been struck by fever. As it came closer, they saw that it was an exceedingly tall penny-farthing, with a man riding on top, and that the wagons were papered with brightly colored posters—so much color, suddenly, that the ground seemed to tremble. Jacob ran to greet the front wagon and a man hopped down. By the time they reached the house, they were talking like old friends.

"Wild Whippersnapper Willy," said the man, doffing his hat with a great bow—"Howdeedoo"—and Jacob fell into such a huge, hysterical laughter that Minna and Samuel found themselves laughing, too. Willy laughed back at them, and though his was the kind of laugh that didn't involve the eyes, it was professional and long-lasting and it satisfied. He wore trousers that ballooned at his knees and cinched tight at his ankles, and a black satin vest, and a white scarf, and the sad effort around his eyes, along with the vest, reminded Minna of the magician. With him were other performers: one very fat man, one dressed as a cowboy, two dressed as Indians, and one with three eyes. This man was impossible not to look at, for he stood no more than twenty feet away, doing nothing but being himself and looking back at them. He seemed unbothered, almost happy, as if nothing in fact was wrong with him, which struck Minna as wrong in itself until she realized that the longer you looked on him, the more normal he started to appear: the longer you stared, his three eyes were not what struck you as odd, but the fact that he only had one mouth, and two feet.

Willy clapped, to get their attention. "Stragglers of the Whippersnapper Circus at your service," he said. "Not Barnum, I'll admit, but you don't look particularly famous yourselves!" They were bound for Mitchell, he said, where they'd meet the rest of the band. They needed a place to rest the night, and Jacob had told them yes, of course, stay here!

"We've little food," Samuel said, and Willy said they carried their own. If they could only wash in the creek, they would be grateful.

"Yes!" Jacob cried. "Yes! And perhaps we'll come see the circus! Perhaps you'll admit us free of charge! Where are you headed after Mitchell?"

"As far as the roads will take us, I suppose!"

Jacob pulled spoons out of his pocket and began to play. Willy whistled along. So much noise so suddenly, Minna's ears began to hurt. Max stumbled out in his nightshirt. He looked at the scene with disbelief, then anger. "I'm not crazy," he said to Willy, as if he knew him as someone else, and could see through his disguise.

"Come back to bed," Minna said, taking Max's arm. "You're shivering."

She tugged him gently, but Max had spotted the three-eyed man. He slapped Minna's hand away, then pulled her to him, grabbing her hair in one hand and covering her eyes with the other, so that her head was squeezed between his sweating palms. "Don't look!" he cried. "The child!" And Minna, unable to see and smelling fever on Max's skin, remembered not only the village dwarf, with the egg in his neck, but his mother, an average woman who was blamed for the dwarf's being a dwarf because she'd looked on another dwarf as she carried him. Minna remembered her confusion, as a child. The woman was old by then, and people ignored her, and patted her poor son on the head, and went to *shul*. It was as bewildering as the circus posters, the penny-farthing, the entire spectacle behind Max's hands. She wrestled free of him—not gently—not trying to seem weaker than she was—until they stood facing each other, their breath coming fast, and Minna said, "I'm not with child," loudly enough so that even the freak would hear.

CLOSE to dawn, she woke to gunshots. One. Two. She ran outside, but there was only a poster on the ground, and in the distance, the uppermost reaches of the penny-farthing rolling away. A third shot rang out.

"Cowards." Samuel stood in the doorway behind her, hastily

buttoning his trousers beneath his night shirt. You could hear the excitement in his breath, his desire to fight somebody, his disappointment at finding only Minna there.

"What do you mean cowards?" she asked.

Samuel shrugged. He'd woken from some dream, she guessed, where he was a hero.

"They were only getting an early start," she said.

"But why the shots?"

"To say good-bye."

"Or they stole something."

"Don't be like your father. There's nothing to steal."

Samuel said nothing. In the gray, blooming light, his bare feet glowed. The ground was cold. She was alert. She wondered, if she kissed him, what would happen. She wished she had a blanket to cover her shoulders, to calm her. She should go inside. But the gunshots were in her stomach still, beating like warm wings.

"They were amateurs anyway," said Samuel.

"I don't know."

"They were."

"Fine."

"You just don't remember the real world."

Minna looked at his face. It was blue-shadowed, almost soft. In Minna's life, she'd rarely talked just to talk, the way she and Samuel seemed to be doing now, without any clear purpose other than to make words out loud and see how they landed. It was pleasant, and silly, and also very serious, for you could not admit that anything you said might in fact mean something.

"What if this is real?" she asked.

Samuel crossed his arms, and looked back at the house. She

guessed that he was thinking of Max, alone in bed, out of his mind. She guessed she should be thinking of Max, too. When Max came back from his fever, she decided, she would stop letting herself think these thoughts, like how Samuel was tall but she could find a way around his shoulders, or how, if he turned back right now and took her hand and kissed her, then it wouldn't be her fault.

He half turned, and took her hand. His had been in his armpit, and was warm. Minna felt a sudden panic. Of course it would be her fault. Whatever happened would be her fault. In Beltsy there had been a girl named Libi, who had breasts like a grown woman, which made the boys silent and the girls mean, until one day she cornered the rabbi's son behind the *shul* and made him touch them. After that the girls were still mean, but the boys followed her and Libi was called a *nafke*. Then the Russians came, and took Libi's brothers away, and that was blamed on Libi, too.

Samuel drew her to him. He wrapped his arms around her. She could hear his blood, in his chest. She leaned into him. But what if Max should wake and call for her, and run outside?

"Samuel," she whispered.

He rested his head on hers. His arms were warm, and heavy. The sum weight of his embrace surprised her; it seemed to demand that she hold him back. She did. She waited. When Samuel finally spoke, it was into her hair.

"Jacob," he said. "They took Jacob."

"No."

"Yes."

She pulled away—embarrassed, disbelieving. Cool air crept into the space between them. They stood, watching the imprint

of the wagon in their minds, until the instant the first birds called
out of the near grass and the pink sun rimmed up above the far
grass, which was the same instant, as if the birds and the sun
knew how to be together far more easily than any people. And
when it was light, they went inside, and saw that it was true.

MAX wept until his fever broke, then he wept again, with
understanding. It was terrifying to see a man sob in such
a way, on his knees beating the floor, on his back hugging his
knees. There was an ecstasy, almost, to his weeping. His beard
ran over with saliva and tears. Minna stared. She couldn't help
it. She wondered if he'd cried like this when Lina left. And if
Minna left, would he do the same? How could you leave a man
knowing it would make him do this? But how could you stay
having seen it? She watched until he gave in to a quieter moaning, then she drew him a tin of water and knelt at his side.

"Please. Motke."

Max drank, wiped his nose with his sleeve, looked up, and
started to cry again. He wasn't looking at Minna, but behind her,
where Samuel stood with folded arms.

"He'll be back," Samuel said nonchalantly. "He doesn't know
what he wants. He doesn't know anything about anything." You
could hear that Samuel wanted to believe this, from the lazy way
he dropped the words. But when he began to pace, his outrage
was visible. "Those people won't even want him. They'll drag
him along for a while, make him carry props, toss him off."

Max shook his head. "You wish you'd gone."

Samuel guffawed. "And be a circus act?"

"You're covetous."

"Don't be ridiculous." But he'd stopped pacing. "Don't say stupid things."

"If I were Otto, he wouldn't have left me."

"Perhaps." Samuel looked away. In his face was a sudden satisfaction. "But then you'd be dead."

"I don't understand," Max cried. "Was he so miserable?"

Neither Samuel nor Minna answered. Yes, she supposed, Jacob was so miserable. Now that he'd left, you could tell. He'd belonged here less than any of them, perhaps. He'd wanted to be happy.

Max said to Samuel, "You'll go away now, too."

"Yes. But only to the colony."

"You'll leave me."

Samuel squinted. "Yes." He spoke with the measured slowness of one beginning a long calculation. "But then I'll return."

"If you had other plans, you wouldn't tell me."

"I'll return." Samuel's voice was quiet, almost intimate, but he didn't lower himself down next to Max. He shoved his hands into his pockets, and composed his face into its blankest, hardest, most handsome expression. "I'm your son," he said.

"How do I know?"

The question hung, unfurling itself.

"I'll go with him," Minna said. "I'll see that he returns."

Max looked at her. His eyes were bright from crying, his mouth open and soft. She wondered if he could see the heat bloom up her neck.

"You won't go anywhere," he said. He took her hand. "The child."

"I told you," Minna said, recognizing as she said it that in his fever he must have confused her confession with the circus, or the circus with her confession, that she could choose, again, to keep it from him. But she was exhausted, suddenly, by making him a fool. "There is no child," she said.

Max stared, his eyes so wide she could see veins in the corners. He swallowed, hard, and threw her hand into her lap.

"I never said there was," she said.

"You never said there wasn't." His eyes filled again with tears. Minna looked away. Would it have been so bad, she thought, to endure him? Then he said, to the side of her head, "You pretended to pray. You pretended to respect me. You're a liar," and his naming turned her shame to courage. She felt Samuel, watching her. Yes, it would have been so bad. No, she did not want Max. She'd never been able to want, or think, or believe what she was meant to. Why had she imagined it could be another way?

"If you want the truth," she said, "in Odessa, they inspected me like a horse."

"Minna."

"Everywhere. They went everywhere."

"This is not necessary."

"You paid them, yes?"

Silence.

"And what money did you use? What food could you have bought instead? If you could do it again, would you choose the food, or the barren wife?"

"Minna . . ."

"They froze my fingertips."

"This is enough."

"I forgive them. I forgive you. You're only people, doing what you must. It's the most common thing to do."

"But—"

"They wanted to know if I was brave, and if I could stand the cold. They tested my patience and my obedience and everything else you must have wanted."

"Minna."

"But see, Motke." Minna turned her palms up. She stretched her fingers into a gesture of supplication, but they were pale, and looked naked. They were naked, she supposed. She folded them. "They never asked if I was honest."

Spring

TWENTY-SEVEN

NEAR the Missoury, the land changed. The ground rose into small hills and fell into steep valleys, and because the grass was shorter, and much of it still brown, the rippling slopes taken together looked like the hide of a great animal. The road followed the valleys for a time, where it was shaded and cold, then mounted hills for a view. But the river wasn't visible until they were upon it, the pitching bluffs suddenly giving way to the wide flat of the water, which was brown with its spring running. They saw the railroad, ending like a broken stick. The town was Chamberlain, the street oddly quiet. It was Sunday, they realized.

A steamboat driver said he had nothing better to do and carried them across for a penny, talking about the railroad problem and the dividing-the-territory problem and the government problem, all the problems facing a steamboat man such as himself, and all the while he talked he asked nothing of Samuel or Minna, not where they were from or where they were going, so they were silent, and in the silence Minna felt a shift, a complicity, for they could have interrupted him, and announced themselves as themselves; they could have insisted that he hear their names, witness their titles, deliver them bound on the west docks as they'd been on the east. But neither of them did. Minna looked to Samuel but he stayed intent on the steamboat man, nodding as if he were a student of steamboats. On either side of his mouth, though, in the grooves there, which had grown deeper through the winter but no less impressive in their symmetry, no less something a man would choose to have if given the choice, here she saw, she was almost certain, the twitches of a smile. She leaned out over the gunwale and looked down at the water, which gurgled and spat as if at a low simmer, and she imagined the snow and rocks and sticks and parts of houses and animals and people and everything else the melt had sloughed off the land. The sun was on the back of her neck and she felt a kind of glory then, a gratitude, in being there on a vessel so outsized for their small purpose, in the press of her ribs against the gunwale and the thrum of the engine down her legs, in the frothed wake the boat sent as they left behind the town and the people in their churches who would know nothing of this crossing.

THE grass was shorter on the other side and the hills taller, and for a while they felt no sun and Minna was cold and chastened. She thought of her mother, that last morning, for it had been morning, just before sunrise, Minna's aunts had made a point of telling Minna this, again and again, as if to warn her even of beginnings. The sky must have been the color of ink, Minna's mother wearing only her dress, carrying nothing. Had she stopped, on the Out Bridge? Minna had kept herself from her mother's leaving; she'd left it unquarried, an accident. But had she used the back door with the whining hinge, or the front door that scraped the porch? It was spring. What had her heart sounded like when her feet started walking? Did she think of herself as a woman leaving a husband, or as a mother leaving children, or as a wife leaving a house? Did she run at any point? And on the Out Bridge, had she stopped, in her dress, carrying nothing, the moon still waiting for the sun? Did she imagine turning back, slipping through the window again, closing it against the dew? She might be in the bed when the man woke and the infant started its howling again and the girl—Minna—what did the girl demand of her?

Or maybe the woman only stopped on the Out Bridge because she was cold and regretted not taking a shawl. And why hadn't she? Had her heart been so loud she'd forgotten? Did she think herself bound for a place where all would be provided her? Or did she want, at least a little bit, to suffer?

Then it was warm again. The hills spread out wide, like fat, soft fists punching the skin of the earth; the road took a straighter course up and down the broad summits. There were flowers, blue and orange and purple and white, on tall stems that reminded Minna of straw, and lack of rain, and made her think of the dampness in the woods behind her father's house, the snow-drops and fiddleheads deep in the undergrowth. You had to kneel to smell their thick, sweet scent. You would be wet all over. The tall, dry flowers here looked scentless, but they were beautiful, too. Minna could feel Liesl's map laid out beneath them: the end of the grid, the opening out, the lack of claims. "This is Indian country," Samuel said, as one might say, without thought, *that is grass*, or *those are clouds*. But they saw no Indians. If they existed, Minna thought, if they were out there beyond and beneath her line of sight, then perhaps they were far more civilized than anyone suspected. If civility was Jews shaving beards and women smiling and children wearing shoes, if it was the ability to disguise oneself, what greater civility could there be than not to appear at all?

Late in the day, Samuel stopped the wagon at the top of a hill. Down below were the colony's sod roofs, and fields. In a large fenced pasture, animals passed each other, too distant to make out sheep from goats.

"That's it?" Minna asked.

"That's it," Samuel said.

They looked.

"Maybe we should wait until morning," he said. And when Minna said nothing, he turned the horse and mule around, drove them back a quarter mile or so, and tied up in the shelter of a small butte.

Samuel broke the last of their bread and passed Minna half. They'd spoken little the whole trip, not when they stopped seeing circus posters in the road, nor during the long days as they drove; not through the two nights they'd already spent in the back of the wagon, still as logs, a full body space between them.

They ate, watching the sun dip below the horizon, then the after-colors—red, orange, green—as they spread through the sky. Minna thought of the circus; of Jacob; she thought she had been too quick, when she first arrived, to detest the Sodokota sun. It was extraordinary, really, once it had disappeared.

The colors faded. Minna laid out the folded blankets in the back—his, then hers—their openings facing away. They drank water; they lay down. The sky was still light. The hawk was still circling. One star appeared, then another.

"I won't abandon him," Samuel said suddenly. "I'll go back."

Minna rolled her head slightly, to examine his profile. It was the same as always: straight brow, straight nose, strong chin—tinted blue, in the darkness. The charge in his voice caught her off guard; she was unsure if he was defending himself, or accusing her. He had no right to accuse her of what she hadn't yet decided herself. Would she return to Max? The question was like a face she couldn't bring herself to look at. What did she intend, this girl lying so straight next to her stepson that she must look, to the hawk, like a young, blameless, fallen tree? The bread had been stale. Her teeth ached. She had a choice. Which Minna used to think was the same as freedom: given choice, you were free to choose, and then you made—you knew how to make—the right choice. But she was coming to think that there were certain things you could only do if you did not quite know that you were doing them, choices you could make only by pretending you didn't comprehend them. Her mother, for instance, on the Out Bridge, starting to walk again: her mother must have told herself, *I'm only going for a walk.*

"You don't believe me," Samuel said. "I won't leave him."

"Of course you won't," Minna said. "How could you?" Though in her mind, she thought, *How could you not?* "You're his favorite."

"No. Jacob is his favorite. I'm the one he needs."

"Is there a difference?"

"You know there is." Samuel turned to face her. "If you knew I wouldn't leave, why come along as my warden?"

Minna was silent. Samuel's eyes glinted, but she couldn't be sure she was looking at their center. Why come? What did he want her to say? Wasn't he supposed to know better than she knew herself?

"You should have stayed with him," he said.

"He didn't want me."

"That's not true."

"He didn't." Minna had told herself this so many times now, she almost believed it. They had both watched Max not wave as they drove off. They had watched him stand with his feet pointing north and west, his shoulders slumped, not moving, then they'd watched him turn his back and walk into the house. He was fasting, because they'd missed the Passover; he would fast until they returned.

"You wouldn't have to do much," Samuel pressed. "He would forgive you."

"Is that what you want?" she asked.

"Say you're sorry. Pray more."

"Pray at all. I'm not what he sent for."

A new star pierced the sky above them.

"You might be surprised," he said.

"What is that supposed to mean?"

Samuel shrugged. She felt and heard it—a shift in the blankets, a rasp against the floor. Even lying down, she thought, he shrugs. And in his shrug was everything she loathed, and desired, his fineness, his control, his beauty, his disregard. She rolled to face him. The blanket caught her. She felt his arm through the blankets, against her stomach.

"As in I *am* what he sent for? Or I might like praying after all? As in you think I've never tried? You think it would be good for my soul?"

"As in you want too much to be someone other than yourself," he said.

Minna watched him. Her eyes had adjusted; she saw him more clearly than if in daylight, for the attention the dark required. He'd trimmed his sideburns again. His curls were short and neat, his cheekbones sharp.

"And you want to be no one," she said.

Samuel smiled. "Well that makes sense," he said, coolly.

"Half the time you talk, you make no sense!" Minna spat. "You might as well be talking to yourself!"

"That's all anyone does. Haven't you noticed?"

Minna thought she might punch him. Then he'd rolled toward her, grabbed her by the shoulders, pressed himself against her. Between them, the blankets bunched—Samuel pulled hers off. He pushed her onto her back, let his weight down onto her, bit her ear. Minna gasped. He lifted himself up again, and bit through her dress, first her collarbone, then her breast, hard enough she cried out. She felt his hand between her legs, the dampness there, felt herself urging her dress up her legs, one foot dragging it up the other calf. Even by herself, in privacy, she'd never felt so close to losing control. She seized him— stopped him—by the hair.

"You're right," she said. "I should have stayed."

"Yes." Samuel shook off her hand. "He barely knows how to cook."

"He's fasting anyway."

Samuel propped himself over her, on hands and knees, his face so close to hers she couldn't see it. He reached behind her neck, undid a button, broke two more, then pulled her dress off by the wrists.

"He'll manage," she said.

"Yes." He bit her neck. "Or he'll go mad."

Minna laughed. She was thinking of a woman's madness, of Galina and Ruth and of the women outside the asylum in their clean white gowns, their fingers painstakingly drawing Odessa's air; and of herself, now, the laughing Minna and the Minna that wanted to cry and the one that hated Samuel and the one that wanted him; and of whether, and how, a man went mad: how Max, in his fever, had been entirely himself, only more so: more unified, more shameless. She thought of him pointing and shouting at the emptiness in her stomach. She could not stop laughing. She was so sorry. Samuel said, "You're cruel," and she grabbed his ears and said, "So are you." Her dress was up around her thighs—Samuel reached for the hem. He lifted it up to her waist and in the same movement stuck his fingers inside her, just like that, no fretting or poking, and Minna wondered what women he could have known—or if he'd been practicing, in his mind, for this. She pushed him away with her knee, undid his belt, his trousers; she kicked them down around his ankles and pulled him toward her. Still his shirt was on, the work shirt he'd bought new, scratching against her stomach as he entered her.

Oh.

And like any moment one waited for, Minna did not experience it so much as she saw herself experiencing it, so that as soon as it was over, her memory of it was already made, and it had been brief, and somewhat violent, and he had made no sound. Even now he made no sound. He lay atop her, perfectly still; he seemed not to fear, like Max, that he would crush her. She took him by the ears again, lifted his head, found his mouth with hers. They had not kissed. But his lips stayed closed, and hard. He pushed off her, and rolled onto his back.

"Samuel."

He didn't move. She laid her head on his chest. His ear, she realized, was still in her hand, the felt of its back side against her fingertip, the rubbery lobe against her thumb.

"Samuel."

She could hear the mule, breathing gently. The familiar buzz-song of insects, farther off. Her teeth ached. Her back ached where he'd pressed her into the floorboards. She ached where he'd bit her, and between her legs, and in her throat, where tears were rising.

She said his name again, but he barely seemed to breathe. He was hiding from her the way children in Beltsy were taught to hide from bears.

TWENTY-EIGHT

THE colony kitchen smelled of wet wood. One girl washed the cutting blocks, another the spoons, a third the buckets. They might have been sisters, or not; all the colonists shared the same sturdy gait, and a way of keeping their eyes raised even as they bent over their work. They moved like birds, clustering, splitting off, clustering again, and talked almost constantly, though they seemed to agree more often than not, which struck Minna as odd, and somewhat irksome—agreeable conversation—and made her feel more strange and miserable than she already was. The girls smiled at her as they passed, but for all their cheerful bustle they did not talk to her or ask her to help, and she began to feel as though they suspected her. They'd noticed the missing buttons at her back, or a desolation in her face. Maybe Samuel's teeth marks were visible in her dress, or she sat on her stool in a certain way. The colonists did not know that she was Samuel's stepmother, but neither were they certain that she was anything as right as his wife; he'd introduced them by name but offered nothing more. It seemed possible that the people would simply think them brother and sister. But now she shrank from the girls' smiles; she felt as though they'd seen her and Samuel in the back of the wagon, seen everything, and what followed: his climbing out; his sleeping on the ground; his taking up the reins this morning without so much as looking her in the eye; Minna stuffing her hand in her mouth, all she could do not to cry. It was impossible that the girls had seen any of this, of course—yet every time they gave her a kind look, Minna's distress mounted. That was pity, she was sure of it, and that, there, that was disgust. They were her aunts, in disguise. *Look, how she proved us right. Look how far she went just to prove us right.*

An older woman set a dozen onions and a knife in front of Minna. "For supper," she said, though dinner had just been served, and Minna looked up, to thank her, for the woman must have seen her about to cry. But she was already crying, and could barely see. She cut quickly, to set off the onion fumes, then slowly, so she wouldn't slice herself. Worse than her shame was her disappointment, which threw her deeper into shame. What had she thought? But she had not thought—that was her downfall. She had thrown herself at him. And he wouldn't even kiss her. All the way down the hill she'd tried to decide if his not kissing her had been out of shock, or the opposite—if he hadn't been shocked at all. If he'd been waiting all this time to reject her. She remembered the doctor who'd told her to smear yogurt on herself and how for a month after that she did not touch herself once, not because she feared the terrible itching again but because the man had seemed so unsurprised that a girl like Minna would itch.

She should never have left Ilya, that last day in Odessa. She should have said, ask me to marry you, and been his wife; then her worst sin would have been stealing a bottle of milk. Ask me to marry you. Galina always said, Make sure they think it's their idea. But Minna had pressed up against Samuel, given herself easily, failed utterly. There were names for what she'd done with him. Even her mother would let a man go first, unless he told her to go first, in which case it would still be his idea.

Minna sucked on her right little finger. The taste of onion made her tongue wet. Her tears ebbed. The kitchen was silent, she realized. They'd left her alone. The room was large and clean and bright, with an up-to-date stove like the one Ruth claimed Leo had gotten her and a full sink as well as a washbasin, and from her stool she could see three of the families' houses, along with two dugouts they used for storage. She and Samuel had been given "the tour" by the colony's leader, a man called Abe who wore suspenders and carried a looking glass as a sort of conductor's wand, waving and pointing it as he rattled off colony statistics. Eleven families, twenty-two cows, twenty-two calves, four yoke of oxen, six mules, four horses, more chickens than they could count, a well for every quarter, one barn, a "Farmers' Hall" for study and debate and prayer, a schoolhouse, a kitchen attached to the hall, one grand piano, four privies. Oh, and a few hogs. The hogs he'd mentioned with a little question mark in his voice, as if some part of him recalled that they might pose a problem but couldn't remember exactly what it was. Minna understood now why Max wanted nothing to do with the colony. They were Jews, but they seemed to have forgotten their fear. They spoke as often in English as in Yiddish. They had rules—it turned out, for instance, that they only raised the hogs, and did not eat them—but the rules were self-written and subject to change, quite literally, for on the wall of the Farmers' Hall there was pinned a long scroll, where next to the item about the hogs, and not eating them, someone had inked in: *most of the time.*

The window closest to Minna was open; through it came the sound of crickets. She'd never believed her father when he said that crickets weren't singing, that they made all their noise with their wings and legs and stomachs, one part rubbing against the others, but now she thought she could hear this in the insects' rhythm, a tripping between frenzy and stillness, and a vibrato within vibrato that no throat could produce. *Stridulation*, she would learn later, in a tall, beautifully illustrated book called *Nature*. But now Abe walked into view, followed by Samuel. They stopped by one of the dugouts. Abe pointed, and waved his looking glass vigorously. From the moment they arrived he'd been trying to convince Samuel to stay. The colony was the future! he said. It proved that Jews could do more than buy and sell—they could work, and make, and provide! Who could hate them now? But they needed men, he said; the fall harvest had gone well enough that the Baron de Vintovich was sending two of their boys off to agriculture school, which would be good in the long run, but in the short, see, well, two boys gone left them short. In the short run, see? Excuse the pun. Women, too, he'd added, looking at Minna, and he seemed sincere, not just placating. A panic rose in her throat as she imagined telling him all the reasons she was not the kind of woman they wanted. She could not bear children, it seemed. She was not faithful. She was not cheerful like the colony girls, nor robust like the colony women. She could not promise, if given twice her share of food by mistake, that she would give any of it back.

Samuel stood with his arms folded, nodding as the man went on. There was his shirt pulled tight across his shoulders; there was the line where his collar met his neck. She'd laid her head against that neck, like a fool.

Stop looking at him, she told herself. Look at the onions. Look at your knees under your skirt. Close your eyes and look at nothing. Hear the crickets. Imagine that you're in your own kitchen; imagine the dream, come true: your own kitchen with a sink, and curtains on the windows.

But she could no more talk herself into the fantasy than she could stop looking at Samuel. It was like testing out a new injury, making it hurt just to confirm that it was still there. She watched his hands. She watched the subtle movements of his neck that told her he was speaking. His stillness, compared to Abe's; he didn't once shift his weight. His trousers, which she had mended. His hands moving to his hips.

Then the woman was back, wiping her boots on the step. Minna moved her pinky from her mouth to her ear, and shook out the tears that had pooled there. She picked up the knife again. There were two more onions to cut, the smallest and most bruised, which she'd left for last.

She cut into one. But before she could start to cry again, the woman was by her side, pointing a short, dirt-caked finger at the wet, white rings, saying, "Now. Isn't that the most remarkable thing. No matter how many hundreds of times you see it. Look at that. An onion's milk."

———

THEY were boarded at Abe's house, on two cots set up next to the children's bed. Night at the colony was loud compared to where they'd been: there were the crickets; the cries of an infant; footsteps on the path; in the Farmers' Hall, someone played the piano. Minna sat up to see if the children were asleep, then lay back down. She shifted slightly, closer to Samuel, then bent her elbow out and slid it toward him.

"What." His arm withdrew.

"What did you tell him?"

"Who?"

"Abe."

"Shh."

"They're asleep."

Samuel didn't answer.

"We can go outside, if you don't believe me." She entertained an image of herself and Samuel walking arm in arm toward the Farmers' Hall, swaying slightly to the music. She would shiver. He would remove his arm from hers, lay it across her shoulders. She was desperate, she thought, deranged—yet she couldn't stop the scene's unfolding.

Samuel turned away, onto his side. "I told him I'm going back. Tomorrow. He's given me supplies. I plan to pay him back."

"And what about me?" Minna asked.

"I didn't answer for you."

"So what will I do?"

"How should I know?"

In his voice was temperance, boredom.

"Do you despise me?" she asked.

"I don't despise anyone."

"That's an awful thing to say."

"There are worse things to do."

Minna said nothing.

"In another circumstance," he went on. "If we were different people, I mean, you would go back. I would be the one to run away."

"Is that what you want?"

"Does it matter?"

One of the children coughed. Minna waited. "I don't know," she said.

"Of course you don't."

"See? You despise me."

"No, Minna," said Samuel. "If I despised you, I would kiss you."

Minna rolled toward him. Her face met his back.

"You can come, if you want," he said. "I won't stop you."

"Samuel."

"I won't tell your husband. I never told him who tore the pages in the *siddur*. I never tell him anything. He's been forsaken enough."

Minna thought of her stove. The cellar she'd dug herself. Her comb, under the mattress. She'd forgotten about it until now.

"So we'll go back, is what you're saying, and everything will be as it was?"

"It's up to you."

"But you could do that," she said.

"I can do anything I choose to do."

"But you must have thought . . ." Minna was thinking of his

face when he'd come to her, at the creek. His simple, undefended want.

"Is that what you want to know? What I *thought*?"

"No. I suppose not."

The child coughed again, snuffled, tossed, settled. The crickets rubbed themselves. The piano player started up a new song. She reached for Samuel's shoulder.

"I thought you'd been sent to ruin us," he said.

T HERE had been a monkey, in Odessa, that sat on various corners and blew kisses to passersby who threw coins. These kisses involved the monkey touching its fingers to bared teeth, then waving and grinning until the passerby waved back, at which point the monkey would fold its lips over its teeth and scowl and pretend as though it had never seen the person, at which point the person had a choice: he could walk away, or he could pretend as though he wasn't offended by laughing very loudly and throwing another coin, only to go through it all over again. Most made the second choice. And Minna would wonder, Why did people do that? What was wrong in them that they should be so rough with their own hearts?

But all night, she could not let go of Samuel's shoulder.

T HE wagon was packed, the horse and mule hitched. The colonists thronged about, shouting to each other as much as to Samuel, who sat on the bench, reins ready in his hands. Stay awhile! The Baron de Vintovich is due to visit! It's a

once-in-a-lifetime chance! Samuel looked back at them with a
quiet impatience on his face, as a nobleman might endure the
attention of peasants, and Minna, standing next to the wagon,
looking up, felt certain that he would never marry. The thought
made her glad, in the lowest of ways. But even as she indulged
her gladness, she saw that his expression had changed, or else her
vision of it had changed, and now Samuel's stiffness on the bench
was that of the lame and his face was searching the colonists with
a furious, urgent fear.

"You thought your mother might be here," she said loudly, for
the thought had come to her loudly, and given her a shock. She
had not often thought of Samuel as the son of a mother.

He looked down at her. "So what?"

So what. She didn't know. She'd meant to accuse him, she
supposed, but of what? So he'd been a child. So he'd known his
mother. So his beautiful mother had been the one he preferred,
even after she'd run away. Minna had not been so forgiving. She
waited for him to shrug, or look away. But he kept his eyes on
hers. She could see him trying not to blink.

"So I'm sorry," she said.

His gaze held. "I never asked you for anything."

"I know."

"I don't want your consolation."

Minna nodded. Her throat hurt. With time, she thought, she
could break his face apart. She could make it half a face, an ugly
face. She would refuse to long for him.

"That's just as well," she said. "I never wanted to console you."

THE team pulled slowly up the long hill. It was still early: the crickets made their sound, the grass was tipped with pink, long shadows followed the wagon. The horse and mule had never looked so alike as they did now. Minna envied them their likeness, and their calm; she envied the clarity of the task ahead of them. She wished Samuel were on horseback, and would disappear quickly. She could feel the colonists watching her watching him. She smiled, held up a kerchief, and began to wave it. She waved excitedly, almost exuberantly. If anyone had known her, they would have known that she was close to weeping. But they didn't know her, so she kept waving. She thought of Ruth's wig, and the dead child she would not speak of. Of the gloves Galina wore to cover her bitten nails. Of her aunt's dark dresses. Of Liesl's mourning, which would be silent. She thought of her mother, who'd left her daughter and gone off to her own disguise, and of Samuel and Jacob's mother, whom Minna had been brought to replace, and of Rebeka, the last morning, her gasping laugh above the tea tray.

Who knew what any of them wanted? Who knew what they were good for?

At the crest of the hill, the wagon seemed to pause. But that must have been the light playing tricks, because the next minute it was gone and one of the women whose son had been sent off to the State Agricultural College rushed up to Minna, beaming, gave her a hearty clap on the shoulder, and offered her his empty bed.

TWENTY-NINE

MINNA might have stayed at the colony. For two weeks she slept in the bed of the boy who was in Brookings learning about manure and horticulture and how to tell the difference between a good cow and a bad cow, and also, it would turn out, how to fall in love with a gentile girl from the town, whom he would marry and settle with in Brookings, where he would open a dry-goods store named Lawson's—instead of Lowenstein's—and seldom use his knowledge of horticulture.

But his parents knew nothing of this yet, so their pride and joy in their son was still intact and they showered Minna with its excess. Their younger children asked why Samuel had left without her and she made up a story about steamboats and rabbis and ranch hands and babies, a story so long and convoluted that by its end, the question had been forgotten. The colony children were brave in a way she hadn't known children to be. There were few rules to obey, or fail to obey. They prayed with the adults as matter-of-factly as they did their chores. They played and studied and ate all together, and ran through each other's houses, and milked the same cows. It was as if any one child had as much right to another family as to his own. The girls Minna's age were not yet married. They took her to make cheese with them, and to bathe. They made fun of large breasts, and small ones, and told their jokes in front of her, and did not sneer when she laughed though they must have known she didn't understand all their English words. They had secrets among them, but you could tell from the way they rolled their eyes and flirted with their skirts that the secrets bore no shame.

It was this, the obvious triviality of their agitation, the way they rehearsed the telling of gossip more than they told it, which put Minna at ease. No one asked her to explain herself. She was made official onion cutter.

Then, one day, the Baron de Vintovich kept his promise and arrived. The colonists welcomed him with great cheers, and a marching band of children banging pots and pans, and that night, they gathered around the piano to hear him play and sing. Some of the children sang along, slapping the piano's sides and stomping their feet, until they were hushed—for the Baron did not look pleased at the accompaniment. Nor did he look pleased at the hushing, which was, of necessity, somewhat loud. The Baron was a short, square man with a pointed beard on his chin and a smile that appeared to cause him pain. He'd descended from his wagon in a long cloth coat, which he wore unbuttoned as if to remark upon its indulgence and which flapped around him as he walked. Now he sat at the piano bench, his feet barely touching the floor, his mouth open so wide you could see his tongue quiver as he crooned, with all the humor of an opera singer: *Like Oscar Wilde I flirt with the girls, I should utterly blush to murmur, The most liberal man that is on the road is the Hebrew clothing Drummer*. Some of the colonists seemed to know the song. They nodded along and smiled and generally made a good effort to cover their alarm, though as it became increasingly clear that the Baron was not a man to notice his effect, their faces fell into wincing. *In winter as well as in summer,* he warbled, *He is out on the road, In his style à la mode, You might think him a sport or a Bummer*. Minna was the only one still smiling. It was funny, really, if you hadn't expected him to be an advanced example of humankind. So za great Baron de Vintovich was a stout, disagreeable man. Minna could have guessed as much. She thought, Good for Samuel, that he didn't have to see this. She kept smiling. She did not think to herself, I am seeking an advantage, but she must have known, some part of her must have understood. And indeed, when the Baron finally arrived at his exalted, ear-piercing conclusion— *His expenses so large, To the firm he does charge, That Hebrew clothing man!!!*—he looked up, and it was Minna's smiling face he saw (for he was the sort of man who could locate praise in a bowl of teeth) and everyone in the room could see him fall for her.

What a phrase that was. *He fell for her*. As though the man had swooned off the piano bench. Yet his ardor was unmistakable. Even the Baron could not summon an affectation to mask it. He stood, and took her hand. Minna felt the color rise in her cheeks. And though there was fright in her blushing, at the fact of his hot, fleshy hand on hers, and embarrassment, for the colonists stared, she continued to smile. The Baron rode in a freshly painted wagon, hired in Pierre, with red velvet seats and a fringed roof. He had a small entourage of bespectacled men to assist him. Most importantly, he was bound for Chicago, to make an offer on a bridge that would cross the Missoury. For the Baron's wealth was not mysterious, as they'd wanted to believe. He was a railroad tycoon.

MINNA bid the colonists farewell from a thick cushion of brushed velvet, her lap covered in a lambskin though the morning was warm, the Baron next to her waving with only his fingers. The colonists looked less stunned now, and more judgmental, and Minna could see that she was not excluded from this judgment. They felt betrayed, she supposed, and confused in their betrayal, for they had never known anything about her nor had she made them any promises. That girl, they might say, do you remember that girl? She guessed she would be a story for them whose details were debated each time it was told. Had she truly been taken with the Baron? Had she been stupid, or shrewd? If she was stupid, did that make her more forgivable? What did she even look like? Did anyone recall?

En route to Chicago, when the train ran stretches of his track, the Baron took her hand and cried, "Here! Now! Do you hear that rail? How smooth? You feel it, yes? Only the best on the Baron's rail." Wink. "One must be ruthless to be the best."

Minna tried not think about the Baron's ruthlessness. She demanded her own compartment on the train, and did not allow anyone but the porter through the door. She murmured nonsense about modesty and allowed the Baron only to touch her

hand. It turned out to be easy to say no in a way that appeared
to promise yes. It was easy to mislead a man who you trusted
would not blink if given the chance to mislead you. In the eve-
nings, they sat at a table set in silver and ate pot pies and fruit
tarts and rolls so light you could eat ten before feeling full. How
marvelous and silly and sad those rolls were. If there was a draft
in the dining car, the Baron would drape his long coat over her
shoulders. He spoke of claims and contracts and "the fucking
government" with its fancy regulations and bought Minna her
first glass of champagne. He told jokes and she laughed. Sometimes she felt a stab between her breasts, a reminder of a task
she'd forgotten, and she would sense all her duties coming to
find where she had gone, knocking at the car windows, tugging
on her skirts. Images of Max eating a cold pancake with his hands
and her father fussily nailing lacy trim onto the birdhouse as
though her mother might return to eat seeds and Galina smearing lip paint onto her cheeks. She thought of herself, as a girl,
leaving the houses she was meant to clean. But she couldn't hold
the pictures still, or summon guilt, or even pity. She pictured the
girls at the colony, who might be pulling warm eggs from nests,
or dipping their fingers in butter, or watching boys, or falling
asleep thinking of boys. She might have stayed, and pretended to
be one of them. But she would never be a girl like that. They
were no more possible than the Baron himself, who in his desire
to kiss her and save her from hunger and want would save her
from freedom as well. She kept smiling at him, laughing. If memory was only a dream, the present, when necessary, could be
dismissed as an addled remnant. You didn't have to count it away;
only to keep your thoughts loose, as in hunger, or heartbreak.

And when the train pulled into the Great Central Depot, you didn't have to explain yourself. You could ask one of the bespectacled men for a not insignificant bit of money, wait for the Baron to become preoccupied with his discovery of a (carefully placed) tear in his coat, and walk, calmly, into the crowd.

THIRTY

MAX died some time before Samuel's return. He might have died as Minna lay under his son, or as she laughed at a joke she didn't understand, or as she let the Baron take her hand for the first time; as she left Max in her slow, cowardly way, he pardoned her by dying. It was a violent, vengeful death, but it began quietly, in the middle of one night, when a mouse chewed through the door's string, severing Max's connection with the railroad tie outside and locking him in the house. Max was trapped for who knew how long, already weak with his fasting, refusing to break a window for who knew what reason except perhaps God, who might have heard his prayers. If so, He sent a cruel answer, for it was Fritzi who kicked the door through, Fritzi who'd been driving cattle northward again, who couldn't help but drive them through Max's land, just to do it and to have done it. When he didn't see Max anywhere outside, then saw the cow's udders hanging almost to the ground, he went to knock, and when Max shouted from the other side and Fritzi lifted the tie and flung open the door, Max's sense was not that he'd been saved but that he was being attacked, and when he saw the hundreds of head of cattle lolling their greedy way through his grass, he ran toward them wildly, waving his arms, screaming. And when the cows did not find him frightening enough to warrant even a dent in their course, Max told Fritzi that he had a gun inside, the very one Fritzi had given to Jacob, and that as long as Max owned this land, Fritzi would not set foot on it again. And Fritzi's arm, swinging his father's rope, that arm might have looked to Max like the arm of one of his sons, for he did not run. Or maybe he didn't run because he knew it would make no difference, that the rope would catch him neatly around the arms and pull him hard to the ground. Fritzi rode—a hundred feet? a thousand?—and Max's head hit a pile of stones.

Samuel found Max in bed, under a blanket, with a note. What the note said, Minna always wondered. Had Fritzi thought only to give Max a scare, or to kill him? Had he believed Max's lie about Jacob's gun still being in the house, or did he only choose to believe it to justify his prank? Did he imagine himself to be a character of a cowboy in one of his books, dragging a character of a Jew?

His note, of course, would not have answered these questions. It would have offered only the facts, and even then, only the facts as he knew them to be and wanted them known. Samuel would have had to fill in the details, and what he left out, or what Ruth suspected he left out, Ruth must have guessed at. For it was Ruth who wrote Minna a letter, after Minna, for the first time in her life, didn't simply disappear but sent back word of her whereabouts.

> We were relieved to receive news—Chicago! Very sophisticated. Not all are cut out for this life. Indeed. I fear I may be the first to tell you that your husband—or was a divorce announced? I do not mean to pry, but people have asked, as they do— has suffered a terrible fate . . .

Ruth described the scene between Fritzi and Max, then concluded:

> . . . I hope you will forgive the messenger, my dear. You are bound to find a suitable husband in the city. (Speaking of which, did you hear of the Baltimore sister who took one of the fraudulent potions that con man was selling? It was meant to find her love, apparently—but she nearly died, she fell so ill.) Thankfully, you are more sensible than that, Minna. I do believe this to be true. And so I will leave you with this tidbit, applicable, I believe, even in the most urban environs:
> "The true economy of housekeeping is simply the art of gathering up all the fragments, so that nothing be lost."
> Isn't that lovely?
> It has given me something to ponder, in any case. Here, the crops grow well. The children improve. Health is in good order. We are sorry for your loss.

T HIS was in July, again—after Minna had discovered the pleasures of boardinghouses, in particular that of moving from
one to the next only to find it the same, the sharp old mistress,
the chalky stains on the doorknobs from where they bumped the
walls, the plain, clean, narrow bed dressed as if in bandage: the
surprise, and humor, and satisfaction, in having one's expecta-
tions so precisely met. She signed the logs as Losk. She could do
anything. Mostly she sat in her various and identical rooms, reading books available for rent at the desks downstairs. In hallway
mirrors she inspected the short, fuzzy hairs growing at her scalp,
replacing what she'd lost in her winter hunger. The wind turned
warm and the old mistresses dropped their fees and the Baron's
money lasted a little longer, then it ran out and Minna pawned
her wedding ring. She expected her palms to sweat, but she was
calm. She watched the dealer spin it around his thumb and de-
clare it impure, copper stained in gold. She thought of Max, who
would not have inspected the ring at all, who would have simply
handed over the crystal doorknob he thought he didn't need, accepted the ring, and walked out. The dealer looked at her with
pity, and without curiosity, and she didn't tell him that she was a
widow, though it would have made her more respectable—
though it was, perhaps, what she'd always wanted: the virtue of
marriage, without the burden of its charge; the assumption of
ruin without its shame. She found that she didn't care what he
thought, perhaps because Chicago was a big city, or because she'd
given up some idea of her own goodness.

The dealer gave her a week's board for the ring, and when that ran out, she returned her last book. She walked through Maxwell Street. She pretended to be aimless, though she knew that she couldn't afford to be, that eventually she would find herself at the shirt factory, lined up like other girls she'd seen, girls who looked like the quiet, sick girls on the boat. And though she dreaded this moment, she decided there would be some rightness in it, in the firm brush of elbows and hips, the falling in step behind another pair of boots, the giving in to the press of the herd toward the door. She thought it might be true, what Samuel had said, that she'd wanted too much to be different.

She paused in the middle of a market square. There was the street that led to the factory. There was the American sun, making the carts and doorways and even the stones underfoot look clean, though they were as filthy as carts and doorways and stones anywhere else. There was the smell of tomatoes, as in Odessa, the summer before. There were men who looked like other men, every one of them like another. She heard her name called. *Minna!!!!* And in the seconds that followed, because she couldn't find a single face turned toward her, and because almost no one in the city knew her name, she wondered if, by letting go of her pride, she'd found faith. She looked up. But before she could find God, or even the sky, her eyes were drawn to an open window, where, next to a tall red geranium, a thick, strong arm was waving. Faga's arm. Faga's enormous bust. Faga's loud mouth opening again to shout her name.

———

MINNA would stay in Chicago a long time. She stayed long enough to find work shelving books at the Public Library, and to pay her share of Faga's rent, and to develop new debts, of her own choosing, and new habits, like that of being late, always, and of wearing hats, everywhere, and of being unusually slow at market to pick which eggs she would buy, and which bread, and which beans. She stayed long enough to receive many more of Ruth's letters, including one that told her how the "crickets" Minna heard at the colony in fact turned out to be the firstborn of the grasshoppers, which one day that summer covered the sun and fell like a hail up to the colonists' knees and ate the children's clothes off their backs and devoured their crops and ran them back to towns and cities to buy and sell and bank; and another letter, the next year, which reported that Samuel had married one of the girls from the colony and made his father's farm a success and that the old mule was still alive. Minna stayed long enough in Chicago to fall totally, helplessly, sick with influenza, and to recover, and to read newspaper headlines about the Baron de Vintovich laying tracks across the continental divide. She stayed long enough to see Little Egypt dance her belly dance at the World's Fair Midway, and to think she saw Jacob in a clown costume only to lose him in the crowd, and to hear a man called Turner talk about the end of the frontier. She stayed long enough to see the century change, and to see her first Indians, in three-piece suits and homburg hats, outside a courthouse, and to sit in the dark of the Bijou Dream Theatre next to a man, watching Bronco Billy Anderson shoot and dance and flee his silent way through *The Great Train Robbery*. And at the end of the film this man, who sold nuts at the market and had asked one morning why Minna looked for so long but always bought the same thing, almonds roasted with no salt, and who Minna would know for many years though she would not marry him, pulled her out into the chilled air that blew off the lake that looked like but did not smell like an ocean. He said, "So that's the Wild, Wild West," and Minna smiled and said, "Yes. It's just like that."

AUTHOR'S NOTE
AND ACKNOWLEDGMENTS

The homesteading of Jews in the American West was part of an historical movement called Am Olam. While many aspects of this book remain true to that history, I have also transformed, discarded and created facts for the purpose of telling Minna's story.

My deepest gratitude goes to those who inspired me: the original Anna Solomon (Freudenthal), to mail-order bride Rachel Bella Calof, and artist Andrea Kalinowski, whose beautiful quilts introduced me to the stories of these Jewish pioneers.

Countless books informed and inspired me, chief among them: Isaac Babel's *The Odessa Tales*, *The Shtetl Book* by Diane Roskies and David Roskies, *Dakota: A Spiritual Geography* by Kathleen Norris, *Dakota Diaspora* by Sophie Trupin, *Sod Jerusalems* by David Harris, *And Prairie Dogs Weren't Kosher* by Linda Mack Schloff, and *Rachel Calof's Story*, edited by J. Sanford Rikoon.

I was fortunate to receive generous assistance from William Lee and Dawn Stephens at the South Dakota State Agricultural Heritage Museum, David Ode at the South Dakota Game, Fish & Parks Department, Michele Christian at Iowa State University, Catherine Madsen and Dovid Braun at the National Yiddish Book Center, Patricia Herlihy at Brown University, the librarians at the New York Public Library's Dorot reading room, Clare Burson, and Peter Manseau.

The "tidbits" in Ruth's letter are quoted directly from Lydia Maria

Child's timeless *The America Frugal Housewife*. The Baron sings badly from a real folk song called "The Hebrew Clothing Drummer." The story of the bride up on the dresser is based on a similar tale in *The Shtetl Book*. For critical details about magic, carpentry, chickens, Yiddish, and international medicine, I'd like to thank Laila Goodman, Jim Dowd, Richard Wyndham, Barbara Burger and Alfred Burger. Thank you to rancher Jim Headley in White Lake, South Dakota, who many years ago helped me see the prairie, and to Chris Ballman, for sending me out there.

Thank you to Yaddo and the MacDowell Colony for time, quiet, and nourishment, and to the Brooklyn Writers Space for being right around the corner.

Thank you to my teachers, in order of appearance: Penelope Randolph, Charlotte Gordon, William Keach, Sharon Dilworth, Nancy Zafris, Chris Offutt, Marilynne Robinson, Ethan Canin, James Hynes, Elizabeth McCracken, and Andrea Barrett. To Connie Brothers, Deb West, and Jan Zenisek. To Julia Fierro at Sackett Street Writers Workshop and Jeff Bens at Manhattanville College.

Thank you to my readers, who were honest and wise: Eleanor Henderson, Amy Herzog, Edan Lepucki, Jessie Solomon-Greenbaum, Lisa Srisuro, and Sarah Strickley.

Thank you to my sisters, Jessie and Fara, for their faith and companionship, and to Austin Bunn, Susan Burton, Deborah Cramer, Elyssa East, Jeanne Shub, Kim Caswell Snyder, S. Kirk Walsh, and Gina Zucker for cheering me on every step of the way.

Thank you to Sarah Stein and Sarah McGrath, for their passion and whip-smart editing. And to Ellen Levine, for her patience and generosity.

Finally, I want to thank my grandparents, Rose and Max Greenbaum and Mildred and Walter Solomon, for the stories they told, and for those they didn't. My parents, William Greenbaum and Ellen Solomon, who made me a writer. My daughter, Sylvia, who has taught me more than anyone, already. And Mike, who supports my work, sustains my heart, reads always and again, and brings me back.